Yankee Daughters

Yankee Daughters

Carolyn P. Schriber

Published by Katzenhaus Books
P. O. Box 1629
Cordova, TN 38088-1629
Cover Design by Avalon Graphics

ISBN-10: 0990797570
ISBN-13: 9780990797579
Library of Congress Control Number: 2016916691
Katzenhaus Books, Cordova, TN

Acknowledgements

The inspiration for the story of *Yankee Daughters* came from my mother's old family photo album. Margaret McCaskey was the youngest of eight girls, all of them born in western Pennsylvania in the nineteenth century. Most of the photographs were taken between 1900 and 1920; many of them were of people I never knew, relatives who died long before I was born. What I learned of them came from my mother's occasional family stories and the shaky reminiscences of elderly aunts. They were not the factual material of biography or history, but they stirred my imagination. I wanted to recreate the world these distant relatives had inhabited.

This book is a novel, and its characters and events, except for certain historical details, are entirely fictional. They should not be construed as having any factual basis in the lives of members of the McCaskey family, except for the following instances.

❧

The map at the top of the front cover is a fragment of a map of Beaver County, Pennsylvania, hand-drawn in 1860 to show the location of every residence and landmark in the county. The farm I have described as belonging to the Grenvilles in the 1890s lies in the bend of Conoquenessing Creek and is labeled as belonging to a J. McCaskey. Near it, you may be able to identify some of their neighbors mentioned in the story and various landmarks such as the post office, the coal mine, the church, and the cemetery.

❧

The pictures on the front and back covers of the book show the real McCaskey girls—my grandmother, my mother, and her seven sisters. The pictures were taken by a local Ellwood City photographer in 1912. They have served me as visual models for the fictional Grenville women in the story.

❧

The limerick about the Kilkenny cats was a favorite of the McCaskey sisters, and I grew up hearing it whenever an argument loomed. The origins of the legend go back as far as the fourteenth century, and the anonymous limerick itself has been popular since the 1800s.

⟡

The details of the women's suffrage talk given by Miss Liliane Howard in Chapter 29 were taken from a pamphlet prepared by the Pennsylvania Women's Suffrage Association and distributed in Pittsburgh in 1915.

⟡

The letters attributed to Sergeant Wilhelm McDevlin in Chapter 34 were actually written by my first cousin once removed, Wilbur Schweinsberg, who served in the Medical Corps during World War I. They were published in the Ellwood City newspaper, and the clippings were preserved in the family scrapbook.

There once were two cats of Kilkenny.
Each thought there was one cat too many,
So they fought and they fit
And they scratched and they bit,
Till, (excepting their nails
And the tips of their tails,)
Instead of two cats, there weren't any.

—Anonymous

Contents

Acknowledgements · · · · · · · · · · · · · · · · · ·v

Rebecca's Journal, September 15, 1886 · · · · ·1
Chapter 1   Did the Earth Just Move? · · · · · · · · · · · · ·3
Chapter 2   What's to Be Done about Becca? · · · · · · · ·11
Chapter 3   The Worse the Passage, the More
             Welcome the Port · · · · · · · · · · · · · · · · ·21
Chapter 4   Take a Deep Breath and Start Anew · · · · ·31
             Rebecca's Journal, October 28, 1889 · · · · ·41
Chapter 5   Mighty Oaks from Little Acorns Grow · · ·43
Chapter 6   A Picture Freezes the Moment · · · · · · · · ·55
Chapter 7   Man Proposes . . . · · · · · · · · · · · · · · · · ·65
Chapter 8   . . . God Disposes · · · · · · · · · · · · · · · · ·75
             Rebecca's Journal, December 1898 · · · · · · ·85
Chapter 9   The Things that Never Die · · · · · · · · · · ·87

Rebecca's Journal, December 31, 1899 · · · ·99

Chapter 10 Sufficient unto the Day Are the
Troubles Therein · · · · · · · · · · · · · · · ·103

Chapter 11 If Truth Be Told · · · · · · · · · · · · · · · · ·111

Chapter 12 The More Things Change · · · · · · · · · · ·119

Chapter 13 Some Paths You Choose; Some Are
Chosen for You · · · · · · · · · · · · · · · · ·129

Rebecca's Journal, Summer 1902 · · · · · · · ·139

Chapter 14 Marriage Changes Everything · · · · · · · ·143

Chapter 15 The Dreams Girls Dream · · · · · · · · · · ·155

Rebecca's Journal, March 1906 · · · · · · · · ·163

Chapter 16 If Wishes Were Horses, Beggars
Would Ride ·169

Chapter 17 A House Needs a Family to
Make It a Home · · · · · · · · · · · · · · · ·177

Chapter 18 Having a Baby Does Not a
Mother Make· · · · · · · · · · · · · · · · · · ·187

Chapter 19 Death Is a Thief Who Comes in
the Night ·197

Rebecca's Journal, December 1910 · · · · · ·207

Chapter 20 Growing Old Is Mandatory;
Growing Up Is Optional · · · · · · · · · · ·211

Chapter 21 Off with the Old; On with
the New ·223

Chapter 22 Love Makes the World Go 'Round · · · · ·233

Rebecca's Journal, December 31, 1912 · · ·243

Chapter 23 Old Soldiers Never Die · · · · · · · · · · · ·247

Chapter 24 Only the Dead Have Seen the
End of War ·257

	Rebecca's Journal, July 1913 ·········· 267
Chapter 25	If You Love Them, Let Them Go ······ 269
Chapter 26	To Each Her Own ·················· 281
Chapter 27	Graduation Is Not the End but the Beginning ······················ 291
Chapter 28	We Always Want What We Cannot Have ···················· 301
	Rebecca's Journal, Summertime 1914 ···· 311
Chapter 29	Deeds, Not Words: Give Women the Vote ·················· 315
Chapter 30	In for a Penny; In for a Pound ········ 327
Chapter 31	You Don't Find Love; Love Finds You ··· 339
	Rebecca's Journal, December 31, 1915 ···· 351
Chapter 32	The Calm before the Storm ·········· 355
Chapter 33	The War to End All Wars ············ 365
Chapter 34	Dear Mother: Words from the Front ···· 377
Chapter 35	Be Careful What You Wish For ······· 389
	Rebecca's Journal, December 31, 1920 ··· 399

Rebecca's Journal

September 15, 1886
Charleston, South Carolina

When I look back over my life, I begin with the Civil War, because it has colored so many of my experiences. I was eleven when it began and fifteen when it ended—a childhood lost. I didn't understand the causes of the war. I knew only the fear engendered by booming cannons and approaching armies, the smashing grief that nearly destroyed my sister when her new husband died in his first battle at Hilton Head, the mixed curiosity and revulsion of seeing my brother return from the war without his right leg.

Next came the aftermath—talks of peace and reconstruction, but acts of terrorism, lynchings, and brutality beyond my ability to understand. Economic crisis and government corruption offered little hope for the future. I spent my young *adulthood desperately trying to figure out a way to avoid having to grow up. And then I realized I was twenty-five, a quarter of a century old, and with not a thing to show for myself. My brothers and sisters were marrying, having children, starting businesses, pursuing dignified careers. I called myself a house cat and took shelter, as my mother had done before me, in books and music. I hid from the world until something physically shook me out of my cocoon.*

Twice in my life, the very house in which I lived was torn out from under me. The first time came in the Great Charleston Fire of 1861. The flames raged across the peninsula in a race toward the river, and they carried our family home with them. When it was over, nothing was left of our Logan Street house except one stark chimney standing in a pile of wood ash. I once heard my father say that the fire ripped him from his cloak of complacency and forced him into a life of action. I didn't understand then, nor did it make sense to me until my own ripping away in 1886, when the Legare Street house crumbled around me in the Great Charleston Earthquake.

Chapter 1

Did the Earth Just Move?

Charleston, South Carolina
August 31, 1886

It was only a small sound at first. Becca Grenville had been headed to bed, but she hesitated at the foot of the stairs as she listened. It sounded like a wagon rumbling over the cobblestones outside. Could someone be arriving at this time of night? She shook her head at the very idea, but she wouldn't put it past her brother Johnny, she decided. She waited for his knock.

Then an explosive boom slammed into her whole body. It was not only a sound—it had weight and strength to thrust her backward against the stairs. She couldn't seem to breathe. Her chest hurt with the effort. She stumbled as the floor rocked beneath her feet, and she fell onto the steps. The kerosene lamp she carried dropped from her hand and shattered on the parquet tiles of the hallway. A small tongue of flame licked at the edge of the puddle of kerosene. The rest of the world had grown very dark, and the sound went on and on.

Am I dying? she asked herself. Is this what dying is like—a pain without cause, a lack of air and light, whirling vision, nausea, fear, and above all, the sound? She somehow had expected dying to be quieter. Then the acrid kerosene smell aroused her, and she struggled to her feet, stamping out the flames that were beginning to spread. Still disoriented in a world that would not stand still, she grasped the newel post at the foot of the stairs and clung there, only hoping that something—someone—would make this heaving, rocking motion stop.

As if in answer to her prayer, the movement did stop, although she could now hear other discordant sounds. Bells were clanging without reason or harmony from church steeples. Invisible people were screaming. Periodic crashes echoed from all sides. Glass shattered. Horses whinnied in terror. Dogs barked and howled.

And then the roaring came again. Becca sank onto the bottom steps, wrapping her arms around her head to blot out the sound, but it did not help. The noise seemed to come from every side, from above and below, even from inside her very soul. Another odd smell—like wet ashes— made her open her eyes. She watched in disbelief as the parlor fireplace spewed dust and smoke and then sank from view, leaving only a gaping hole in the floor.

This time, the shaking stopped quickly, but Becca was too terrified to move. She simply sat there, staring into the void, until a voice roused her.

"Miz Becca? You be all right? Miz Becca?"

"I'm in the hallway, Sammy. I'm here."

The old stable man limped toward her through the gloom. His pant leg was torn, and scratches on his arms were bleeding.

"What happened? Do you know what's going on?" she asked.

"I don know nuthin, Miz Becca. De horses be throwin fits in dey stalls, an I come out fuh see what wuz goin on. Den part uh de stable roof come off an hit me on muh head. When I dun pick muhself up, de whole world wuz kickin round, like one uh de horses."

Becca fought to regain her wits. The presence of the old black man who had managed the family stables for as long as she could remember was reassuring, no matter what he might be telling her. Sammy Hawkins had started life as one of her grandmother's slaves, but he stayed on after the war was over and all the slaves, including Sammy, had been freed. "Dis be muh home," he had told Jonathan Grenville, "an dese be muh animals. Dey needs me fuh take care uh dem, an I needs dem fuh give me sumptin fuh do." He had stayed on even when the Grenvilles moved to Beaufort, leaving only their daughter Becca to maintain the Charleston residence. "I wuz born here an I aim fuh die here," he argued when Jonathan once again tried to get him to go off on his own.

Sammy and Becca had established a comfortable routine. He had turned the loft above the stables into a cozy home for himself. He did his own cooking and spent his free time doing as he liked. Becca paid him a monthly wage to care for the animals and do odd jobs around the house, but they seldom interacted. When something needed fixing, he took care of it without comment or instruction. They waved to one another and exchanged pleasantries as one might do with a friendly neighbor, but they both avoided discussions that would draw attention to their servant-employer relationship.

Now, however, Becca was absurdly grateful to see him there in her hallway, providing reassurance that one thing, at least, had not changed in the last few minutes.

"I aint never seed de ground shake like dat," he was saying. "Is it de end of de world?"

"I think we've just had a terrible earthquake, Sammy. I've read about them, but I've never experienced one before. They don't usually happen around here. It seems to be over now, and we're both still breathing, so I think we'll be all right."

"Well, dere be lots uh stuff wrecked, Miz Becca. When I come in tru de back door, I seed dat in de dinin room, all de plates an cups an glasses be scattered in pieces all over de floor."

"Oh, yes, there will be lots of damage," she said.

"What we gonna do? Yo mama gonna be mad bout all dose good dishes."

"Yes, I'm sure she will, but we can't see how much damage has been done until dawn, when it gets light—as I assume it will."

"Yo be sure de sun gonna come back up?"

"Yes, Samuel, I'm sure." And she suddenly realized that she was smiling again. "This has been awful, but we're going to be all right, I promise. You best go on and take care of those scratches on your arms. We'll get through this night and things will look better in the morning."

Once Sammy was gone, however, Becca was not so sure. Remembering something she had once read about being safest in a doorway during an earthquake, she dragged a small chaise longue to the arch between the ladies' parlor and the central hall. Grabbing an afghan from the back of the sofa, she bundled herself into a tight ball and determined to stay awake throughout the night. As her terror drained away, however, she drifted into an uneasy slumber, only to be awakened by someone pounding on her front door.

"Miss Grenville! Miss Grenville! Hello? Are you in there? Can you open the door? It's Alex Croft—from next door. I'm a friend of your brother Johnny. Henrietta McLeod's son-in-law. Please. Let me know you're all right!"

Clutching the afghan around her shoulders, she struggled to lift the security bar on the door. "Alex? I'm here, but I can't get the security bar out of the latch. It's jammed."

"Which way does the door swing open?"

"Inward."

"Then let me see if I can pull it toward me to give you some extra leeway."

With their combined efforts, the bar finally slid away. Becca held the door open for Alex; she was once again relieved to have made contact with someone. "How did you get here, Alex? Don't you live over on Meeting Street?"

"Yes, I do, and the red brick monstrosity I inherited from my parents held itself together pretty well during that earthquake. I brought my wife, Rachel, over here to be sure her mother was all right, but they both insisted I check on you as well. Are you all alone?"

"I'm afraid so, except for Sammy, out in the stables. But we're fine."

"Not from the looks of the outside, you're not. Every one of your chimneys has collapsed, and the sleeping porch out back is just dangling from a few supports."

"Oh, dear! I knew this fireplace was destroyed, but I didn't think . . ."

"You're certainly not the only one with damage. From what we saw on the way over here, it looks like every house in Charleston has been shaken off its foundations."

"That bad?"

"Worse, I'm afraid. There were several streets where we could not walk through the debris, and the public buildings, even the Fireproof Building and Hibernian Hall, have major damage. From the talk out on the streets, it appears all the water lines—the gas mains, too—have been cracked and broken. Someone said that nearly eighty meters of railroad track at the station have been displaced or twisted, and near one intersection, there's a locomotive on its side from being thrown off the track."

"What have we done to deserve this?" Becca looked at him, with tears finally starting to form. "I've been hoping it was just a bad dream, but it's not, is it?"

"No, my dear, I'm afraid not. What has happened to your family? Why are you living here all alone?"

"My choice," she shrugged. "I thought I was being brave and independent. Well, at least I saved them from sharing this horrible night."

"So where are they? You can't stay here, you realize. Most families are already moving into the streets and parks for fear their houses are going to fall down around their ears and crush them. But living on the street is no place for a young woman on her own."

Becca was shaking her head. "Where are they? You want a roll call? Mother and Father moved to Beaufort to run a school there, and Mary Sue and Eli live close to them on St. Helena Island. At the other side of the state, Eddie and his wife and Charlotte and her family are living on our farm in Aiken. Johnny's in Washington, DC, serving as an aide to Senator Hampton, and Robbie . . ." Her voice cracked a little. "Robbie went to Savannah in 1883 to take a job as a law clerk. He caught yellow fever there and died. And Jamey? Well, Jamey married a girl from western

Pennsylvania and went to live on her farm. We're all scattered to the winds, and this is the only place we have in common. I was supposed to take care of it, so they would have somewhere to come home to. No one ever asked where I would go if I had to leave here."

"But this isn't your fault. And there's no way you can put this place back together again. It's too big a job for a single woman."

"Maybe so, but I can hold things together for a little while, until I can contact everyone and find out what they want me to do."

"Becca! You can't . . ."

"Why can't I? Where are you going to go, Alex?"

"I don't know. We'll be staying with Mrs. McLeod for the time being."

"So she's not moving, either!"

"Well, no, but then she's a tough old broad, Rebecca, and don't you dare ever tell her I called her that! You still have a life ahead of you, and Charleston is not going to be a hospitable place for you to be living for a long time to come. You need to—"

"I need to live my own life, Alex. I thank you for your concern and for your help in getting my front door open. But I'm staying put until . . . until I find somewhere that I'm needed."

Chapter 2

What's to Be Done about Becca?

Franklin Township, Pennsylvania
September 1886

Katerina found Jamey sitting at the kitchen table, his head in his hands, as he bent over a small stack of papers. "Is that one of those round-robin letters your mother sends to the family?" she asked.

"I'm afraid so, and this one is worse than most."

"How so?"

"Most of Mother's news ends up being nothing but family gossip, but this . . . this is a family disaster, and my siblings are not demonstrating their finer sides."

"What's happened?" Katerina pulled up a chair and sat close to her husband, a comforting hand on his arm.

"An earthquake, believe it or not. It hit Charleston a couple of weeks ago, and from what she describes, pretty well wiped out the entire city."

"Oh, no! Your sister?"

"Becca's fine, she says, but the Legare Street House is a total loss—all the masonry, every chimney and fireplace, crumbled. The upstairs sleeping porch now occupies the back yard. No way to heat the house in cold weather, no cooking facilities, gas and water lines out, windows shattered. Becca is sort of camping out in one of the parlors, where the damage is least severe, waiting to hear what the family wants her to do."

"The family wants her to get out, I hope!"

"I thought that, too, Kat, but the situation is more complicated. Apparently, the local hotels all have major damage, and there are already some 40,000 people living in tent cities in the parks and even in the streets. Boat transportation out of the city is booked solid, and train travel is still hit or miss because of damage to the tracks. There's no place else for her to go, without simply abandoning the house."

"And that would be bad because . . .?"

"Because it's not just her house. Our parents inherited it with the stipulation that they cannot sell it. They allow Becca to live there and keep an eye on the property. If she abandons it, she destroys part of the family inheritance. On the other hand, she can't do anything with it beyond continuing to live there. She is not in a position to make any repairs, even if she could find available workmen, which she can't because of the sheer amount of work to be done all over the city."

"What does your father have to say? Surely it's his house to . . ."

"Not really, because according to that same legacy, when Father and Mother die, all their properties are to be sold at auction and the proceeds distributed evenly among all their surviving children. So it boils down to a decision among the six of us. What do we want her to do about the property we are all supposed to share and share alike?"

Katerina was shaking her head. "What kind of twisted mind puts such complicated restrictions on a family?"

"My grandmother Dubois is to blame, and you would have had to know her to begin to understand. This is just the way it is, and it's all strictly legal, so there's no use in complaining. It's unfortunate, however, that dear old *Grandmère* could not see far enough into the future to know how difficult her arrangements would become."

"What do your brothers think?"

"Well, Johnny's advice is short and sweet. He says Becca should have our lawyers arrange to have the property condemned as a hazard to public safety. Then they could tear the house down, the insurance company would have to pay up, and Becca could take that money to go somewhere else and start a new life. I'm inclined to agree with him."

"And Eddie? He's always seemed to me to be the one with the best business sense."

"Eddie wants to wait and see what happens." Jamey shuffled through the pages to find Eddie's addition to the round-robin letter. "He says that earthquakes usually come in clusters and that there have already been several aftershocks. There's still the possibility that one of those tremors will succeed in bringing the rest of the house down. I think he's also suggesting that Father and Mother could die in the next few years, which would change everything."

"That's terrible!"

"I don't think he means it as wishful thinking. It's just his practical side. Our parents are in their sixties, and Father's health has been none too good lately. Eddie has always been opposed to betting against fate. He prefers to assume that time will do its worst."

"And what is poor Becca supposed to do in the meantime?"

"Well, he says—and Charlotte seems to agree—that they can take Becca in for a while at the farm in Aiken. Mother and Mary Sue both have said much the same thing. Everyone is willing to find a temporary home for Becca— 'squeeze her into one of the children's rooms' is the way Mary Sue put it."

"And that's horrible, too! Becca's a capable, functioning adult woman. There's no reason to treat her as if she were some kind of nuisance half-wit simply because she doesn't have a husband!"

"I think you're overstating that a bit, Kat. They are trying to be kind."

"But they're thinking primarily of themselves and what will least inconvenience them for the shortest amount of time."

"Do you have a better idea?"

"Uh, no, not at the moment, but give me some time to think about it."

❦

After supper and bedtime for the children, Jamey and Katerina sat down again at the table to renew the discussion.

"I know what I want Becca to do," Jamey announced.

"Just like that?" Katerina smiled and shook her head at her husband's self-assurance. "The baby of the Grenville family is going to solve all the problems his older brothers and sisters can't handle?"

"Yep. 'Cause I've always been the different one, the burr under the family saddle."

"Let's hear the great plan!"

"I agree with Johnny. I want her out of that house, and then I don't care what happens to it. I want Becca to move here."

"Here? You mean we'll be the ones to squeeze her in with all our own babies?"

"No, hear me out. I do want her here. Becca was always my favorite member of the family because she paid attention to me. Granted, she was usually telling me to stop doing something, but at least she was noticing me.

And when I tried to be good, which I also admit was none too often, it was meant to please her, not our parents or the older children. So, reason number one: I would enjoy having her around. I love her dearly. Reason number two: I worry sometimes that our daughters are growing up without knowing any of my family. I'm convinced that every little girl deserves a doting aunt who will love her unconditionally—one she can turn to when she feels like running away from home. And if our girls could only know one of my siblings, I would want it to be Becca, who has the best heart of them all. And reason number three: I have the perfect solution to providing Becca with a home of her own."

"Found a magic wand, have you? If so, I'd like a rabbit out of a hat for tomorrow night's supper."

"No magic wand, I'm afraid, but I do have a surveyor's rod."

"What?"

"Do you remember several years ago, there was a minor kerfuffle with the Hazens over a small piece of property in the woods between our two farms?"

"Vaguely."

"They were building a small cabin in those woods for Mrs. McNabb, Mr. Hazen's mother-in-law. She had been living with them, and Hazen was desperate to get her out of his house. Then it turned out that the property line marker was off by some ten feet, so that the cabin was actually sitting on our land."

"Oh, yes, you were quite magnanimous about it, as I recall. You admitted that it was a small spot you were never going to put into cultivation because there was a creek running through it. So you told them to leave the marker where it was, and we would not make a fuss about a small cabin sitting on the land."

"Quite so. And it turned out to be a pleasant little cottage, perfectly situated to blend in with the surroundings. Hazen painted it, decorated it, hung curtains, did everything he could to make it welcoming. But when it was time for Mrs. McNabb to move in, she put up such a fuss about being kicked out and banished to the woods that she worked herself into a massive attack of apoplexy. She died a couple of days later and never even got to see the cabin. It's a major sticking point between Mr. and Mrs. Hazen. They slapped a padlock on the front door, and it's been sitting empty ever since."

"Oh!" Katerina's eyes did not reflect the smile on her lips. "I'm sure that would be a lovely spot for Becca. But I doubt that Mrs. Hazen will let her husband sell it."

"Actually, they don't have much choice. It's built on our property, so legally it's already ours. I'm going to drop by and have a little chat with him tomorrow. I'm guessing that if he is offered a fair price for the contents of the cabin, he'll sign it over in a minute."

"But then you'll have to talk Becca into moving all this way. I can't imagine that she would want to do that. How would she get here?"

"I also intend to check train schedules. Maybe even purchase her a ticket."

Katerina put forth no more arguments, but her tightly compressed lips might have warned Jamey that she was not happy about his proposal to bring a new family member into their private circle.

❧

After several days of inquiries and negotiations, Jamey was ready to write a letter—one that would change their lives, and Becca's, forever.

> *My dearest sister,*
>
> *I hope this letter finds you well and coping with the deplorable conditions under which Charleston is currently struggling. As I am sure you know by now, our entire family has been searching for solutions to the problems associated with the Legare Street House. We all seem to be agreed on two points. None of us particularly cares that the house be preserved for the future. And we all want you to be once again safe and secure in your living arrangements. I have seen offers from all our family members to have you come and live with them, but I have the offer I hope you will be unable to resist.*
>
> *Put simply, I want you to come to Pennsylvania. I am entirely happy with my situation here, except for the lamentable absence of any member of my own*

family. I have five little girls who are growing up without knowing anyone in the Grenville family. My fondest wish for them is that they have at least one wonderful, caring aunt, to whom they can run when the rest of the world seems to be working against them.

And here's what I have to offer you. There exists, in a lovely patch of woodland adjacent to my farm, a cottage designed, built, and decorated for a creative and independent woman such as yourself. The woman for whom it was intended was never able to live in it. Now, due to several odd twists of fate (and I do believe in fate), that cottage has come into my possession and is standing empty. I would like you to see it and decide for yourself if you could be happy living there.

To that end, I have taken the liberty of attaching a train schedule and a voucher for one passenger's travel from Charleston (or as close outside the city as the trains are able to run), carrying you to Augusta, Atlanta, Chattanooga, Cincinnati, and finally to Pittsburgh, where we will be waiting with welcoming arms as soon as we know the date of your arrival. The whole trip should take no longer than three days total.

Please accept this offer. Come and spend as much time with us as you like. We have plenty of room in the farmhouse for a visitor, or we can open the cottage for you. Meet your sister-in-law, Katerina, and your five nieces—Nora, Martha, Millie, Lillian, and Ruby. Get to know this area. Experience the beauties

of autumn in the hills of Pennsylvania. And then de-cide if this is the right move for you. I hope it is.
Fondly,
The baby brother who has, I assure you, grown up quite nicely,
Jamey Grenville

Chapter 3

*The Worse the Passage,
the More Welcome the Port*

*A*nd so it was that on this cold and windy October day, Jamey Grenville paced the train platform at Pittsburgh's Allegheny City Station. His stomach was twitching. It felt as if it were full of those childhood butterflies that had always plagued him when he suspected someone—usually his sister Rebecca—was going to yell at him about something. He had been priding himself on how grown-up he was, but Becca still had the power to reduce him to a sniveling adolescent.

Becca's train was not due for another half-hour, but he could not bear the fetid atmosphere inside the station. I'm glad Katerina couldn't come along, he thought. She would take one deep breath of this poisonous air and be ready to start scrubbing things. I can hear her now: "Look at that, Jamey. This floor is so dirty my shoe is sticking to it. And the closer you get to one of those God-awful spittoons, the deeper the crud gets. What's wrong with you men that you can't even aim your spit?"

He smiled as he realized that he could imagine her exact tone of voice. That's how domesticated I've become, he thought. Not only do I know what she would say in this situation; I can actually carry on whole conversations with her. I would tell her not to blame me because I don't chew tobacco, but she'd brush that excuse away and go on to comment on that unwashed-body odor that permeates everything and the cloud of coal smoke that makes up a whole layer of Pittsburgh's atmosphere. She'd cringe at the sight of harried mothers dragging screaming children across this dirty floor. She would pull away when a beggar grasped her sleeve and then drop a penny into his outstretched hand, all the while carrying on a monologue about how well-raised people ought to behave.

I wonder how she and Becca will get along? They both love me, I know, but I'm not sure whether that will make them partners or rivals. And how will Becca react to our little hardscrabble farm? She's had her years of farm life in Aiken, so she won't be too surprised at barn smells or squawking chickens, but she's also used to the gentility of Charleston. She's sure to find the North harsher and less civilized than her beloved South. Oh, rats. I'm beginning to sound as disapproving as Katerina.

A whistle split the air as the engine with its high smoking funnel rounded the final bend and chugged to a stop at the platform. Jamey had trouble locating a lone woman in the swarms of businessmen who pushed their way off the train. But there she was, head still held high, valise firmly grasped in one hand, eyes bright with anticipation as she surveyed the crowd. They spotted one another at the same moment, and nearly identical family grins reassured them both that this was a homecoming of sorts, even if it was happening under strange circumstances.

"Jamey! You're all grown up!"

"You were expecting to be met by a pimply adolescent?"

"No, but that's what you were the last time I saw you ten years ago. And now look at you! Oh, is your wife here?" She looked around expectantly.

"No, if we all had come, there wouldn't have been room in the carriage to pick you up. With four little girls and a baby underfoot, she has her hands full. But they'll be waiting eagerly for us to get home. Do you have a trunk?"

"Two of them, actually, right over there. I hope I haven't brought too much, but I realized that I might be leaving Charleston for the last time."

"I hope that will prove to be the case."

With relatively little fuss, they managed to get the trunks loaded into the carriage. Jamey was eager to leave Pittsburgh behind. "You'll have to visit the city sometime and get to know its cultural offerings," he said. "They have a good reputation for theater and musical productions, but they're still lagging a bit in the niceties of everyday life. For now, though, I'm anxious to introduce you to the natural beauties of Beaver County."

"It's hillier than I imagined. We're going steadily up-hill, aren't we? Poor horses!"

"It's up and down. We don't have actual mountains, but these are the foothills of the Appalachians, and you'll see that the hills are separated by lots of small rivers, all of them running into the Ohio River, which heads west on its way to the Mississippi."

"Are you suggesting that this is the Wild West I've heard about?"

"Well, I don't know about the 'wild' part, but, yes, this is definitely the West. The frontier does not lie far away, and settlers still leave from here in their Conestoga wagons to explore what lies beyond."

Becca leaned over to look into the nearest valley. "There is a river right down there, isn't there?"

"That's the Beaver River."

"There's that name again—the county, the river. Are they named after the hat?"

"No, dear heart!" Jamey was laughing gently at her. "We have real live beavers—lots of them—from whose glossy brown coats tailors make those beaver hats. You'll see, soon enough."

A few minutes later, he pulled on the reins to slow the horse team. "As we round this bend, I want you to look off to your right, at the edge of the river."

"Oh! What in the world? What are those things? Ewww. They look like gigantic rats."

"No, no. They are classified as rodents, but of a different sort. They're not scavengers. See the wide, flat tails? They're beavers, and when they slap the water with those tails, every animal in the vicinity knows there's trouble coming. And look at the trees around here. Notice anything different?"

"Well, somebody's been cutting a lot of them down, but the chopped-off part is sort of pointed rather than flat."

"That's the beavers at work. They chew through the trunks and then carry the treetops down to the water to build their own underwater homes. Theirs is the only job I know of where the workers get to eat their work. If it were a little later in the day, we'd be seeing deer along here, too, whole herds of them."

"It's beautiful country, Jamey. I understand why you're happy here. But it's going to take me a while to get used to it. It's quite different from South Carolina, you realize."

"Of course. What's bothering you the most?"

"It's so . . . big."

Jamey could not help but laugh, and she reached out to cuff his ear, just as she had done so often when they were children. It was a poignant moment for both of them, and they exchanged warming smiles. Becca fell silent for several minutes, and Jamey let her follow her thoughts wherever they were leading. Finally, she was ready to try to explain herself.

"You know how in Charleston, the houses are built really close to one another and then walled off to keep them separate? When you walk down a Charleston street, the buildings loom up, and the houses and gardens hover right at your shoulder. You can see for a few blocks, if the street lies straight ahead, but you don't see anything beyond the buildings to either side. It reduces the city to a manageable size somehow. The city is whatever you see right in front of you. The only place you can go, if you want to look off in the distance, is to the edge of the harbor. And then you only see water for as far as your eyes can focus. There's nothing else out there.

"But here—every time we come to the crest of one of these hills, I look off in the distance and see more and more land—folds and ripples of land, fading off in the distance like some Renaissance landscape painting. But it keeps going, seemingly forever. And when I look around, I feel very small and out of control. I don't know how to process this much land—how to find a place for myself in its vastness."

Her voice quivered, and she quickly turned her head away, but not before Jamey caught the glimmer of tears welling in her eyes. "I'm sorry. I don't mean to sound ungrateful for all you are doing for me. But it's been a long trip, and a terribly emotional one. I've left everything I knew behind me, and now . . . now I don't even know how to look for something new to replace what I've lost."

Jamey waited for several minutes before he answered her. "You're only seeing the hills at the moment, Rebecca. For some people, seeing this part of the world for the first time, the vastness of the mountains is intimidating. For others, it represents unlimited opportunity to start afresh. So what do you look for? That will depend on what you want to find. Remember one thing—you can't have hills without valleys between them. Look now for the valleys. They are there to shelter you."

"How did you get to be so wise, Jamey Grenville?"

"Experience. Life."

Becca looked at her brother with a new respect in her eyes. "You really have grown up well. It almost makes you worth all the trouble you caused as the baby of the family."

"I'm still growing up and still learning, I hope, although I thank you for the vote of confidence. But I must remind you that no one sees me as 'the baby of the family' here. I'm a well-respected family man—something of a patriarch in my own right."

"I'll try to remember that." Becca was smiling again, her qualms about this trip temporarily erased by the need to get to know this new side of her brother. "You know, I've never heard the story of how you came to meet your Katerina and how you ended up here. Mother and Father, typically for them, were unwilling to discuss the matter with the rest of us."

"Well, it was the summer after that Christmas we all spent in Aiken—1878, wasn't it? I had one more year of college to go, and I was working for Eddie, helping with the peach orchards to earn some extra money. Katerina McDevlin was in Aiken, too, spending the summer with her cousin Gretchen's parents."

"Is she a Mennonite, like Gretchen?"

"No, but at one time her mother was. Wilhelmina McDevlin and Gretchen's father were brother and sister. Wilhelmina—Schwimmer, she was then—left the church and her family to marry her Scotch-Irish suitor, Andrew McDevlin, but she wanted her daughter Katerina to visit her Mennonite relatives and get to know her heritage so she could choose for herself. Kat wasn't much taken with the Mennonite ways, so we ended up spending a lot of time together around the Schwimmers' cheese-making operation to give her some breathing room. Then her parents were killed in a freak accident. Something spooked their horse, their carriage tipped over, and they went over a cliff."

"That's terrible."

"It was. Kat had two younger brothers at home, so she had to head back immediately to take care of them and to deal with the funerals and other issues. I couldn't bear to let her face that all by herself, so I came along. Once I saw her family farm, I knew we could be happy here. So we got married, and then I told our parents—not a popular decision, as you can imagine—but it was exactly what I wanted and needed."

Becca was still pondering the story when they pulled into the farmhouse yard. From the doorway came four little girls, all shouting "Papa! Papa!" Jamey leaped down to keep them from trampling one another and hushed them. "Mind your manners, girls, and say hello to your Aunt Becca."

The transformation was instantaneous. "Hello, Aunt Becca!" echoed from every throat. Then Kat was coming toward them with the baby in her arms. "You must be Rebecca. I'm Katerina. Welcome to our home. I hope you'll make it yours."

"Thank you. I'm grateful to be here at last."

Jamey put a protective arm around his sister's shoulders and spoke quietly in her ear. "Welcome to my valley."

Chapter 4

Take a Deep Breath
and Start Anew

Franklin Township, Pennsylvania
October 1886

Jamey was relieved to see that Rebecca and Katerina had seemed to warm to one another at their first meeting. Was it the presence of the children, Becca's first experience with being an aunt? Was it the bracing mountain air? The sheltering of the valley that seemed to cradle the small farm within the shadows of the eastern hills? Becca was not quite sure, but she felt the tension that had plagued her ever since the earthquake begin to drain away. When Katerina reached out a hand, Becca let herself be led into the warm kitchen, where she was soon ensconced in a comfortable rocker with a cup of tea at her side and somehow, mysteriously, a purring kitten on her lap.

"I don't know if you're used to having pets in the house," Katerina said. "If she's bothering you, I'll have the girls take her outside, but cats are simply a part of our lives around here."

"No, no! I love it. She's making me feel very welcome."

"You are welcome, Rebecca. Jamey has talked so much about you that I've always felt that I knew you, but having you here is a real pleasure for all of us. I'm only sorry that it took such a disaster to bring you to us."

"Sometimes it takes a disaster to shake us out of our complacency. Without the earthquake, I might never have gotten to meet your beautiful girls—or you."

While Becca sipped her tea, Katerina bustled around the kitchen, taking an iron skillet of fragrant corn bread from the oven and placing it on a warming hob, while periodically stirring a cast-iron pot that was giving off a bouquet of tantalizing odors.

"What smells so good?" Becca asked.

"It's just a beef stew with plenty of vegetables from our garden. We don't have much and we eat simply, but nobody has ever gone hungry in my kitchen. Oh, and there's an apple pandowdy for dessert."

"A . . . a what?"

"An apple pandowdy!" Katerina laughed at her citified sister-in-law. "You'll get used to our country ways and Pennsylvania Dutch recipes soon enough. A pandowdy is like an apple pie, except you cook the apples in an iron skillet with just a top crust. And then about halfway through

the baking time, you break up the crust and shove the pieces down into the bubbling apple juice so they soak up all
that sweet goodness. It looks a mess, but add a dollop of
cream on top, and you'll beg for mercy!"

"I'm sure I will. I'm afraid I'm not very creative in the
kitchen. I'll have much to learn from you."

Becca watched as Katerina finished her dinner preparations. She seemed to be several places at once, deftly balanc-
ing plates and corralling children at the same time. Rebecca
was happy to have some quiet time to observe her sister-in-
law. Katerina was plainer than Rebecca had expected her
to be. She was tiny and slight of figure, but strong at the
same time. She wore her light brown hair pulled severely
back from her face and tucked into an untidy knot, as if
she might have just managed it with one hand while doing
the laundry with the other. She had a pair of wire-framed
spectacles balanced on her nose, and her pale blue eyes were
overshadowed by her heavy brow. Her collarless dress was
clean and well-ironed, but unremarkable in either style or
pattern. And over it she had tied an all-purpose apron, whose
pockets bulged with several unidentified objects. Rebecca
smiled to herself at the sight of the apron, remembering the
traditional white aprons of her Mennonite in-laws.

Taken at first glance, Katerina was the last girl Becca
might have chosen to catch her brother's eye. She had been
expecting a much different woman, and yet, there was something rather appealing about this one. She had a look in her
eye that suggested she was not above a bit of mischief. Her

lips curved upward in a secret smile. She hummed as she worked, revealing a beautifully resonant voice. And when her eyes lit on one of her daughters, her entire face softened with love. Jamey's a lucky man, Becca decided.

Mealtime was relaxed and fun. The girls plied their aunt with questions about what she liked and what she did with her time, until Katerina told them to let Aunt Becca eat her dinner. They hushed, each one pressing her little lips together in obedience but sneaking sideways glances to watch the new family member. Jamey wanted to be brought up to date on the family activities. Katerina hushed him, too, suggesting that it was a topic best discussed once the girls were in bed. But when the adults pulled their chairs closer to the fire, the warmth and good food lulled Becca into dozing. Understanding that she had had a very long trip, Katerina led her to a small dormer room upstairs and tucked her into a feather bed topped with a much-laundered quilt. She fell asleep instantly.

❧

In the morning, Becca found her way back to the kitchen and discovered that she was the last one up. Jamey was just headed out the door. "I'm meeting the hired hands in the north field to stack hay bales," he told Katerina. "If you could bring the big wagon out there in an hour or so, we'll be ready to start moving them to the barn."

"I'll be there as soon as I get the lunchtime soup on the simmer," she replied.

Jamey ducked out, barely missing Nora, who came in with a pail of milk, and Millie, carrying a small basket of eggs. "That red chicken is hiding her eggs again," Millie reported. "I thought she was pretty when we got her, but she sure is ornery!"

Katerina grinned without turning around. "*Schön, wie schön tut,*" she replied.

"Yes, Mama, we know! Pretty is as pretty does," Nora replied.

"Do the girls speak German?" Becca asked.

"Not really, or at least no more than I do. I grew up hearing my mother make wise pronouncements in German, so I have quite a repertoire of useful nuggets. Saves time when I want to lecture—or when I'm thinking something that I shouldn't say out loud. I can say '*Du bist ein Dummeresel*' with a smile on my face, and no one is insulted."

"And it means—?"

"You are a dumb a . . . uh . . . a stupid donkey, to put it nicely."

Becca laughed in understanding and then changed the subject. "You all sound awfully busy this morning. Is there anything I can do to help?"

"With the haying? No, I wouldn't recommend it. But if you could keep an eye on the girls this morning while I'm needed out in the field, I would be grateful to you. They shouldn't be any trouble, but one never knows when one of them is going to need something that Nora can't handle."

"Of course. I'd love that. It will give me a chance to get to know them better."

Becca could not look at these tiny versions of Jamey without smiling to herself. She watched their faces and saw traces of the Grenville family in every one of them. Nora, at age eight, is the most like me, Becca thought. She is already a caregiver for her smaller sisters. Millie, age five, was the perpetually cheerful one, laughing off small insults and injuries with a charm that reminded Becca of her sister Charlotte. Lillian was just a year younger than Millie but her polar opposite. She was quiet, watchful, waiting for something. Another Mary Sue, perhaps? Little Ruby was only two, but Becca already saw in her the impish troublemaker that her father had been in their own family. Then, of course, there was seven-year-old Martha.

"Is there . . ." Becca hesitated, not sure whether she would be touching a too-sensitive nerve with her next question. "Is there anything I should know about Martha?"

Katerina took a deep breath before answering, "Well, she's slower than the other girls, but of course you've already noticed that. Her birth was . . . difficult. She arrived unannounced in the middle of the day, when I was all alone in the house—too quickly for me to summon help. She was born with her umbilical cord wrapped tightly around her neck. I unwrapped the cord as fast as I could but not fast enough. She was blue and not breathing. In desperation, I shook her and blew into her mouth. Eventually, she gave a weak cry and started to breathe on her own. But her inability to breathe in those first crucial minutes has left her with several problems." As Katerina recounted the story, her face was curiously empty of emotion, almost as if she had deliberately shut down.

"She has been slow to walk and even slower to talk. Even now, she barely communicates, her vocabulary limited to words such as mama, papa, eat, sleep, or no. She seldom cries or laughs. For a while, I worried that she was deaf or blind or both, because she did not respond to sounds or movement. We've talked to the doctor about her, but he has no help to offer. Now, for the most part, we simply accept her as she is and let her grow at her own pace. She won't give you any trouble. Just don't expect her to interact with you."

"Perhaps . . . in time?"

"We try not to think in those terms, because . . . well, because she may never change. She's just . . . Martha." Katerina's voice was harsh as she rejected Becca's attempt to sound encouraging. Then she shook herself, as if trying to shed the burden she carried. "She'll be fine."

❦

In the following days, Becca came to adore her young nieces. She had often heard people say that there was a special bond between an aunt and her nieces, but because her only aunt, her mother's sister Annaliese, lived far away, she had never experienced that kind of relationship. Now Jamey's girls turned out to be everything a new aunt could have hoped for. They bonded almost instantly. The girls looked at Becca with adoration in their eyes. They fingered her Charleston-bought gowns and studied her hairstyles. They brought her small tributes—bunches of bedraggled flowers plucked from the woods and clutched in grubby fists. They willingly ate her amateur attempts at making sandwiches for lunch and assured her that, whenever she was ready to bake them some cookies, they would be eager to help. If Becca had been a bit more attuned to Katerina's reactions, she might have recognized a touch of resentment at the amount of time the girls were spending with their newly discovered aunt. But Becca was still something of an innocent when it came to the family dynamics, so she let herself revel in their sweet attention.

Jamey had been right about his daughters' need to connect to their Grenville roots. The girls particularly enjoyed hearing stories of Becca's and Jamey's childhood—tales of holidays spent with their Dubois grandparents, summer vacations on Edisto Island, the fun they had in their Logan Street house before it burned in the Great Charleston Fire. Even Martha seemed to enjoy hearing about the Aiken farm, the peach orchards, and Uncle Eddie's peacock. Now and then, she would creep closer and rest her cheek on Becca's forearm as she listened. And Becca cherished such moments. Still, she realized that her presence in the house put an additional burden on Katerina, so she asked to see the cottage Jamey had told her about.

Jamey drove her over in his little farm wagon the next Sunday afternoon. Her first impression was that it was a house for elves, surely not big enough for a woman who often towered over the men in a crowd. But once inside, she discovered it was perfect—large enough to hold comfortable furnishings and cozy enough to wrap itself protectively around her—her own private valley, perhaps.

"It's lovely, Jamey. Someday I must hear the full story of how it came to be built. But not today," she added. "Today, I just want to discover what all is here. Look! It has a small parlor with its own fireplace, a roomy kitchen with a fat wood-burning iron stove and a round family dining table, a bedroom with lots of storage space, and an adjoining bathroom with its own pump. How clever!"

"The gentleman who built it equipped it with every imaginable creature comfort—the rocking chair by the fireplace, softly padded chairs and sofa in the parlor, the wide iron bedstead, handmade quilts, and sturdy but decorative pottery plates and cups. He was hoping to satisfy his mother-in-law, although he should have known that would be impossible."

Becca wandered outside to inspect the window boxes just waiting to be planted, a plot for a vegetable garden, a rose trellis, a wishing well, and, in the back, a stable with room for a small horse and surrey. "It's like a fairy tale come to life," she said.

"I've saved the best for last," Jamey said, leading her back inside and opening a side door. A multi-windowed sunroom attached to the south side of the cottage provided wide vistas of autumn's brightest leaves and a rippling creek just beyond the yard. "Mr. Hazen's mother-in-law was an artist," Jamey explained. "He thought she would enjoy this studio, but she refused to consider using it. So now it is yours, and you are welcome to use the desk and the books, the pencils and sketch pads, as you see fit."

"I've always dreamed of being a writer," Becca admitted. "I even started keeping a journal—still write in it now and then. I thought perhaps I would try writing a novel when I took over the Charleston house, but I never found the time. Maybe here, I can actually do it."

Rebecca's Journal

October 28, 1889
Magnolia Cottage

*I*t's hard to imagine that I've been here for three years now. When I moved into the cottage, I thought of it as a temporary landing, a place to collect my thoughts and decide what I wanted to do with the rest of my life. That first fall season was lovely, and I was content.

Then came winter and the snow. Oh, we had seen snow flurries in Aiken once in a while. The weather would turn cold, the wind would pick up, and perhaps the roof would catch a few flakes. But then the sun would come out, and the snow would be gone. I thought of it as frosting on a cake, not a wild barrier to survival. Pennsylvania snow is different. The first snowfall caught me entirely by surprise. The first flakes were beautiful and fluffy, clumping as they fell. But then they *began to pile up, and the winds swirled them around and deposited them in ever-deepening drifts. By the next morning, the world was white and the snow piled so deep on my front porch that I could not open the door. I thought I would surely die, buried under this deadly white shroud.*

Then Jamey arrived—ever-faithful Jamey—making his way across the fields on something he called snowshoes. He brought a shovel and cleared my paths to the mailbox, the road, the henhouse, and the outhouse. I was grateful, but I still expected a quick melt. It didn't happen. Thus I met my first real winter, as other storms added to the piles and the snow turned to ice. By March, I was ready to walk to Charleston, if that meant I could get out from under these drifts and back to the winter warmth of the Atlantic coast. And that didn't happen, either.

Instead, I was charmed by the spring melt-off, the buds bursting from the bare trees, the birds flocking back, the first tiny mushrooms and snowbells stretching through the ground cover to promise the coming of warmer days. And I've been here ever since.

During that second year, I learned my way around town. I met the postmistress, the schoolteacher, and the milliner who designed hats and embroidered lacy handkerchiefs in her spare time as she waited for customers. I joined the Ladies Aid Society at the local parish church and made friends among the other spinsters in the area—of whom there turned out to be a great many. And before I even realized what was happening, the North Sewickley community became my new home.

Chapter 5

Mighty Oaks
from Little Acorns Grow

Magnolia Cottage
May 1, 1890

Becca was sitting on her front stoop, hoping to catch a small breeze passing through the yard. On her lap lay an unused sketchpad and a soft pencil. Last night, she had thought this might be the day she could start to write her novel, but when it actually came time to put pencil to paper, she found she had nothing to say.

Instead, she watched as her new kitten rolled and tumbled in the grass. Tabitha was a beautiful silver tabby (hence her name) with pristine white paws and a white tip to her tail. At the moment, she was fully engaged in trying to catch a fly, which seemed to be having as much fun in the game as the kitten was. The fly would try to land on her nose. She would shake her head to knock him off and then pound on the spot where she thought he had landed. Once or twice, she was sure she had been successful, but that presented a new problem. The fly was on the ground, and the kitten's paw was on top of the fly. Now what to do with it? Becca giggled to herself as she watched. After what seemed to be an interminable wait, the kitten lifted her paw and looked underneath it. And away flew the fly, only to do a couple of loops and come back to start the game all over again.

Almost without thinking about it, Becca picked up her pencil and began to draw the furry ball she was watching. Sometimes, the only distinguishable features were the four paws with their pink pads in the air. At other times, it was a tiny pointed tail sticking straight up, the kitten's rear wiggling in anticipation. Without thinking or second-guessing herself, Becca almost covered the page with kitten poses. Then she looked at them in surprise. They're not half-bad, she thought. I never knew I could draw.

She looked at the kitten more closely, and this time, she found she was unconsciously noticing shapes and proportions: the head a circle, the almond-shaped eyes lying along the bottom of an imaginary diameter, the small muzzle— almost a figure eight—at the bottom of the circle, and the pointed ears as an extension of a continuing line from muzzle to cheek. She was only entertaining herself, or so she thought.

A jingle of bells drew her attention, as a small cart pulled by a reluctant mule came around the bend. Eleven-year-old Nora, the oldest of Jamey's daughters, was astride the mule, teasing him with a wand from which hung several bells on leather straps. The mule flicked his ears at the sound and tried to walk faster to escape the annoyance. And from the cart came shouts and giggles: "Go, Mortimer! Giddyup! Tickle him behind his ear, Norry."

Grinning broadly with delight in her newfound ability to drive, Nora waved. "Hi, Aunt Becca! We've come to bring you a picnic lunch. Or at least Momma is bringing the picnic lunch. I just had the job of getting all these urchins over here without losing any one of them in the woods." She slid to the ground and tossed the reins around a small tree. Then, one by one, she unloaded her charges. First Martha, who needed a hand and a steadying grip from Millie to help her get down from the cart. Next came Lillian and Ruby, sitting at the edge of the cart and then sliding off. And last, Nora lifted three-year-old Gloria and swung her in the air as she lowered her to her feet. "Are you glad to see us? You're not too busy, are you?"

"Oh, I'm never too busy for you girls. I love having you drop in like this. You know you are always welcome. It's a little early for lunch, though, isn't it?"

"Not for us. We've been up since way before sunrise."

"Why? Did something happen?"

"Oh, Aunt Becca, it's May Day!"

"Uh . . ." Becca was still looking puzzled.

"Don't you know? On the first day of May, you have to get up very early and wash your face in the dew on the grass. That's how you can be sure you'll be beautiful!"

"Really? No, I guess I missed that lesson. It's one of your mother's sayings, isn't it?"

"Sure. She says we all have to do it every year so we can be certain we'll catch a good husband when we grow up."

Becca tried not to let her disapproval show. "I'll have to ask your mother about that. Did you say she's on the way?"

"Yes, she's bringing the picnic hamper, but she said she'd rather walk than ride with old Mortimer here. So we came on ahead."

"Ah, there she is now, coming around the bend. Perhaps I'd better go and see if I can help."

But Katerina shrugged off any effort to share her load. "This is your surprise, Becca. You hadn't forgotten it's your birthday, had you?"

"Oh! I guess I had. Once you turn forty, you are officially allowed to quit counting birthdays."

"Not when you have children around," Katerina laughed. "Nora and Millie have been talking about this for weeks."

"Well, come inside and unload your treasures. I'm dying to know what we're having for lunch."

"This big jar has lemon juice and sugar in it. I thought we could add your water—save me from carrying it all the way over here."

"Water, I can manage."

"Then deviled eggs, meat salad sandwiches on biscuits . . ."

"Oh, I love those! You're going to have to teach me how to make the filling."

"All you need is an old meat grinder and a couple of young'uns to crank the handle."

"But what do you put in it?"

"Leftover cold meat—whatever's available. Today's version grew out of Sunday's pot roast. Then lots of sweet onion, celery, dill pickles, whatever happens to be lying about. And something to bind it together a little. Today, we used old mashed potatoes, but it could be salad dressing, sour cream, or plain milk. Then you chill it and let all the flavors sort of soak themselves up. Easy."

"And delicious. Ah, carrot sticks, too, I see."

"Yes, because I insist on the girls eating their vegetables. But there's also a reward of sugar cookies and little apples at the bottom of the basket."

"A feast fit for the angels. But, speaking of angels, where are they?"

"Still in the yard, I guess. Probably playing with your new kitten. Girls? Time for lunch."

Katerina turned toward the door to emphasize her call, then stopped, staring at the front porch. There on the top step sat ten-year-old Martha, her straggly head bent over a piece of paper, deep in concentration. For Martha, the pose was extraordinary.

Katerina moved quietly to her daughter's side. "What is that paper you have, Martha?"

The little girl turned to display the page on which Becca had been doing her cat sketches.

"Ta-di-ta," she said.

"What? *Du bist ein strobelkopf*," she said with a smile, as she tousled the little girl's hair. "You're my own little simpleton, aren't you?"

"Tadita, Tadita!" Martha was pointing to the sketches and then at the yard. "Tadita!"

From behind her, Becca gasped. "Tabitha?"

Martha smiled. "Tadita." She nodded.

"Thank you, darling. You recognized her, didn't you?"

Becca and Katerina exchanged wide-eyed glances. What they were witnessing seemed an amazing break-through. For the very first time, this little girl had made a connection between the marks on a piece of paper and a live object.

Becca knelt beside her. "That's very good, Martha. Would you like another picture?"

Martha nodded, and another smile broke through.

"What shall I draw for you?" Becca wondered out loud.

Martha shrugged.

Knowing how limited her talents were, Becca hesitated and then drew a long wavy line with a bit of a head at one end — a dot for an eye and a curve for a mouth. "How about a worm?"

"Wum!" Martha shouted and nodded vigorously.

The excitement in her voice drew the attention of the other children, and they clustered around to see what was going on. As they watched, two opposing curves became a fish.

"Fiths!"

The shape of a half walnut shell needed only a head and some feet to reveal its own name.

"Tuttle."

Tears filled Katerina's eyes. "I didn't even know she understood those words," she said. "You seem to have mysteriously unlocked something in her mind."

"I wish I really knew how to draw," Becca lamented. "I'm about out of talent here."

"You could draw a flower, couldn't you, Aunt Becca?" Nora suggested. "You know, just a circle in the center with petals around it, a stem, and a couple of leaves."

"Fwower," came Martha's response. And so it went, through a tree, a house, a cloud—simple line drawings that allowed a child to make a connection between a word and its object.

They were all so engrossed that lunch was forgotten, until Jamey's booming voice broke through the spell. "Hey, where is lunch, Birthday Girl?"

The interruption startled them all. Then everyone was talking at once, and Martha was tugging at her father's arm, saying "Wum!"

As he often had to do in a household full of women, Jamey held up both hands in surrender. "That's enough, all of you. I can tell you're excited, and that's wonderful, but this is Aunt Becca's day, and I made a special trip in from the cornfields to have a bite of lunch with all of you. Can we get on with the important issue of eating and save the earthshaking news until later?"

Becca grinned at her irrepressible brother. "This time I'm grateful for your single-minded interest in food, brother dear. These girls are about to exhaust my meager abilities. Let's work on these meat salad sandwiches. Then I'll try to explain what's been happening here."

Katerina was about to say something, but Becca patted her hand. "I know, Kat. You want to keep this excitement going, but I think it will be best to stop now, before our little girl gets tired of it. That way, she'll be more willing to go back to working with the images later." Becca hurried inside, ignoring the anger-filled glance that Katerina aimed at her back.

❧

Becca sat up very late that night, trying to understand what had triggered the breakthrough in Martha's understanding. Then she had to face the more serious question of what to do next. I know nothing about how children learn, she thought. But maybe the children's teacher will have a clearer understanding of what is going on. I want to do anything I can to help, but I don't want to make a crucial mistake.

The next morning, she walked over to visit with Katerina while the children were all busy elsewhere.

"I know Martha went to school for a few days and then stopped. What happened? Can you tell me?"

Once again, Katerina forced herself to respond normally to this new relative who kept pushing her way into the family. "She was terrified. Nora and Millie tried to sit with her and help, but apparently all she did was cry—not loud, but quiet tears running down her cheeks, sniffling, shoulders shaking. Mrs. Dunning is a wonderfully kind woman, but she couldn't do a thing to help, either. Finally, she brought Martha home and asked me not to send her again. She said the struggle was just too much for the child to bear."

"How sad!"

"I was heartbroken for her, because I had hoped being with the other children would help her somehow, but it was not to be. She's happy here with me when school is in session. At least that's something to cling to." Katerina wanted to drop the discussion right there.

"Of course, but . . . uh, would you mind if I talked to Mrs. Dunning about her?"

"*Einige Dinge verändern sich nicht.* Some things never change!" Katerina frowned with irritation. "She's my daughter, and I love her the way she is. You needn't interfere and try to fix her."

"I'm not trying to fix Martha. I'm only trying to help myself understand. Something important happened yesterday, Kat, and I want to see it continue. But I don't know much about children. I thought Mrs. Dunning might be able to offer some suggestions as to what happened and what we should do next. I've met her several times at church, and she seems approachable."

"If you think it will help, go ahead, but I won't hold my breath."

On a hunch that a dedicated teacher would be at work even in these summer months, Becca went home by way of the one-room schoolhouse that served the small North Sewickley settlement. As she expected, she found the teacher with her skirts hiked up around her waist, on her knees, hand-scrubbing the floors of the schoolroom.

"My goodness! Do you have to do all this work around here?"

"No one else is about to do it," the older woman said with a small laugh that held little humor. "I try to get things in good shape during the summer, because there's no time once this room is full of children."

"I still don't think it ought to be part of your job. Can I help?"

"No, Miss Grenville. It's kind of you to offer, but I'm about through for today. I work in small sections. A little at a time gets it all done. Truth is, I'd welcome a chance to get up off these knees." She stood slowly, arching her back to try to relieve the stiffness in her body. "Is there something I can help you with?"

"Actually there is, but I hate to impose on your time."

"Like I said, I need an excuse to quit scrubbing floors. We can go out on the porch, if you'd rather. It smells better out there, without the fragrance of lye soap and carbolic acid."

Briefly, Becca described the breakthrough the family had seen in Martha the day before. "I'm excited that she seemed to understand, and it was the first time I had ever seen her smile. But I don't want to make a mistake and undo any progress we've made. I thought you might be able to suggest the next step."

Mrs. Dunning leaned back in her chair and stared off into the distance for several minutes. "It is important, Miss Grenville. You are absolutely correct. I'd like to think about the problem for a day or so, rather than rush you through some quick advice. Children like Martha are so special. We're only now beginning to realize that they have more potential than we once assumed. Let me work on the problem and talk to a couple of people I know. Can we talk again, perhaps next Friday?"

"Certainly."

"Good. Come by any time. And bring some of the drawings with you, if you don't mind. You'll find me still on my knees. Maybe I'll be praying for guidance while I'm scrubbing."

Chapter 6

A Picture Freezes the Moment

*B*ecca arrived at the schoolhouse right after breakfast the next Friday, the drawings carefully folded into a small cardboard box. "I brought all the drawings we used last week, but I'm afraid they're not going to tell you much. They're really primitive. I've never had a drawing lesson of any kind, and the children were pressing me to keep coming up with new objects. They're just rough pencil sketches."

"But very good! It has only taken you a few lines to suggest the object. Our own human eye then supplies the rest of the detail. Fascinating! Are you sure you've never had any training?"

"None at all. But it has occurred to me, as I looked back over them, that their simplicity might have been what appealed to Martha. What do you think?"

"I think you and I are on identical tracks here." Mrs. Dunning smoothed the drawings as she talked. "There are no extra details to confuse a child. In this case, that's the key. But come back to my inner sanctum, to what the township fathers laughingly call an office and I would identify as a rather large closet. I've just brought the kettle in from the hearth, and there's a pot of tea brewing. I want us to be comfortable as we explore this problem."

"Oh, this is cozy—no extra details for distraction here, either," Becca quipped.

"Well, you're right on that account." Mrs. Dunning busied herself for a few minutes laying out the teacups and sugar cubes. Then she pulled up a rocker opposite Becca's chair. "Now, then, here's what may be going on."

For the next several minutes, she laid out the sources of her information—a children's doctor, a book on birth injuries, and another on the teaching of "difficult" students. "Doctors don't know what happens when a baby isn't able to breathe right away at birth. Some recover without damage. Others 'fail to thrive,' as the doctors say. In other words, they wither away and die. Martha seems to fall somewhere in the middle of those two extremes."

"But you can't tell us why she doesn't talk, why she seems totally detached from the world around her?"

"No, I can't, but we know that children like her frequently have difficulty making sense of their world."

"Yes, I know that Katerina was worried for a while that Martha might be blind or deaf, because she didn't respond to noises around her."

"When, in fact, the exact opposite is probably true."

"How so?"

"These children have brains that process information much more slowly than in normal people. But while they are, for example, trying to identify a single sound—What was that? Where did it come from?—the world keeps bombarding them with new sounds, until they simply have to stop hearing even the first one."

"How frightening!"

"Indeed. Imagine a kitten that can move so fast, you never see it. The most you can see is a gray blur swirling around you. Then comes a screech, and a scratch opens up on your arm. It starts to bleed, and it hurts. But you didn't see what caused it. All you know is that the blur is still around you and that, when it is, you sometimes get hurt. So you pull away. You roll yourself into a ball and hide your head, while the kitten, whatever it is, keeps blurring past you."

Becca was shaking her head, not in denial but in a wish not to hear more. Yet she was beginning to understand the terrible world in which her niece lived every day. "But the pictures of Tabitha? How did they help?"

"Simple—a picture freezes the moment. The whirling dervish stands still. The kitten materializes into a recognizable shape."

"When we first noticed Martha with the kitten sketches, she was sitting quietly, almost poring over those pictures."

"Absorbing them. Learning from them, as she could not learn from the real Tabitha, who refused to be still even for a moment."

Becca was quiet for a long while. Then she looked up with a new question. "But after she saw the pictures, and after she identified them as Tabitha, she pointed to the real kitten. Something else changed."

"Ah, that's the real turning point, isn't it? After she understood the picture, she knew what to look for, and the blur resolved itself into a real kitten. She was, in effect, teaching her brain to isolate an image."

"So what's next?"

"Well, first, you and the others around Martha will have to learn to slow down the things that are bombarding her senses—all of them. I would recommend that her parents try to shelter her from loud noises, for example."

"Easier said than done in a household with six daughters under the age of twelve. There's a new toddler now, you know—little Gloria, and she's a screamer."

"They'll have to try. Bright lights can be a problem, too. Flashing or flickering candlelight can be disorienting. Then, of course, the other senses. I'm guessing she hates sharply flavored foods, vinegar, spices, even too much sugar. Smells. She avoids the barn, doesn't she? And skin sensations."

"Yes, she hates wool, even when that's the only thing that can keep her warm."

"It's pretty obvious that that's what's going on. If her parents can slow down her life, they will give her time to sort out her experiences."

"Can you explain that to them? I'm in a difficult position here. Katerina reacts badly if I suggest anything about how she is raising her children. Why, I'm not sure. Maybe she resents the fact that the girls come to me when they are angry with her. But the upshot is that she may refuse to act if I'm the one to tell her. I think she'd listen to you."

"I can certainly try, and I'll keep your name out of the discussion, if you think that will help."

"Yes, please. And in the meantime, is there anything I can do to further this language breakthrough? I've been practicing drawing other items from nature. I'm getting pretty good at mushrooms and ladybugs, but animals are a real challenge."

"Keep practicing. The more you do, the more you'll get the hang of it. And two other things you may want to add— but add very slowly. First, color. These sketches are all in lead pencil, which is fine, but she's going to have to live in a world of color. If you can get access to some pastels, you might try tinting some of the pictures. No bright red flowers, of course, but maybe a soft pink one. A nice tan little worm."

"All right. That I can do. What's the other thing?"

"Stories."

Becca let out a huge sigh. "I've always wanted to be a writer, but I find I'm not much good at grown-up stories. Do you think children's tales would be easier?"

"They need to be very simple and short. For instance, Mr. Worm finds that the rain is filling up his underground home. So he crawls out onto the lawn. But now a bird is looking at him as if he's lunch. So he hides under a large toadstool. The bird goes after a bug instead. Think of it like this: A problem arises. The hero faces the problem. The solution causes a new problem. The hero wins. End of story. It gives her a line of thought to remember and teaches her a lesson about figuring out what to do with problems. All excellent training. And I think you'll be very good at it."

"I'll give it a try, but I'm not as sure as you are."

"Bring me the first few things you write, and we'll go over them. Everything takes practice, my dear. Even when you're all grown up."

That afternoon, Becca decided to start training herself to see her world through the awakening eyes of little Martha. Instead of standing in the yard and taking in the whole picture of her fairytale cottage, with its manicured yard and the woods surrounding it, she walked close to individual objects and focused on them, one at a time. Instead of seeing a rose bush, she plucked a single petal, felt its velvety surface, gently traced the veins that gave it life, smelled its faint fragrance. She noticed an overturned mushroom and watched an exercise in persistence as a tiny spider crawled over the gills of the underside, climbing the membranes one by one, toppling over the top, and then starting the climb on the next one. She scooped a small handful of pebbles from the path and spread them out on the palm of her hand, noting which ones matched in color, which were smooth, and which were broken. She felt as if her own little world had shattered itself into thousands of tinier worlds, each one harboring secrets she had known nothing about.

She closed her eyes and listened, until she could pick out the individual sounds that made up a formerly un-heard chorus around her. Songbirds trilled their messages from tree to tree. A bumblebee hummed its way through the marigold patch. Dried oak leaves, still clinging to their branches, rattled against one another as if discussing whether or not it was time to make that last long leap to the ground. A cricket crossed the path, stopping to send out a Morse code of clicks. Cicadas deep in the woods rattled their shells and advertised their presence for miles around. A grasshopper produced a buzz by rubbing his legs together.

Finally, a squirrel caught her imagination by stopping in the middle of her lawn to chatter away, as if scolding her for being in his path. She watched him for a long time, being care-ful not to move. Satisfied that she was not a threat, he went on about his business. Under one oak tree, he gathered acorns and stuffed them into his mouth until his cheeks stretched and bulged. Then, leaping quickly across the open grass, he scurried up another tree and disappeared. Becca stared at the bark of that tree until she could see the crack that must open into a nest. Patient waiting rewarded her. The small nose poked out of the crack. The little head turned sideways, and a paw reached out and took hold of the tree bark. Bit by bit, the squirrel extracted himself from his hidey-hole. Tail twitching, he carefully surveyed the whole yard before slithering down the tree, back across the grass, and opening wide for his next mouthload.

"There's a whole story!" Becca exclaimed to Tabitha, who had been watching the exercise with fearful curiosity. "That's the key. The stories are out here. I only have to find them and then write them down."

After a quick dinner of leftover soup, Becca turned her attention to another problem. She had told Mrs. Dunning that she didn't know how to draw. That was certainly true, but how did one learn? she wondered. One answer was surely to draw from observation, but that would be nearly impossible with a squirrel for a subject. He was too quick to allow her to see details.

She sighed with impatience at her own incompetence and thought of little Martha. She would surely love a story about a squirrel; her word for it would be something like "kwerly." But how to stop those quick movements, so Martha could see him? How to draw a picture? Frustrated again, she looked around her rooms, and the answer was suddenly obvious. In the parlor was a bookshelf that held multiple volumes of an encyclopedia. Why? Becca could only imagine a persistent salesman showing up while Mr. Hazen was moving furniture into the house. Perhaps the books had even come with their own bookcase. Whatever the story behind the story, there they were, and when she opened the *S* volume, it took no time at all to discover a line drawing of a squirrel—several of them, as a matter of fact, in different poses. She studied the pictures for a long time, noting geometric shapes and proportions. The tail is as long as the whole squirrel, she noted, and the little paws have four fingers each. The ears are tiny, there's no bridge to his nose, and his eyes are set on either side of his head, instead of in front.

As Becca studied the pages of the encyclopedia, she began to understand more than just squirrel anatomy. This book is doing for me exactly what I want my book to do for Martha, she realized. It has stopped my world from spinning long enough to let me see the details I might have otherwise missed. It was not a particularly original thought, but for Becca it seemed to be fitting in the last piece of the puzzle.

"I can do this," she told Tabitha. "I'll start in the morning. You keep an eye out and let me know if Mr. Squirrel shows up in the yard. Maybe some day, I can write a wonderful children's book and help Martha at the same time."

Chapter 7

Man Proposes . . .

The Grenville Farm
1892–1893

*T*he girls had learned Becca was working on writing a book about a squirrel and were eager to help. Most days, they could be found clustered around her large desk, picking through the squirrel sketches and making helpful comments.

"What kind of animal is this?"

"I think it's a beaver," announced Millie.

"It's not a beaver," Becca assured them. "It just looks big because there's nothing else in the picture to show his size."

"No, it's definitely a beaver. Look at those teeth and that broad tail."

"I'm not writing a story about a beaver."

"Why not? Beavers make great stories. They cut down trees and build underwater houses and hold den meetings." Lillian was always the defender of the oppressed.

"Maybe so, but I'm writing about a squirrel."

"That's a squirrel? With a beaver tail?"

No, squirrels have big tails, too. And big teeth. They are both rodents."

"Woden," Martha said, making Becca laugh at the Norse mythology parallel.

"Yes, but squirrel tails are fuzzy. You need to learn how to draw fuzzy!" Ruby was the one with the advice.

"And squirrel teeth are pretty small. I've never even seen a squirrel's teeth."

"You've never seen one with his mouth open."

"No, but his whole mouth isn't very big. His teeth would have to be pretty small, or they wouldn't fit behind his lips."

"Squirrels don't have lips."

"Yes, they do, but they're really small."

Becca surrendered. "Why don't we make some cookies?"

After several more attempts at drawing unsatisfactory squirrel pictures, she decided to return to Mr. Worm. "Mrs. Dunning outlined a story about a worm for me. I'm going to do that one first, to be sure I'm creating the kind of book she thinks will help Martha," she explained.

"I'm not sure I'm going to like that story," Nora said. "After the last time it rained, all the real worms crawled up out of the ground and onto the road. Then the sun came out and fried them. They ended up all black and flat and dead."

"What's dead?" little Gloria asked.

"Wum!" Martha shouted from across the room.

"This 'wum' is going to crawl onto the nice, cool, damp grass. He'll be fine."

"Until that bird eats him!" Ruby chortled.

"That's why he will hide under the mushroom," Lillian explained.

"Mushrooms don't grow in the grass."

"These do! Really, girls, you're not helping me much."

"But, Aunt Becca, you're writing for children. We're just trying to show you how children think of things," Nora said.

"Believe me, I'm learning."

Once fall arrived and the children went off to school, Becca thought she might have more time to be creative, but she had forgotten about fall chores on the farm. Katerina was apologetic about interfering with her writing time, but she frequently needed help with putting up the jams and jellies, canning vegetables, and laying in supplies of winter roots. The two of them began to enjoy their time together, happily chatting away about recipes and old family stories, and Becca was happy to help.

On one particularly chilly morning, Katerina went off in search of another pair of socks, complaining that her feet were cold. Then she plopped down on a kitchen chair, commenting that she was already having trouble reaching her feet. "What am I going to do by the time winter really arrives?" she laughed.

Becca looked up from removing the stems from a basket of green beans and then took a second look, as Kat stood up and placed both hands on the small of her back, a gesture any woman would recognize. "Kat Grenville!" she said. "Are you carrying another baby?"

Kat grinned back at her. "Yes, and I'll share a secret if you promise not to breathe a word to Jamey."

"What? Surely you've told him."

"Oh, he knows there's a baby. What he doesn't know is that it's a baby boy!"

"Really? How can you be sure?"

"The signs are all there. Like my cold feet this morning. And the size of my waistline. I've always carried my girls without showing for months. But with this one, I'm only about four months along, and I already look like I've swallowed a watermelon. That's why I've been wearing aprons so often. Look!" She lifted the apron and smoothed her skirt over a distinctly round belly.

"He's riding low, too. I spend most of my days and half my nights running to the outhouse or reaching for the chamber pot."

"Why haven't I noticed before this? Every time I've been around you, you seemed to be feeling well."

"Oh, I am! And that's another sign. With the girls, I was always sick, right from the beginning. But with this little fellow, I feel great. I haven't gained a whole lot of weight, but I'm always hungry, and I can eat anything without a problem."

"Jamey is going to be thrilled."

"I'm sure you realize how much. He's wanted a son for so long. Every so often, he tells me that he's the last hope of the Grenville line to keep the name going. Oh, he loves his daughters, but when Gloria was born, he joked that maybe we ought to just give up and call her Grenville. But I don't want to get his hopes up. He's not going to recognize these signs, so we'll let him wait to be over the moon until his son appears."

"Well, that'll be another mouth to feed. We'd best get on with making things like applesauce!"

The next months passed swiftly, and in January, little James Grenville Jr. made his lusty, wailing entrance into the world. The ecstatic father jumped straight into the air when Becca emerged from the birthing room to tell him his son was waiting to meet him. The girls received the news with a little less enthusiasm.

"What'll we do with a boy around here?" Ruby pouted. "He'll get his own room, and the six of us will get crammed into the attic in layers."

"Oh, don't be so dramatic, Ruby. We older girls will be getting married soon, which will reduce your crowded conditions. You'll survive. I think it will be interesting," Nora said.

"Maybe so, but Mama and Papa will still love him best. I didn't see Papa jump that high when Gloria was born."

Despite her initial reluctance, even Ruby came to love little James. The girls cooed over him and argued about whose turn it was to have the privilege of rocking him or feeding him. They seemed to speak the words "my brother" in perpetual italics. That spring, it seemed that nothing could dampen the happiness in the Grenville household.

❦

Then came hurricane season. Jamey and Becca were still attuned enough to the South Carolina seasons to be aware that they were approaching the stormiest part of the year. But it was easy to forget about the heaviness in the air, the cloud buildups out over the Atlantic that presaged a storm at sea. In Pennsylvania, the newspapers did not even report warnings coming out of shipping lanes. There was no reason to worry about a hurricane in western Pennsylvania—unless you had family living in the path of one in South Carolina.

The Great Sea Island Hurricane of 1893 hit on Sunday, August 27, and the news did not reach the outside world for days. The reports did not reach Beaver County, Pennsylvania, for more than a week. Jamey first learned of the devastation when he purchased a copy of the following

Sunday's *Pittsburgh Post-Gazette*. The headlines were frightening enough to stop him in his tracks:

Sea Islands Wiped Out
City of Beaufort Destroyed
2,000 People Feared Dead

He hurried home, knowing that he would have to break the news to Becca.

"That can't be, Jamey! The Sea Islands wiped out? No! They've withstood storms for centuries." Becca stood with her arms wrapped around herself. She was shaking her head in denial.

"There's not much doubt about the truth of the stories, Becca. The paper is simply reprinting eyewitness reports from the Charleston and Savannah papers. But that doesn't mean that anything has happened to Mother and Father, or to Mary Sue and Eli."

"But it says here that St. Helena, Hilton Head, Daufuskie, Parris, and Lady's Island were all devastated. Lady's Island is where Mary Sue and Eli have their horse stables. Annie Moreau lives and teaches at the Penn School on St. Helena. And it says that there are some 20,000 people left homeless in Beaufort. What are we going to do? We have to find our family."

"We can't just go rushing off. Apparently, the Red Cross has rescue missions there already or on the way. The last thing they need is a bunch of distraught relatives underfoot. I'm going to wire Johnny. He may have more information because of his connection to a South Carolina senator."

When he arrived at the telegraph office, he found there was already a message from Johnny waiting for him:

KEEPING TABS ON HURRICANE SITUATION. CASUALTY REPORTS COMING TO SENATOR HAMPTON'S OFFICE. NO GRENVILLE OR MOREAU NAMES AMONG THEM. MAY ALL BE WELL. JOHNNY.

"This is good news, Rebecca. We have to be strong—and patient. If anything had happened to Father, Johnny would have been told. Say your prayers until we hear more."

❦

It took another three weeks for a letter to arrive from Susan Grenville. As had been her practice ever since the family had scattered in 1877, she sent the latest news in a round robin letter, with copies to each of her children.

Dear children—Johnny, Charlotte, Eddie, Becca, and Jamey—one and all.

I hope this letter finds you all well and not too worried about your beleaguered Sea Island relatives. Despite the inflammatory newspaper articles, our situation is not too bad. The storm hit on Sunday night, when people were home tucked into their beds. That was probably a good thing, for most families knew where everyone was. There was little or no warning before the 16-foot storm surge hit the shore, wiping out docks and small buildings right along the coast. Then came the winds and the downpours of rain. By morning, it was over, but it left a trail of destruction behind it.

Our house is situated on a small rise, which was enough to protect it from the flood, but your father's schoolhouse, located on the other side of the street, suffered major damage. We cannot yet be sure, but it will probably have to be demolished. As for Mary Sue and Eli, most of the buildings at Grenmore Plantation are the original structures, which were built on stilts, as is the custom in these sea islands. The design looks odd in dry weather, but a storm such as this proved the wisdom of such a design. The storm surge was able to flow under the buildings, and as long as it did not meet any resistance, it passed without damage. The Grenmore Stables are also located on high ground, so they missed the brunt of the wave. Some of their marsh ponies are missing, Mary Sue tells me, but Eli says they are used to storms and will wander home eventually.

We all have ample food stores—a carry-over, I suppose, from the war days, when we spent so much time putting up produce on the farm to feed ourselves during the winter. At any rate, we have not needed to avail ourselves of the rations being distributed by this new Red Cross organization. We leave those supplies to those in greater need than ourselves.

My only concern at this stage is your father's emotional state. Poor, dear man. All he has ever wanted to do is live in peace and teach young people about his beloved history. I had really hoped that this new Grenville Academy would be the fulfillment of his lifelong goal. Instead, it has once more been twisted out of his grasp. Classes have, of course, been suspended, as has most business hereabouts, but if the school building is as badly damaged as we believe it to be, it will be impossible to reopen. Your father is seventy-five years old, I would remind you—well past his biblical allotment of threescore and ten, as he so often tells me. This time it may be too late to start over.

Please do not worry about us, dear hearts. We are safe, and we will soldier on for as long as it is possible. Your loving mother,
Susan Grenville

❧

"You see?" Jamey said. "I told you everything would be all right in the end."

"No, Jamey," Becca replied. "Everything is not all right, and this is not the end. If I understand our mother, she is gently preparing us for worse to come."

Chapter 8

. . . God Disposes

*A*s usual, Becca was correct. In Beaufort, the situation remained dire. People driven from their island homes by the storm had flocked to Beaufort, only to find the streets impassable because of accumulated debris. The Red Cross efforts, led by Clara Barton, floundered, hindered by a second hurricane that hit Charleston in mid-October. That storm disrupted the distribution lines that had been providing relief supplies. Eventually, the centers for food supplies had to be moved out of Beaufort and onto the smaller islands to lure refugees back to the places they had abandoned. Sending people home relieved the pressure on Beaufort, but it did not solve the problems of the refugees. It would take almost a year for beleaguered sharecroppers to drain submerged lands, plant new crops, and rebuild homes and barns.

But the Grenvilles did not have that long. Becca received several short letters from Mary Sue, who was worried about their father's decline. "He has lost all interest in the world around him," she wrote. "I can't tell why. Maybe the disinterest is caused by some unidentified illness. Perhaps he is making himself sick because of his despair. Whatever is going on, he doesn't eat, he doesn't talk, he doesn't bathe. He's growing a beard because he can't be bothered to shave, and Mother says she doesn't trust herself to take a razor to his neck." By Christmas, he was refusing to get out of bed, and on the New Year's morning, Susan found him dead on his pillow.

"Do not try to come to Beaufort," Susan instructed her children. "Affairs are so unsettled here that it will be impossible to hold the usual funeral rituals. We shall be lucky to find a dry spot of ground on which to bury him. Please remember your father as he was at his finest. I myself will be trying to forget what he was like in these last few months. I do not want you to be witnesses to the ravages of time on his body."

Mary Sue and Eli took Susan into their home on Lady's Island when the governor of South Carolina politely but coldly informed her that the house in which the schoolmaster and his wife had been living must be returned to the possession of the State of South Carolina. But now it was Susan who fell into a state of despair. She and Jonathan had been a couple for so long that she could not deal with life without him. Within months, she, too, became ill, apparently from one of the swamp fevers that had gained new strength after the hurricanes had done their worst. She breathed her last in June.

The Grenville children floundered in their new condition of orphanhood. Two wonderful guiding figures in their lives were suddenly gone. There seemed to be no center to hold them all together.

"Maybe I should have stayed in Charleston and tried to repair the old Dubois house," Becca worried. "Then at least we'd all have somewhere to go to be together."

"You know that would have been impossible, dear heart," Jamey said, trying to soothe her conscience. "Besides, it wouldn't help now. By the terms of Grandmother DuBois's will, every bit of our parents' property reverts into the hands of their attorneys, who are to put it up for public auction."

"Oh dear, I had almost forgotten. How are we going to handle that?"

"There is nothing to handle, at least for us. The Middleton Law Firm will take over. I'm guessing that Eddie or Charlotte, or maybe both of them, will have to go to Charleston to arrange a preemptory bid on the Aiken lands. Everything else will simply go under the auctioneer's hammer, and once the lawyers have gobbled up their share, the remains will come to the six of us in equal shares."

"How sad it is to watch a family and its estate disintegrate before our eyes," Becca mourned. "To think that two lives can be reduced to a few figures written on a piece of paper."

⁓

And still the Fates were not through with the Grenville family. One day in September, the Grenville girls came home from school bearing a note from Mrs. Dunning. "Teacher said to be sure to give you this, Mama," Nora announced.

"A note from your teacher? Which one of you has been misbehaving?"

The girls stared back at her with wide, innocent eyes. "We didn't do anything bad, Mama, but they are closing the school."

"What!" Katerina tore open the note and skimmed its contents. Mrs. Dunning explained that one student had come down with diphtheria right after school opened. Now five more had symptoms. "This has all the earmarks of an epidemic," the note went on, "and because exposure can often spread the disease, I have decided to close the school until all cases have disappeared from our community. In the interim, I will be scrubbing everything with carbolic acid in hopes of eradicating any contagion. If any parents wish to take on the task of teaching your children at home, I will be happy to supply guidance. Please be aware that the closure may last through Christmas."

Katerina sighed. Oh, dear. I cannot hope to teach all six girls, she thought to herself. Whatever will we do? She sent the girls out to play, which would allow her some time to mull over her options. Maybe Becca, she thought. But she might never have worked up the courage to make such a request if Becca had not chosen that moment to drop by for a visit.

"I hope I'm not intruding," she said. "I know it's silly, but since Mother's death, I've been feeling more and more alone in my little cottage. I know she was never there, but I always felt I could talk to her in my imagination. Now she's gone, and I seem to bounce off those walls. Can you stand some company while I get my head together?"

"I think we're all feeling a little bit that way," Katerina said. "Even though I did not know Jamey's mother, she has left a hole in my heart. Although, I admit, right now I'm not very lonesome."

"What do you mean? If you're busy, I'll . . ."

"No, no. I'm happy to see you, but I am wrestling with a problem of my own. Here, read this note. The girls brought it home from school today."

Becca read silently. At one point, she gave an audible gasp.

"What's wrong?"

"Nothing. I just had an idea. Why don't I take charge of teaching the girls while the school is closed? I have no experience, but I'm sure Mrs. Dunning can point me in the right direction. Would that help you?"

❧

Becca thoroughly enjoyed her mornings with the girls. She suspected that she was learning more than they were, but with the older ones helping the youngest, all went well. Even Martha usually tagged along and was happy to sit at the table, drawing pictures that only she could understand. On one frosty November morning, however, only five of the nieces showed up. Millie herded her charges out to the sun porch, explaining, "Nora said to tell you that she was afraid to leave Mama and little James alone at the house. Mama's got the morning sick again, real bad, and the baby was off his feed this morning. He has a nagging little cough, too. It's nothing serious, but Nora's a worrywart."

"Your mother would say, '*Vorsicht ist besser als Nachsicht.*' Foresight is better than hindsight," Becca reminded her. "Tell you what. Let's make this an essay-writing morning. Then I'll go check on the rest of the family."

"What do we write about?"

"Well, let's see. We have several holidays coming up. Why don't you each write about the holiday you like best— Thanksgiving or Christmas or New Year's Eve?"

With the girls safely occupied, Becca ducked out and hurried over to the family farmhouse. She met Katerina as she was coming from the outhouse, looking pale and shaky. "You look a little rough around the edges, my dear. Can I help you?"

"Oh, don't worry about me. It's the usual. But I can tell you one thing—this next baby is definitely going to be another girl. I'm violently sick every morning, and sometimes well into the afternoon, too. What have you done with your pupils?"

"They're writing essays this morning, and Martha is drawing 'wums,' as usual."

They found Nora in the kitchen, rocking her little brother near the wood stove. Little James was usually bouncy and boisterous after breakfast, but this morning he seemed content to loll in Nora's arms, his cheek resting on her shoulder. "He's very sleepy this morning," she said. "I don't think he feels well."

Becca put her hand on the child's cheek. "He feels warm, too."

"Maybe it's because they've been sitting by the fire," Katerina suggested.

"No, I don't think so. He may be coming down with something, Kat. Perhaps I should go for the doctor."

"No, please, don't. I . . ." Kat looked away, her bottom lip caught in her teeth. "We can't afford the doctor right now."

"Kat, if money's the problem, I can . . ."

"No. No. Jamey would never allow that. If the baby gets worse, we'll call the doctor but not yet. He just has a little cold coming on."

Little James had only a cough and a low-grade fever at first, but then he began to refuse food, choking if he tried to swallow. He fought for each breath. The glands in his neck began to swell, and the little cough became the croup. Katerina did her best to take care of him, but she was often too ill herself to give him her full attention. When his skin took on a bluish pallor, however, they called in the local doctor.

Dr. Higgins took one look, pried open the little boy's mouth, and pronounced him to be suffering from the dreaded diphtheria. A grayish, leathery membrane had grown in the child's throat, shutting off most of his air supply. The doctor simply shook his head. The child had only a 50/50 chance of survival, he warned, and there was no known cure. The outcome would be in the hands of God.

"Is it my fault for waiting so long to call you, Doctor?" Katerina didn't really want to hear his answer. In her own mind, she was clearly to blame.

Dr. Higgins did his best to reassure her. "You must not blame yourself. Diphtheria is a horrible disease. Once it takes hold in someone this young, there is really nothing to be done. I feel as helpless as you do. I've watched you nurse your family through many illnesses, Mrs. Grenville. You are as talented and caring as any nurse I know. You've done everything correctly. But sometimes the best is simply not good enough."

Katerina continued to struggle against the inevitable. She tried to suck out the membrane, as she had once seen her own mother do, but it was firmly attached. Similar attempts to poke a hole through the fibrous membrane also failed. It had grown too thick and had firmly embedded itself. A neighbor mentioned that her husband had seen doctors cut into a child's windpipe to admit air, but if the operation failed, it would mean certain death. Jamey would not allow that. "He's my only son," he protested.

Still the child lingered. In the second week, he began to suffer a pounding heart rate. His parents watched in horror as the blue veins in his forehead swelled and throbbed. Then the muscles of his eyes became paralyzed. He no longer followed their movements or seemed to recognize anyone. On the evening before Thanksgiving, little James Grenville Jr. died. The children, who had been clustered around his crib, stared in terror. It was their first experience with a death that had touched a person rather than small animals or insects.

"Are we all going to die, Mama?" asked Gloria in a shaky little voice.

Katerina looked around, desperately wishing someone else had to answer that question. But that was the price of being a mother.

"Yes, my darling. Every creature must die at some point, but you will not die until you reach God's appointed time. And meanwhile, you have a long and happy life ahead of you."

"Well, I don't think it's fair. James didn't even get a chance to have a birthday party. God certainly didn't know what he was doing in this case." Ruby threw the little doll she had been holding across the room and stomped out.

"Don't blaspheme, Ruby," Katerina cautioned automatically.

"She should be saying a prayer for his soul, instead," Lillian pointed out.

"Oh, Lillian, you're so virtuous I can't stand it," Nora said with a shake of her head. "Come on, girls, I think we should all go to bed now and give Mother and Father some time alone with James."

As they headed for the stairs, it was their father who cried out, "How long, oh Lord, will you torment us? My father. My mother. And now my son? What more will you strip from me?"

And Katerina's blood froze as she contemplated how much they still had to lose.

Rebecca's Journal

December 1898

*A*s I look back on that terrible two-year period, it seems to me that Jamey's wife, Katerina, was our mainstay. She always had one of her German proverbs to sum up the situation. This time it was "Man muss die Dinge nehmen, wie sie kommen," which means literally, "You have to take things the way they come." And that's what she did.

At the time, I remember wondering how in the world she could keep from cursing God and raging against her fate. Losing one's child has to be the worst possible disaster. Parents are not meant to outlive their children. But, of course, some do. And they must suffer in a way that most can never understand.

Jamey was deeply affected, I knew. Beyond his own personal desire to raise a son, he felt a responsibility for perpetuating the Grenville family name. Our brother Johnny had *shown no interest in ever getting married. He had given up all such notions as a result of his injuries during the Civil War. Eddie and Gretchen, for reasons no one understood, had not been able to have children. And Robbie had died too young. So Jamey was the only son who could provide a name-carrying grandson for Jonathan and Susan Grenville, and he, in his turn, had produced only female children. He loved the girls, but he felt like a failure, nonetheless.*

Jamey spent long hours in the barn and in the fields. He was working too hard, I feared, but he hated to be unoccupied. The girls missed their time with him, but somehow they seemed to understand and respect his needs. We all took our guidance from Katerina and soldiered on, treating life as if it had not collapsed around our ankles. We were Stoics, rising above personal suffering for the greater good of the family.

Only months after Baby James's death, Katerina gave birth to little Fiona—another girl, but robustly healthy. I worried about the newest baby, wondering if Katerina would be able to love her as strongly as she had always loved her other daughters—and her son. There was, I feared, a real chance that she would turn her emotional attachment off after the experience of losing little James.

I resolved to be ready to step in, if necessary, to provide the mother's love that Baby Fiona might lack, but there was no need. Katerina was stalwart. She carried on with her responsibilities. If she cried, no one witnessed her tears. Life went on. And with the changing of the seasons came the promise of better times to come.

Chapter 9

The Things that Never Die

The Grenville Farm
1896-1898

*I*t was a long and cold winter. The sun rose late and set early in those Pennsylvania hills. Ice crystallized along the edges of the local rivers, and then the water froze over entirely. Becca worried about the small woodland animals that came to her creek for daily drinks. What would they do for water? For a silly moment she thought about putting out a pan of water for them—then realized it would quickly freeze as well. So maybe that's why so many of them hibernate, she decided.

Hillsides that had been lush and green now displayed only dried grasses and bare branches that seemed to scrape the low-hanging clouds. Bird calls had long since faded away, except for the occasional screeching of a crow that disapproved of the world. Fresh vegetables were a thing of the past. Meals were repetitious renderings of root vegetables and cabbage soups.

The girls had gone back to school, and Katerina had spent the last weeks of her pregnancy confined to the house for fear of falling on a slippery step. Becca filled her days with sketching lessons and pages of fanciful imaginings about the secret lives of local bugs and other critters. Were her stories any good? She had no idea, but she was starting to notice that the words were flowing more easily.

Mrs. Dunning had explained a few of the design elements of children's literature. Brevity was a virtue, Becca had learned. The younger the child, the shorter the attention span. Children firmly believed that animals had the same feelings as they themselves did, so it was all right to let the storybook animals talk, play games, or eat something tasty. Body noises were hysterical. Magical solutions were perfectly logical. Animals could get angry and fight with one another, but every child wanted the reassurance that all would be friends in the end. Children believed that bad folks never win and that little people can triumph over big ones. With all those thoughts firmly in mind, Becca's imagination was learning to run free.

In the old farmhouse, grief over little James's death kept the Grenville family subdued for most of the first winter. They rose before it was light, did their chores, went off to school or work, came home in the dark, ate a quick supper, and went to bed early so they could keep warm under the quilts. But change was coming, and as the weather warmed, so did the family's spirits.

⌘

Back in Charleston, the Middleton Law Firm was proceeding with arrangements to auction off the Grenville properties. Arthur Middleton wrote to Johnny, the oldest son of Jonathan and Susan, inviting him to come home from Washington, DC, and help oversee the final settlement of three family wills. Not surprisingly, Johnny refused, pleading important national business that kept him firmly committed to Senator Wade Hampton's office. Instead, he suggested his brother Eddie.

Both Eddie and his sister Charlotte agreed to travel from Aiken to Charleston to learn what was being done with their parents' and grandmother's lands. Charlotte, in turn, took on the round-robin responsibility of keeping the other siblings informed.

> *Dear Brothers and Sisters,*
>
> *Eddie and I have spent all day in that stuffy lawyer's office going over paperwork. Here's the breakdown, as we see it.*
>
> *The house in Columbia was destroyed by fire during the last year of the War of the Rebellion, and the*

city finally had the remains bulldozed and the property confiscated. There is no case to be made for a claim against the city.

The Aiken farm, of course, will have to go to auction, but Arthur Middleton assures us that if we put in a preemptory bid, the auctioneer can immediately declare it sold. So in effect Eddie and I shall buy it from ourselves and then each of us will receive one-sixth of the selling price back as our rightful shares. The rest of that price will come to the four of you, so you may say, thank you.

The Ashley River Road Plantation has fallen into disuse and disrepair. The Middletons likewise have allowed their adjoining rice fields to go to waste. There is simply no profit to be made from rice any more. The auction will offer the land for sale, but we do not expect to get much for it.

The same is true for the rice plantation on the Combahee River. If there are no bidders, the lands will simply revert to the state, which will at least relieve us of owing any more taxes upon the property.

The Edisto Island Plantation, however, is a different story. Despite the damage done by the recent hurricanes, long-staple Sea Island cotton is still much in demand. The freedmen whom Father allowed to live on their plots and raise their cotton without having to pay anything but a minimal rent have done well for themselves. Mr. Middleton assures us that most have diligently saved their money and will be buying up their land with their profits. We should see a tidy sum from the place, and at the same time we can know that we have helped bring to fruition Father's dream of settling free blacks on his land.

The warehouses and storefronts in Savannah are expected to sell to their current renters and leaseholders. Wherever possible, the auctioneers will see to it that those now occupying the property can have the first shot at claiming it for their own.

And that leaves the Charleston house. Eddie and I visited it yesterday. How sad it looks! Although it has not collapsed, as everyone feared it might back in 1886, the property is a total loss. Any attempt to make the major repairs needed would probably bring the whole structure down around our ears.

It should be possible, however, to retrieve a few keepsakes, if there is anything there that one of you would like. The house has been well-guarded, so there has been no looting. The china, glassware, and lamps are all destroyed, but the silver remains. The family portraits may have some cracked frames, but the paintings themselves are undamaged. And of course, some of the furniture is still usable. We have agreed to give the four of you first choice, if there is anything you would like us to pack up and send to you. If other valuables then remain, we shall try to sell them before the wrecking ball moves in.

Oh, one more item. Becca, we tried to find out what happened to old Sammy the stable hand, but he has vanished—perhaps he just wandered off after you left, or, sadly, died and was given a nameless pauper's burial. I'm sorry.
Your Loving Sister,
Charlotte

❧

"Is there anything you want, Becca?" Jamey asked. "You lived there for so many years after the rest of us were gone . . ."

"No. I would just as lief put that period of my life behind me. I'll tell Charlotte to sell it all. I don't even care about the money, so long as we know that Father's dream of seeing freed peoples become property owners is helped along."

"But you've been living on some of those rents. Your cottage is free and clear, but what will you do for spending money once those payments stop?"

Becca tried to appear as serious as Jamey was, but she couldn't suppress her grin. "I'll manage," she said. "In fact, I have something of a surprise for all of you. If I can wangle an invitation to dinner tonight, I'll tell you all about it."

"What's your big news, Aunt Becca?" Nora asked as soon as Becca arrived. "You're not getting married, are you?"

"Don't be silly, my girl. I know you're involved in a courtship right now, but then, you're eighteen. Your old aunt is long past that stage."

"Then what?" Millie demanded.

Becca held her peace all through dinner. Then, reverting to an old Grenville family tradition, she tapped her spoon on her custard dish and signaled for quiet.

"I do have a small announcement to make. You'll remember, perhaps, that the girls' teacher, Viola Dunning, promised to look over the stories and pictures I've been making for Martha. She's been a wonderful resource and has taught me much about writing children's books—so much so that I have accumulated quite a collection of fanciful animal tales."

"Wum!" Martha added.

"Yes, Mr. Worm has featured prominently. At any rate, with my permission, Viola showed some of the stories to a bookseller she knows in New Castle, and he, in turn, liked them so much that he contacted a publisher in Pittsburgh. The long and the short of it is that I have a publishing contract."

"No!"

"Really? How wonderful!"

"Yippee!"

The older girls were laughing in delight, but ten-year-old Gloria looked puzzled. "What does that mean?"

"It means that the Clarksdale Publishing Company of Pittsburgh will take my handwritten stories and put them into book form. Each story will have its own book. They'll copy my pictures and put my name on the front cover as the author. There will be a whole series of books, and I'll get a small amount from each copy they sell. The first one to come out will be *The Adventures of Mr. Worm*. I'm going to be a real author!"

"Can I have one of your books?"

"Of course. You girls will get the very first books to come off the press, because they will be dedicated to you. But there's a lot of work to be done first. It's pretty scary to know that strangers will be reading my stories, so I'll want to do some rewriting and polishing. And then the process of printing the books . . . Well, actually I have no idea what all is involved, but I know it will take a fairly long time."

Jamey was leaning back in his chair, hands behind his head, beaming broadly at his sister. "I always knew you were pretty clever," he said, "but when I arranged to get you that little cottage, I never dreamed you'd turn it into an author's studio. Why, you'll be Beaver County's most famous citizen! We've never had a real author around here."

"Perhaps I'd better plan a book called *The Beavers of Beaver County*," she laughed.

"You really could, Auntie Becca," said Ruby. "I remember that I liked your first beaver pictures, even if they were supposed to be squirrels."

The evening ended on that happy note, and Becca returned to her Magnolia Cottage, grateful that she had been able to give the family a few minutes of carefree pleasure. Their conversations had been so much fun that she had failed to notice that Katerina remained silent, her thin lips kept tightly pressed together to keep a caustic comment from slipping out.

⌘

In the end, there was little left of the DuBois-Grenville inheritance. When the final settlement checks arrived, both Becca and Jamey felt a frisson of renewed grief. Three lives—those of Elizabeth DuBois, Jonathan Grenville, and Susan Grenville—had been reduced to these scraps of paper. A few hundred dollars went into the bank accounts of each of the six surviving Grenville children to blend anonymously into the other small amounts there.

The year had one more surprise in store. Jamey showed up one afternoon while Becca was hard at work at her desk. "Come with me, Sister. You are needed at the Ellwood City train station."

"What in the world is going on?" she asked, "and why are you driving that big wagon?"

"I received a note from the stationmaster this morning, telling me that I need to bring you and a heavy wagon to meet him. All I know is what my instructions say. Climb aboard. We evidently have business to take care of."

"Who would be sending me something?"

"I don't know, Becca."

"And why would we need a wagon to carry it? It can't be the new books. They wouldn't be that heavy."

"Let's wait and see."

"I don't even want anything. There's no room in Magnolia Cottage for extras."

"I gather that no one felt a need to ask for your permission."

"But what if it's something I don't even want?"

"Then I will tell you that you are behaving like an ungrateful and spoiled child. I am allowed to do that sort of thing, even if I am your younger brother."

Becca fussed all the way into town, until Jamey finally told her to hush. "We won't know until we get there, and we'll get there faster if you'll be quiet and let me deal with the horses."

At the depot, the stationmaster was waiting next to a large crate. "This is addressed to Miss Rebecca Grenville at Magnolia Cottage. That you? You need to sign here."

"Yes, sir, but what . . .?"

"Not my business to know what's in the boxes that come through here. All I'm here to do is load it onto your wagon."

Becca squirmed on the way home, trying to get a better look at the crate. "It's from Charleston," she said. "It must be from Eddie, but I told him I didn't need anything . . ."

"We'll see soon enough," Jamey promised. At the cottage, he grabbed an old claw hammer from the wagon bed and started to tear away the packing boards.

"It's . . . it's . . . Oh, Jamey, look, it's Mother's old melodeon." Tears sprang to her eyes as she realized that music was the one thing she had most missed from her former life.

Jamey carried it into her parlor and opened its folding compartments. "There you are. Guess Eddie knows you pretty well! I'm going to leave you alone with it for a while to let you practice. Then Kat and I will bring the family over for a concert. The girls are going to love this."

Kat herself, however, was less than enthusiastic. "How nice for her. One more thing she can do better than anyone else."

⌘

Becca pulled the stool close and sat, wondering if she even remembered how to play the instrument. Tentatively, she pressed a key, but no sound came forth. "Oh," she explained to Tabitha the cat, who was prowling around, full of curiosity. "I forgot you have to pump the pedals first to build up pressure in the pipes." She worked the pedals gently and then harder, with Tabitha giving a slight jump whenever they squeaked. When her knees threatened to give out, she pressed her fingers to the keys and was rewarded with a booming major chord. The cat fled to the mantel, where she sat, glaring down at this strange object making all those noises.

Trying to let her hands move from embedded memory, Becca began a slower, more rhythmic pumping as she ran through the major and minor chords she remembered. Then her fingers began picking out melodies, and suddenly, all the days she had spent in her mother's parlor came flooding back. This is the real inheritance, she now realized—this love of music, this appreciation of beauty passed from mother to daughter. These are the things that never die. And this is an inheritance I can pass on.

Rebecca's Journal

December 31, 1899

*T**here have been several happy occasions to brighten my days in the past two years. The eighth Grenville daughter appeared, managing to get herself born before Mr. Worm did. Sarah Jane is a delicate blonde baby, already showing signs of beauty to come and displaying a charming smile. Her sisters call her Baby Sally.*

Nora found herself a husband among the young blades who have been hanging around the farmhouse. Henry Southerland is the new high school teacher in Ellwood City—a serious young man with a distinct scholarly bent. Father would have loved him.

And Millie, too, is already caught up in the cycles of courtship, although in my opinion, seventeen is much too young to be thinking seriously about marriage. She seems to have set her cap for a young man employed in the local coal mine. To everyone's surprise, Jamey is much impressed by the work ethic of Joseph Sweitzer—and Jamey is not an easy father to please. Katerina, of course, is thrilled. She constantly tells her girls that their ultimate life's purpose is to become a wife and mother. Sometimes I think she says that just to get in a jab at my spinsterhood, but I try not to react.

I have found, however, that the whole business of closing our parents' estates has forced me to face my own inevitable decline. Jamey worries that he leaves no son, but at least he has daughters. There will be no one descended from me. Katerina is right about that. Perhaps that's just as well—I'm entirely too selfish and impatient to put up with the challenges of a family. Oh, I love my nieces, but I also get to send them home whenever they get on my nerves. Still, I haven't much liked the thought of my life disappearing into the Great Void, with nothing to show for it.

However, the other day, Viola Dunning dropped by. "How's the birthing process going?" she asked.

"What?" I stared at her, sure that I must have misunderstood.

"The birth of your first book," she explained. "That's what it is, you know. The Adventures of Mr. Worm *is your first-born 'child,' and you will labor hard over its birth. And then you'll have to send it out into the cruel world to be judged on its merits, and you will worry constantly that it will be picked upon or ridiculed. But in the end, it will be a rich inheritance*

that you leave to children yet unborn. It's how you will be remembered. What could be better?"

I've been thinking about memories a lot lately. Perhaps holiday seasons lead everyone to reminisce a bit about childhood, families, happy times and sad times, surprises, and disappointments. This year, though, my memories have a more intense flavor because we have reached the end of a century. The proponents of fin de siècle *excitement encourage us to look forward to a bright and shining new world—undreamed-of opportunities, untold advances in every endeavor, and solutions to all the world's problems are only a date away. Or so they would have us believe. I know enough history to understand that time is a human invention. When 1899 gives way to the first day of the twentieth century tomorrow, nothing much will actually change. The sun will set and come up again. We'll all be one day older, and all the same joys and sorrows will color the way we view our world. But I worry that, in our hurry to leave the nineteenth century behind us, we'll turn our backs on the lessons we should have learned from the past.*

Jamey's young daughters wanted me to come to their house tonight for a New Year's Eve party. I refused, to their vast disappointment, because I don't feel like celebrating. I want this night to be one of contemplation. I want to remember the bad times that I have experienced, so that I will have a better understanding when the next wave of suffering arrives, as it surely will. I want to remember the good times, too, for the comfort and reassurance those times bring. I need to be alone, for I would not want to burden the young with the fear of as-yet-unseen dangers. And I would not want to add my own terrors to those of others who are dealing with their own personal demons. Some moments are not meant to be shared.

And now the clock is striking midnight—that bewitching hour that everyone has been waiting for. The past is dead, they say. Well, that's true enough. The future is bright, they promise. I pray it will be so.

Chapter 10

Sufficient unto the Day Are the Troubles Therein

North Sewickley Cemetery
May 26, 1900

In the years immediately following the Civil War, Katerina's mother had begun a tradition that the family spend the last weekend in May tending their ancestral plots in the local cemetery. It was partly a memorial to all the lives lost during the war, but it was also a time to bring the family together, to remember all those who had passed, and to imprint the children with a tradition of respect for one's ancestors. Now that Katerina was the matriarch of her own family, she was determined to carry on the tradition.

On Saturday morning, she was up early to pack a picnic basket. This promised to be an all-day project. The younger girls were in charge of rounding up the various tools they would need—hedge shears, blankets for sitting on, shovels, hoes, rakes, and scrubbing brushes. Nora and Millie had been carefully nurturing some starter plants; now they packed them up for transplanting. When Becca saw how loaded the old wagon was, she laughed at all of them. "You look like you're getting ready to found a new town, not just clean around a few grave sites," she said.

"You'll be glad we have all this before the day is over," Katerina assured her. "You have no idea how many family members I can find up there on the top of that hill."

The North Sewickley United Presbyterian Church had chosen its location well—on Chapel Road, just south of Ellwood City and west of Connoquenessing Creek. Their cemetery lay to the east and was located on the highest hill around.

Becca, still accustomed to the flatlands of South Carolina despite all her years in the hills of Pennsylvania, wrinkled her brow when Jamey announced that they would have to leave the wagon and horses at the foot of the hill. "That road is just too steep and twisty for the horses to pull us and the wagon," he explained.

"I wonder the same thing every time we come here. Why didn't they put the cemetery on flat land? It looks like there would have been plenty of room south of the church, and then people wouldn't have to carry the caskets and everything else uphill."

Jamey shrugged and shook his head, but Katerina was quick to jump in with an explanation. "You two were raised in the Episcopal Church, but this is an old Presbyterian tradition. John Calvin taught his followers that God wanted them to create 'a City on a Hill,' so that their light would shine as a guide to others. And burying good Presbyterian souls way up here gives them a head start by placing them this much closer to heaven."

Becca refrained from pursuing the matter when she remembered that the newly turned grave of little James would be among those they would be tending. Some things were better left unsaid.

The girls scurried on ahead, undaunted by the climb, and Katerina was not far behind. Becca picked up the picnic basket and waited for her brother to gather his load of tools. They brought up the rear of the procession, and Becca thought she understood why Jamey lagged behind. It would be a bitter time for him to visit his only son's grave. Still, she looked over her shoulder several times, wondering how he could be moving so slowly. Maybe he just wants to be alone, she thought. Then a clatter, followed by a wracking cough, made her turn around. Jamey was bent almost double, the tools around his feet, as his chest heaved. Shaking his head, he waved at her with a dismissing gesture, telling her to go on ahead. Then he doubled over again with another bout of coughing.

"Jamey! What's wrong? Are you ill? Or did you choke on something?" Becca put her hand on his cheek to get a look at his face, but he only made another strangled sound and pulled away.

"Leave me alone. I'm fine," he gasped. "I have a bit of catarrh, that's all. Nothing to worry about. Go on ahead. I'll catch my breath here for a minute and be right up."

"It sounds more serious than that," she argued.

"There you go, being the know-it-all older sister again." He gave a weak laugh, which brought on another bout of coughing. He whipped a handkerchief out of his pocket and turned away from her as he coughed, but he was not quick enough to hide the telltale stain of blood at his mouth.

"Jamey! Dear God! You're coughing up blood. You need a doctor."

He shook his head stubbornly. "I've seen the doctor. He's no help."

"What did he say?" When he simply shook his head at her, she stamped her foot. "Jamey! Talk to me!"

"He says it's a mild case of consumption—nothing to worry about."

"That is something to worry about. People die of consumption."

"I'm not dying—not yet, at any rate. He says it will be years before it becomes debilitating, particularly if I watch what I do and don't exert myself. So I don't want Kat to know. She worries as much as you do, and she has enough to deal with without worrying about having a sick husband."

"You don't give her enough credit. How do you think she reacts when she sees your bloody handkerchiefs?"

"She doesn't see them. She simply thinks I lose a lot of them."

"Oh, Jamey. I'm so sorry. I'll help you keep your secret, but only if you promise me that you'll let everyone know what's going on if you get worse."

"Agreed! Now we'd better catch up with the rest of the family, or they'll think we've fled for good."

❦

Although Becca had been dreading the day, the cemetery work actually proved to be quite pleasant. There was something cathartic about rooting out overgrown weeds and replacing them with flowering plants. The girls flitted around the graves, calling out when they recognized a name on one of the stones.

"Look, Mama, here's someone named Electa McDevlin. She must have been related to you. But she died a long time ago."

"That's my father's sister. She died as a teenager."

"What kind of a name is Electa?"

"A stonecutter's mistake. It was supposed to be Electra after the Greek heroine, but they couldn't afford another new stone, so they just left it. Mother always said it didn't matter that much, because God already knew her name."

"Little James's grave looks lonely. There's no one else around him." Ruby still had her talent for saying the wrong thing.

Katerina pressed her lips together to control her tears. Then she forced a smile. "But there will be. When we purchased his plot, we purchased several others, so that we can be buried alongside him. Someday, this sunny spot on the hill will be full of his family."

"Us, too?" Gloria asked, her eyes wide.

"I don't know, dear. We won't make those choices until we have to. Now, come with me to the other side of the road. There is a cluster of McDevlin graves over there, along with a nice patch of pine trees where we can spread out lunch."

Much of the afternoon was spent retelling old family stories. A rough slab of stone with only the name "Nancy" scratched into it puzzled the girls. "It's just lying there. It's not even on a grave that you can tell. No last name, no dates. Somebody was really expecting a lot of God if they thought He would keep track of everyone by just a first name," Jamey commented.

"Ah, but in this case, they were sure He could. Nancy McDevlin was my father's grandmother and the oldest settler in North Sewickley. She was also the first occupant of this cemetery, buried at the very top of the hill in a place of honor. And she didn't need anything else on her stone, because everyone knew who Nancy was. If ever a settlement had a matriarch, Nancy was it. By now, of course, she's been forgotten by all but me, and now you. But if one of you girls remembers her and passes the story on to your children, her memory will linger on, dates or no dates."

When the last of the work was finished, Katerina pulled Jamey aside. "Would you take the girls and Becca home now, and give me some time alone here at the cemetery?"

"Are you sure, dear? It's already been a long and emotional day."

"Which is precisely why I need some time to myself. I won't be long, I promise. But there are a few more visits I need to make. It's bad luck to come to a cemetery and not pay your respects to all the members of your family, you know. I need to go by my parents' plot. And then I'll walk home to stretch out these muscles that have been crouched down most of the day."

Once the family was gone, Katerina strolled among the stones, trailing her fingers over the names of people she had known long ago. She stopped at her parents' headstones. She had not brought her children there because her brother had promised to take care of the plot. But even though he had done a good job, she would have felt remiss if she had not visited. She dropped to her knees and bowed her head for a long while.

"How I miss you, Mother," she murmured. "I'm doing my best to live the kind of life you would have wanted for me, but it's hard—very hard. The farm is not doing terribly well under Jamey's management. He was fine with it for a while, but now . . . now I suspect something is wrong. He's working fewer hours, but even so, he comes in absolutely exhausted. He's tried to raise more cash crops, like corn and wheat, but he really doesn't produce enough to make it worthwhile for customers to buy from him. And so much of our land goes to feed the family. We used to get monthly revenue from his parents' property, but that stopped when they died. Yes, we got a cash settlement, but it won't match the revenue we used to have coming in.

"I'm frightened! I'm terrified that something will happen to him . . . that he will turn out to be really sick and die on me. And then what will I do? I'm trying to remember the stories you told me about your own mother and how she had to take over and run the farm when her husband died. Could I do that? I don't know, and there's no one else to tell me how to do it. What if? What if? How do people keep on going in the face of complete uncertainty? Did you give me that training somewhere? Is it in me, waiting to come out when I need it?"

From a treetop somewhere behind her, she heard the soft notes of a bird's evening song. He seemed to be saying, "Rest. Rest. I'm here." And then another non-voice from somewhere deep in her soul whispered the words she really needed to hear. *"Jeden Tag seine eigene Plage hat.* One day at a time. One day at a time. Sufficient unto the day are the troubles therein."

Chapter 11

If Truth Be Told

Becca's front door burst open, slamming against the wall as Katerina stormed in. "You knew!" she shouted. "You knew and you didn't tell me!"

"Kat, I . . ."

"Don't give me that wide-eyed, innocent look. You knew Jamey was ill. You knew he needed medical attention. Did you think it would just go away? Or did you think I was too weak-kneed to deal with it?"

"No, Kat, I . . ."

"We are supposed to be a family. We don't keep secrets from one another."

"I didn't think of it that way. I—"

"Don't make excuses. You come waltzing into our lives, criticize the way I'm raising my daughters, and now you're sticking your nose into my marriage. I'm tired of having you always interfering in our family matters."

"When have I ever intruded where I was not invited?"

"Oh, only a hundred or so times, in all sorts of subtle ways. You get invited to all our family get-togethers, and you sit there, listening to everything that's going on and making judgments about us. I can watch your face and know exactly what you are thinking. You get a sheepish-looking grin on your face and catch your lower lip with your teeth whenever one of our girls dares to defy our wishes—as if you're cheering them on. And your eyebrows pull together whenever you don't approve of something I say to one of them. Makes you look like you have a giant caterpillar crawling across your forehead."

Becca almost laughed at that image, but this was not a time to make fun. Instead, she simply stored the idea away, thinking it would make a good book some day. "But I've never contradicted you in front of the girls."

"No, I'll give you that. But I always wonder what you say to Jamey in private. You're always there, somehow, coming between him and me. And now you've gone too far, deliberately hiding something from me that I have every right as a wife to—"

Becca held up both hands to stem the flow of accusations. "Katerina, I did know, but not until a few weeks ago, and Jamey made me promise not to tell you—to let him break the news when he thought the time was right."

"You . . . you . . . you should have understood . . . I needed to know . . . I . . ."

Katerina broke off as a flood of tears overpowered her righteous anger. She sank onto a kitchen chair, her head in her hands. Becca sat quietly beside her until the sobs subsided and Katerina began to breathe more slowly. Becca brewed two cups of tea and then pulled her chair close.

"I've never wanted to come between you and my brother, Katerina. I love you both, and if I've made you unhappy, I'm terribly sorry. I . . . do you want me to move away? I'll do that, if you tell me it will help to make up for all the hurt you have suffered on my account."

"No, I don't want you to leave," Kat answered, sniffling a bit. "Jamey wants you here, and I want whatever makes him happy. But . . . I want you to understand that in the larger scale of things, my husband's welfare and our marriage come first. Next come my girls, those bewitching individuals he and I created from our own bodies. I would lay down my life for any one of them. After that come my brothers, who came into my care while they were still little more than children. And then somewhere at the bottom of my list of people I care about, if I scratch around a bit . . . there you are . . . the thorn in my flesh . . . the woman against whom I always seem to be measuring myself . . . and coming up short." The words dripped with bitterness.

"Why would you ever feel that way? From where I stand, you have everything—a husband, eight beautiful daughters, a rich family life that surrounds you with love. And I?" She let the question dangle as her own eyes glistened with tears. "I have a cat."

Katerina couldn't manage to hide the beginnings of a sneer as she shook her head. "You have a cat and a fairy-tale cottage that is always neat and clean and a career as an author that is going to make you rich and famous. Furthermore, you have the enormous luxury of being able to do whatever you want without thinking of anyone else. My girls adore you, and you them, I know. But when you grow tired of them, or when they get sick or dirty, you send them home for me to take care of. You get all the benefits and none of the responsibility. No wonder I hate you."

The word hung in the air for what felt like an eternity before Katerina spoke again. "I didn't mean to say that. I don't hate you. But I guess I do resent you."

"And I think I understand why, particularly in this situation. I don't know if we can ever fix things between us, but for now, let's concentrate on Jamey, since the one thing we share is our love for that irritating man. When did you find out?"

"Last night. I woke in the dark to hear him coughing. He had gone to the kitchen to keep from disturbing me, but . . . oh, Becca, I thought he was going to die right there. The coughs were so deep, and he couldn't get his breath.

His face looked dark, and his eyes stared at nothing as he struggled. I didn't know what to do for him. I put a kettle on to get some steam going, like we do when the children have croup, but he kept pulling his head away. When the spasms finally passed, he was exhausted from the effort. That's when I demanded to know how long he had been feeling ill, and the whole story came spilling out. He was too tired to resist."

"I saw something similar at the cemetery when we were cleaning the graves, but it passed more quickly. Did he do something particularly strenuous yesterday?"

"He was haying all day. Maybe the dust . . ."

"And the heavy lifting. He's going to have to start taking it easy, I'm afraid."

"But who will do the work? He'll say he has to."

"Now that you know, he won't be keeping up the pretense that he's still twenty years old. The two of you should be able to work something out."

"But there's nobody else to help. I've tried, but I'm just not strong enough for some of the tasks, like haying. And the farm's not prosperous enough to allow us to hire help. I don't know what we'll do. And if he dies . . ."

"Stop. Don't buy trouble. Let's look at the short term. What do you need right now?"

"A couple of strong sons would be nice. Or even a couple of sons-in-law would help." Her laugh had not an ounce of humor in it.

"You have Nora's Henry . . ."

" . . . who's a dreamer, a thinker, a head-in-the-clouds observer of life. He's nice enough, but his hands have fewer calluses than mine, and he's in a classroom all day."

"What about Millie's new husband—Joseph?"

"Jamey has always had high hopes for him, but when he asked him if he'd be willing to take over part of the farm, he absolutely refused. He said his grandfather Sweitzer went broke on a family farm, and his father tried running a sawmill and failed at that. Both times the family came close to starving. Joseph says he'll never do something venturesome. He'll settle for being sure he gets a day's pay for a day's work. He plans to keep working in the coal mines until he can get taken on at the mill."

"You have a brother, don't you?"

"Two of them, but one's in Philadelphia doing God-knows-what, and the one living in New Castle has his own clothing store to run. He once offered his son as a summer farmhand, but he's pretty young—eleven or twelve—the age where he would eat more than he could produce."

"The farm already feeds you, I know. Ours did during the war when we had nothing else to rely on."

"Yes, of course it does, but that's the simple answer. It ignores the fact that chickens don't lay eggs and cows don't give milk unless you feed them. You have to have money to buy seeds if you're going to grow vegetables. And then there arell all the other expenses—clothes for the girls, farm equipment, flour and sugar that we don't grow, the roof that needs new shingles, doctor bills." Her voice cracked.

"Oh, Becca, I'm just starting to realize that the doctor bills will only get worse as time goes on. How will we pay for the care Jamey is going to need?"

"You don't owe money on the farm, do you?"

"No, we inherited it from my parents. But to tell the truth, I don't know much about our financial matters. Jamey always handles those."

"Then he'll have a better understanding of the coming problems than you do. I'm sorry if this sounds like I'm interfering with your marriage, but I can't help it. You and he will have to sit down and work things out. Maybe you can sell off part of the land to support the rest. Talk to him, Kat. That's what married people do. And talk to Dr. Higgins, too. I heard him once compliment you on your nursing skills. You may be able to give Jamey all the care he will need. But find out exactly what the future holds, so that you can start preparing for it."

Chapter 12

The More Things Change

The Grenville Farm
1901

*B*ecca's first children's book was published in the spring of 1901. *The Adventures of Mr. Worm* arrived in the mail on a warm May morning. Becca tore away the wrappings with her heart pounding uncontrollably. What if it was a terrible book? What if her pictures looked foolish? What if no one ever bought the book? Her hands shook as she stared at the cover. Mr. Worm grinned back at her. Her own name—Rebecca Marie Grenville—declared her to be both author and artist. She had been afraid that the story was too short, but in print, it stretched itself across some thirty-two pages. And the back cover suggested that there would be more adventure books to come.

A letter from her publisher was enclosed. Mr. Clark wrote that the book had proven popular when they announced its publication at their spring book show:

You seem to have tapped into a fertile market. The new century is bringing with it a general feeling of prosperity, and that translates into parents being able to buy their children toys and books that they might not have had themselves. We had initial orders for five hundred copies, and some of our outlets are already reporting that they need to restock the title. This is excellent news, and you should look forward to receiving your first royalty check around the first of July. In the meantime, please work on your next title. We would like to have The Adventures of Curly the Squirrel *ready for the winter market. You can also start making plans for a ladybug book and a hedgehog adventure.*

Becca let her breath out with a whoosh. A hedgehog? Whose idea was that?

In her own mind, however, Becca had already settled on a way to use her good fortune to help the family. She allowed the money question to rest for a few weeks. Then she approached her brother.

"I have a proposal for you, dear heart, although you may consider it more of an ultimatum. Whatever your reaction, I have already made up my mind, so just hear me out. I've been thinking a lot about my own mortality after Mother's and Father's deaths, and I have come to realize that I have quite a few unpaid debts. I'll feel better if I settle them once and for all."

"Debts? You? Whatever for?" he asked.

"My house, for one. When I came to Pennsylvania, I was not sure I wanted to stay, so I took up your offer of a place to live as a temporary solution. Of course, I fell in love with the cottage, with your family, and with the area as a whole. But now I have lived in your little house for going on fifteen years, and I have done so rent-free. I am embarrassed by that. I should have made an effort to repay your generosity long ago."

"Nonsense, Becca. You're talking foolishness. I wanted you to come here for my own selfish reasons. Magnolia Cottage did not cost me anything, and you owe me nothing."

"That's not so! Don't lie to me. I asked Mrs. Hazen about it a few days ago, and she confirmed that you paid them for all the furnishings of that cottage. But whatever your original costs, the cottage and its surrounding woodlands are valuable today, and I want to purchase them from you at their fair cost. I'm no longer here because you need me. I'm here because I want to live here. I'll never go back to Charleston. There's nothing there for me any longer. And I want to own my own home."

"You can't afford to . . ."

"Oh, but I can. All these years, I've saved my money. And now the children's books are going to be bringing in a tidy additional sum. I can well afford to buy my own house, and it's Magnolia Cottage I want. Don't fight me on this, Jamey. I have the money, and I owe it to you. And you and your family can surely use it now. I intend to visit the bank in the morning and start making arrangements to have the property deeded to me."

"I can't let you . . ."

"Yes, you can, and you will. I'm your older sister, and I expect you to do as you are told."

∼⤫∼

The months continued their swings from highs to lows with dizzying speed. Nora gave birth to her first daughter, Eva Katerina Southerland, and shortly thereafter, Millie and Joseph produced a son named Homer Rudolph Sweitzer. He was followed only eleven months later by Glenda Marie Sweitzer. "Three grandchildren in the first year of the new century," Jamey joked. "I can't keep track of all our girls, let alone their offspring. Before long, we'll have to wear name tags to family dinners." Katerina's answering smile was tight-lipped.

Within the Grenville household, tensions remained high. The older girls had been told of their father's illness, although Fiona and Sally were still too young to understand the full implications. Lillian simply grew quieter and more serious than usual, but Ruby, as was typical when anything interfered with her life, was resentful. "What's going to happen to us if he dies?" she demanded. "Will there be enough money for us to go to school and get married and have nice things? Or are we going to just sit here and starve in the cold and dark?"

"Ruby, my darling child, I do wish that once in a while you would think of someone besides yourself!" Katerina snapped back at her.

"Well, nobody else pays any attention to me. If I don't look out for myself, I don't get anything," she pouted.

⟡

Perhaps because of that unhappy exchange, Katerina paid more attention than usual when her brother Heinrich offered a solution to the Grenvilles' financial problems. "Send the girls to stay with us in New Castle for a while. There's a great demand these days for young women who want to go into service. I can easily find them jobs that furnish their room and board and give them a small salary to send home besides."

Katerina promised to think about it and then broached the topic with Becca. "Time for you to become my faithful advisor again," she said. "My brother wants me to send the older girls into service, and I'm seriously considering it."

"I don't understand," Becca replied. "Service? What kind of service?"

"Cooks, housekeepers, lady's maids, governesses, those sorts of jobs. They'd become part of a rich family's staff, which would guarantee them good meals and housing."

"Servants? You want to turn your daughters into somebody's servants? To be relegated to below stairs, subject to the whims of their upper-class employers, and humiliated by being forced to do the dirtiest, most unpleasant tasks of running a household, like emptying the mistress's chamber pot and scrubbing the stains out of his lordship's undergarments? We got rid of slavery a long time ago."

"It's not slavery, Becca! That's an unfair comparison coming out of your own upbringing. I keep forgetting that you and Jamey grew up in a very different society than we Northerners did. They are not being assigned tasks because of the color of their skin. Nobody's going to own them. They'll be employees, earning wages in exchange for needed services."

"But what do you expect them to gain from this, besides the obvious paltry wages?"

"Exposure. Experience with how the rest of the world lives. The chance to get to know interesting people. Maybe even meet an eligible bachelor."

"There it is! You're still thinking in terms of finding husbands for them, aren't you? Well, I have news for you. Wealthy gentlemen only marry chambermaids in fantasies and fluffy novels."

"Spending a few years in service is quite common in Northern society, especially among the upper crust. The girls would live with their employers during the week but be able to come home on their days off. The real goal, Heinrich's wife tells me, is to teach the young women in service how rich people live—to teach them fine manners, how to set a lovely dinner table, how one conducts oneself in public. It's almost like a finishing school, she says."

"It's being a servant. That's all it is, no matter what kind of pretty words you use to dress it up. And it's likely to mark the girls for life."

"Now I think you're the one who's exaggerating. I'm going to try it with the older ones."

"Not including Martha, surely?"

"No, of course not. No one would want her. She'll live at home for the rest of her life, but I can help the others find a new way in the world. Lillian and Ruby are both old enough to leave home, and who knows? Maybe they'll find rich husbands along the way."

"That's your only goal, isn't it? To find them rich husbands?"

"And what's wrong with that? We have one of those wise old sayings for that: *Es ist so einfach, in der Liebe mit einem reichen Mann zu fallen, wie sie mit einem schlechten ein.* It should be just as easy to fall in love with a rich man as it is with a poor one. Around here, they'll drag home another schoolteacher or coal miner. Maybe, in a big city, they'll meet a banker or a lawyer. And that will be good for all of us."

"You're assuming that they have to marry someone. Why can't you allow them to grow into interesting human beings in their own right? Besides, I thought you were hoping for a farmer son-in-law."

"Not any more. I'm looking for a way out of this farm, not a way to get further buried in it."

"What does Jamey think? Surely he isn't going along with this idea."

"I haven't told him. He has enough to worry about just trying to breathe."

⸎

To everyone's surprise, Ruby was eager to leave for New Castle. When she stopped at Magnolia Cottage to bid farewell to her aunt, she was excited and upbeat. "I'm hoping I get a really fancy family. I can hardly wait to see their furniture and china and silver pieces. Needing to polish a few things is a small price to pay for living in luxury."

Becca sighed as she watched the naïve young girl skip down the road. She'll learn soon enough, she thought.

Things were quieter around the Grenville farmhouse, now that four of the girls were out on their own. Gloria was in school all day, and the two little ones, Fiona and Sally, had learned from babyhood to entertain themselves. One noticeable change was that Martha had begun to do more. Now that she was out from under the shadow of her sisters, she demonstrated that there were many chores she could handle—sweeping floors, setting the table, washing dishes, folding laundry, feeding barnyard animals, and, with a little supervision for a while, gathering eggs. Katerina smiled as she watched her disabled daughter become more confident.

At church, Martha had found a new friend in a quiet young man named Paul Davidson, who had recently purchased land on the far side of the Grenville spread. He was building himself a house, cultivating unused fields, and trying to increase his holdings of livestock. That goal brought him to the Grenvilles now and then to purchase chicks, a piglet, a calf, or a few goats. Jamey was happy to accommodate his needs, but the real winner was Martha, who firmly believed that Paul came to the farm deliberately to see her. And maybe he did.

At church socials or during the visiting hour after services, Paul often offered his arm to Martha and strolled slowly with her, helping her keep her unsteady balance.

"I really appreciate you being so nice to Martha," Katerina told him one day when her daughter was out of earshot. "I'm afraid it's been a long time since anyone paid her special attention."

"I had a sister with similar problems," Paul explained. "Speaking slowly, helping her practice her words, and giving her a hand over the rough spots were things that came naturally in our family."

"What happened to your sister?" Jamey asked.

"She died two years ago, and I miss her terribly. That's why I was drawn to Martha, you see. She seems lonely, and so am I. We help each other."

Chapter 13

Some Paths You Choose; Some Are Chosen for You

The Grenville Farm
Christmas 1901

When the girls came home for their Christmas break, each of them had news to share. After a family dinner at which all the sisters were together again, Lillian asked for their attention. She was bright-eyed over the fact that she had found herself a beau at the church her employers attended. She had gone with the Ledbetters that first Sunday only to be polite, she said. She had never heard of the Church of the Lord's Truth and was more than a little curious about it. Within a couple of weeks, her questions had caught the attention of a young man named Frederick Cummings.

Frederick was a butcher's assistant by trade. During the day, he drove a meat wagon, making deliveries to local groceries and eating establishments. He could often be spotted on local streets wearing a bloodstained apron and toting a leg of mutton on one shoulder. On Sundays, however, he became a one-man welcoming committee at his church. A visitor was sure to attract his attention and be given an intensive lesson on what it meant to belong to this fine organization, which he was sure was the one true church.

Lillian was an early target for his ministrations. "We are Pentecostals," he explained. "Do you know what that means?"

Lillian laughed up at him. "I haven't the faintest idea," she confessed.

"Well, then, it's time for a quick Bible lesson. Jesus promised His disciples that the Holy Spirit would someday come upon them, and that's what happened on the day of Pentecost. The disciples were all gathered in one spot, and suddenly they witnessed tongues of flame coming out of the sky and touching the heads of each of them. And they began to speak in languages that they did not know, but they understood one another perfectly. God's real church was born on that day, and the disciples were able to go out and preach the Word and gather converts to the true faith because they spoke all languages."

Lillian was staring at him in surprise. She had never heard someone talk about religion so passionately. "And you call yourself a Pentecostal. Does that mean that you . . .?"

"Yes. Yes, it does. God favored our own little congregation with the same spiritual outpouring several years ago, and since that day, we true believers have been able to speak in unknown tongues and cast out demons."

"You can really do that?" Lillian was agog with admiration.

"Of course. If you come to one of our revival meetings, you'll see it happen for yourself. We have been given something called 'charismata,' which are gifts of the Holy Spirit. The gifts of revelation are wisdom and understanding. The gifts of power are faith, miracles, and the ability to heal. And the gifts of utterance allow us to prophesy and speak in tongues. That is why we are also called Charismatics."

"When I asked Mrs. Ledbetter what kind of church the family attended, she didn't use those words," Lillian said. "She said it was evangelical. That's a term I've heard, but I'm not sure what it means, either."

"Evangelism is simply preaching and teaching the Word, and spreading our faith through missionary efforts, such as revivals. So, we are Pentecostals, Charismatics, and Evangelicals, all at once."

"Can I really see you do these wonderful things?"

"Of course you can. I want you to. We have a tent revival meeting at the edge of town every Wednesday night. If Mrs. Ledbetter will allow you to take a couple of hours off, I will come and personally escort you to our next session."

Lillian saw many things she could not explain that night. Flames did appear to dance over the heads of some participants in the services. A woman suddenly jumped from her seat and began to shout words Lillian could not understand. Then the woman appeared to be overtaken with emotion and began to cry, with others joining in to cry and shout with her. A preacher walked up to a crippled boy and held out his hand. "In the name of God," the preacher shouted, "I command you, Demon, to leave the body of our brother Nathan!" The boy stood and straightened his legs for the first time. Then he took several steps before falling to his knees, shouting, "Thank you, Lord!"

The climax of the evening came when a preacher approached a basket and lifted out a huge snake. Frederick leaned over and whispered to Lillian, "That's a poisonous cobra, but it will not bite a true Charismatic." The man wound the snake around his shoulders and then lifted it heavenward before putting it back into its basket.

Lillian was convinced. "Can women share in this power?" she asked Frederick.

"Not directly," he said. "The disciples were all men. But a woman who is touched by the flames of Pentecost can be a helpmeet to her Charismatic husband as he brings prophecy and spiritual understanding to his people. Do you think that is something you would like to be able to do?"

"Oh, yes." Lillian was barely breathing in her anticipation. "I think this is what I've been looking for all my life."

"Then we must make your wish become a reality."

❧

Lillian finished her tale and sat back, beaming, waiting for her parents' approval. Instead, she met with silence. Nora and Millie, who had been listening with pained expressions on their faces, stood and asked to be excused because it was time for them to return to their homes and small children. Jamey reached for his pipe. Automatically, Katerina said, "You know you shouldn't be smoking, dear."

"Sometimes it deadens the pain," he replied.

Ruby made a strangled noise that sounded like a laugh gone bad.

Finally, it was Becca who drew the telltale breath and launched the family reaction. "Dear Lord, tell me you haven't gone off and married this fellow, Lillian!"

"No, of course not. Not yet. One doesn't just go off and marry one of the Anointed Ones. I have lessons to study and tests to take. The Elders will have to approve any step we take. Oh, and of course, Frederick will expect to come here and meet you himself and formally announce his intentions, if I am approved as his helpmeet. I only wanted you to know that I have met my true soul mate and that this will all take place some time in the future."

"When do you learn how to pull rabbits out of a hat and saw naked women in half?" Ruby asked, no longer able to contain her amusement.

"Don't be unkind, Ruby," her mother cautioned. "But Lillian, we will want you to think long and hard before you get any more deeply involved."

"I can't believe you're all against me! But maybe this is one of my tests. In which case, I shall prove my steadfastness. Now, if you'll excuse me, I think I'll go read my Bible for a while."

"I don't think I can equal that performance," Ruby said, breaking the uncomfortable silence, "but this may be as good a time as any to tell you my own news. I assure you it's not nearly as farfetched."

"Go ahead, my dear," Jamey invited.

"Well, to be blunt, I got fired. The Easterlings hired me as a seamstress to make dresses for their young daughter. It wasn't hard work, and it was actually fun to have access to all that fancy material and lacy trimming. But it really wasn't what I wanted to do. I was hoping to be in a position to observe their dinner parties and fancy dress balls. Instead, I was locked in the attic with a needle and thread. One day, I got the idea that if I knew how closely my own figure matched that of young Miss Easterling, I could use myself as a model and save her some fitting time. So on a day when the family members were all out of the house, I went into Miss Easterling's wardrobe and started trying on her clothes. To my delight, most of them fitted perfectly."

Her mother grimaced, anticipating what was coming. *"Du bist ein Dummeresel!"* she murmured.

Ruby paused to take a deep breath. "And then I got caught. There I was, all decked out in one of Miss Easterling's ball gowns, when she walked into the room. She immediately started screaming at me, and her parents came running to see what was the matter. All I could do was stand there and look guilty, although I didn't see what was so terrible about what I had done. It wasn't like I had gotten the gown dirty or anything. But it didn't matter. They fired me on the spot, told me to go pack my things and get out of the house."

"Of course they did," Jamey scolded. "Your behavior was inexcusable. You broke their trust and violated that girl's privacy. You're lucky they didn't accuse you of theft."

"What does Uncle Heinrich think?" Katerina asked.

"I don't know. I didn't tell him. When I left the house, I walked downtown and started looking at some of the local shops. Then I saw a sign in the window of the local traveler's inn. It said they were looking for a serving wench to work in the tavern. So I headed in, picked up a towel, and started to clear some of the tables. Evidently, that impressed the owner, because he came out and asked if I was applying for the job. I told him I was, and he handed me an apron. Easy as that. I left one job and found another. And this one is much better. I get my own room in the boarders' section of the inn, I can take my meals as soon as all the customers have been fed, and I meet all kinds of interesting people. Some of them tip well, too."

"I'll bet they do!" said Becca, rolling her eyes.

"It's a perfectly honorable profession, Aunt Becca."

"Uh-huh."

Jamey was shaking his head in disbelief. "Dear Heaven! We have one daughter planning to become the wife of a snake-handler, and the other is a barmaid, sloshing beer on men's shoes. I don't know which one is worse."

"You're only sixteen—much too young to be working in a tavern. I want you to come home," Katerina said.

"No, Mother, I won't. I like what I do, and I'm old enough to make my own decisions. I'm staying in New Castle. You told us all that we needed to go out and find husbands to help out the family finances. Well, that's what Lillian and I have been doing. I don't see what you have to complain about."

❧

Katerina had long made it a practice to refrain from buying trouble. She had decided many years earlier that worrying did not help solve problems, while ignoring a problem sometimes allowed it to shrink to manageable proportions. So once Lillian and Ruby returned to New Castle, she put their situations firmly out of her mind. She had enough to worry about as she watched Jamey continue to struggle with his health problems.

She had followed Becca's suggestion to have a long discussion with Dr. Higgins about Jamey's needs, and the doctor had responded with a suggestion of his own. "Why don't you learn how to be a practical nurse?" he said.

"You mean, go back to school? I can't do that!"

"No, no, a practical nursing certificate only requires that you work under a doctor's supervision to learn how to provide basic care, most of which you already know from your own experiences. You must be able to cook nourishing and palatable foods fit for an invalid. You do. I've seen you make a mean custard! You must have a basic understanding of cleanliness and neatness—making beds and such tasks. You must be familiar with common home remedies, like a simple cough syrup or a cooling salve for a burn. And you must have enough common sense to know when your expertise has reached its limits and it is time to call in the doctor."

"Well, after having nine children, I've learned most of that, I'll admit. But . . ."

"No more protests. You can get a few weeks of experience accompanying me to visit your neighbors, and then you can apply for your own license. The clerk will ask you some basic questions, and I will have to sign a form certifying you. Mrs. Higgins got her certificate recently so that she could help me with my patients, and she would be happy to work with you on what to expect during that examination. It'll be a worthwhile experience for you, and it will increase your confidence in taking care of your husband."

"I don't have a lot of free time, Doctor Higgins. My youngest is only three, so I can't just go off to take care of someone else's family."

"You need to do this now, Mrs. Grenville, while your husband is still strong enough to keep an eye on the child. You'll be glad you did when the time comes for him to need your full-time care. And beyond that, it will assure you of a way to earn your own living after . . ."

Katerina closed her eyes and shook her head to stop him from completing that sentence. But she also understood the validity of his argument. "All right. I'll do it. Where do I start?"

Rebecca's Journal

I'*ve been thinking a lot about how our lives change, most of the time catching us unawares. Katerina is working very hard at her practical nurse training. I see her with books on anatomy and collections of home remedy recipes. She is often gone at night, sitting with one of Dr. Higgins's patients. And she sometimes talks me into pretending to be injured so that she can practice her bandages and tourniquets. I'm sure she never thought she would become a practicing nurse, but she has accepted her new role with grace.*

Recently, Dr. Higgins stopped by the farmhouse with a gift for her. He had a small black satchel, which he had tricked out with all the medical equipment she might need—a thermometer, a mortar and pestle, bandages, an assortment of ointments and homeopathic pills, and even a stethoscope to be used to listen to a patient's heart or lungs. It makes me smile to see her so excited about her new skills and at the same time so nervous about her upcoming testing period. How we have both changed over the years!

My own changes astound me. Who would have ever thought that little Rebecca Grenville would grow up to be a children's author! What an extraordinarily farfetched idea that would have been in the 1860s! I hated other children. My two younger brothers were a constant torment to me, particularly Jamey. And I despised childish things. That dollhouse Grandmother Dubois gave me for Christmas in 1861 was ridiculous, in my eyes. All those tiny little pieces of furniture—I was supposed to enjoy placing them in the rooms and rearranging them to suit whatever season it happened to be. Silliness! Pure silliness!

All I ever cared about as a child were books and music. But the books I coveted were thick and dusty, pilfered from my father's library and read in secret by candlelight. I wanted to be able to write books like those. I imagined heroines who rose above family circumstances to find true love with rich and titled noblemen. I wanted those noblemen to be strong and handsome and brave beyond compare. If I had my druthers, I would set the scenes in an English castle on a hilltop somewhere above the moors, in a landscape buried in snow. An evil butler would lurk behind every closed door, and fearful serving girls would scurry about, dusting the chandeliers.

As for music, I envied my mother's talents at her melodeon. I tried my best to master the art of touching the keys *gently to convey my innermost emotions, as she could. Mother played only classical pieces during my childhood. Sometimes, she helped me to master the études that every student must learn, but I didn't see much sense in playing scales. I wanted that instrument to laugh with me and weep with me. I was never very good, but I could play to please myself. I learned to scorn the more popular pieces that my friends liked.*

 I remember hating the very idea of art, too. All those dismal portraits of Mother's ancestors that hung in our dining room haunted me. At every meal, I felt as if some disapproving old woman was looking over my shoulder and criticizing the way I chewed. I sat through Father's history lectures and found them even more boring when they were accompanied by lessons on the artistic styles of the ages. I never saw art as a way of conveying emotion the way words or music could.

 No wonder I never tried my hand at painting or drawing! Jamey says that I used to draw little designs on my school papers. He laughed when he described our childhood tutor, old Mr. Wilson, chastising me for scribbling little pictures between my arithmetic problems. I don't remember doing that, but Jamey says I once drew some thick numbers and added faces to them, just to annoy our teacher. Perhaps so. But no one—including me—ever expected me to be making a living from drawing pictures of ladybugs and crickets.

 I suppose what I really disliked was being a child. I wanted to be an adult, able to control my own destiny. Ha! How little I knew of the world! By the time I got my wish to become an adult, everything I thought I knew about the world had been turned upside down. And ever since, I've been trying to find that perfect world I thought was out there, waiting for me.

And now here we both are, Katerina and I, two women well into middle age, living not in a castle on the moors but in the Pennsylvania woods. Not a contented grandmother, knitting little booties, but a bed-pan-emptying nurse. Not a writer of bodice-ripping English romances but the creator of little stories for children about bugs. Not a famous musician but gaining some notice as an artist. Would any of us, I wonder, be willing to grow up if we knew we would turn out to be the polar opposites of everything we ever wanted to be?

Chapter 14

Marriage Changes Everything

The Grenville Farmhouse
1903-1905

*E*ven in the isolated hills of western Pennsylvania, news of the astounding innovations and unexpected disasters of the early twentieth century managed to upset the kilter of everyday life. Becca was fascinated by the stories of Carrie Nation, storming into saloons to close them down. She herself had no strong feelings about the issues of temperance, but she could not help but root for a powerful woman taking on a world controlled by men. Local newspapers were full of stories about oil discoveries in Texas and the opening of the first theater to feature moving pictures instead of live performances. The first attempts to manage the heat of summer by adding something called "air conditioning" had Katerina fanning herself harder and wishing it could be put in private houses as well as public buildings. Jamey was more interested in the news that the first wireless messages had been sent across the Atlantic and that a couple of bicycle-shop owners were trying to accomplish a manned airplane flight.

Then came word of President McKinley's assassination and the realization that the world had become a smaller place and that ordinary people had greatly extended their horizons. "A Polish anarchist shooting the American president at an exposition of modern discoveries? I'm not sure I like the direction all these newfangled ideas are leading us in," Jamey fussed. "I'm already feeling old and outdated because I can no longer work around the farm the way I used to. Now the whole world seems to be spinning out of control and moving beyond my understanding."

❧

Almost as if in response to Jamey's complaint, Paul Davidson arrived at the Grenville farm one fall evening. "I've come with a business proposal," he announced. "I couldn't help but notice that you have left most of your fields lie fallow this year."

"I'm afraid that's so," Jamey replied. "I simply don't have the stamina for farming anymore. Eventually, that land will have to be sold off."

"I'm not in a position to purchase it, but I can make you a temporary offer that may be of help to you. I have a very small farm. I could easily plant and harvest most of your fields alongside my own, particularly if the fields were given over to grains that do not take much cultivation in midsummer. I would be willing to take on that responsibility and then split the income from your lands with you, fifty-fifty. My labor and your land together would create a profitable venture for both of us."

"It's a generous offer," Jamey said. "But why would you do that? You hardly know us."

"It's the sort of thing a man would do for his father-in-law."

"What?" Jamey shook his head as if to clear his hearing.

"You see, my offer also comes with a proposal of marriage."

"Marriage? To whom?" Now Katerina was the puzzled one.

"I would like to marry your daughter Martha, if she will have me."

"Martha? No! She's not capable of being someone's wife. This is a ridiculous idea." Katerina was on her feet, ready to show the young man the door.

"Please. Hear me out, Mrs. Grenville. I explained to you once before that Martha reminds me of my late sister, who suffered from some of the same disabilities. Martha and I have become great friends, I thought with your approval."

"Friendship is one thing. Marriage is quite a different proposition."

"In my opinion, all marriages ought to be built on friendship. I've gone out walking with Martha for over two years, and I've seen her blossom. Surely you have noticed that her vocabulary has improved, along with her interest in the world and her ability to carry out her chores. Our friendship has given her a reason to become everything she is capable of being."

"I'll give you that. Your friendship has been good for her. But I don't understand what you hope to get out of this arrangement. She can't be a wife to you in the full sense of the word. She can't even cook or do heavy cleaning."

"Mrs. Grenville, I live alone and have done so for several years. I take care of all my own needs, including cooking and cleaning. I assure you that I am not trying to buy a servant. What I cannot provide for myself is companionship—someone to come home to at the end of the day, someone to share a smile with, or a laugh. Martha and I would be good for each other."

"But there are other issues," Jamey said. "I hesitate to bring this up in mixed company, but you must have physical needs that she would be unable—or unwilling—to accommodate."

"I promise you that I would never force myself on her or do her harm in any way. Look, I'm not going to argue this further with you. I hope you'll take some time to consider my offer. Talk to Martha. See how she reacts to the idea. Check my background, if you need to. Do whatever you have to do, but don't just slam the door on the idea."

Jamey and Katerina sat speechless for several minutes after Paul left, mulling over what had happened. Katerina broke the silence. "He's right, you know."

"About what?"

"A lot of things. We have never talked about what to do with Martha—about what happens to her when you and I are gone. Who takes care of her then?"

"I guess I assumed Becca would . . ."

"Becca's older than we are, dearest. So eventually, it would fall to one of our other daughters to take her in."

"Her sisters, who are doing such a fine, upstanding job of managing their own lives at the moment?" Jamey snorted in disgust.

"All right, then. So she needs a husband. No sense going to look for someone when a volunteer is banging away at our door. Paul's right, too, about asking Martha how she feels about him."

"Do you think she'll understand? Or be able to tell us how she feels?"

"We can only try." Kat went to the doorway to the kitchen and asked her daughter to come to the parlor. Martha made her way slowly, looking a bit fearful. It was not often her parents summoned her for a talk.

"Martha, do you know what marriage is?"

The girl shrugged and then pointed to her parents.

"That's right. Your Papa and I have a marriage. It means we live together and raise a family. Do you think you would like to be married someday?"

Again, the girl simply shrugged to show she didn't know.

"If you were going to get married, who would you want to marry? Any young man in particular?"

She frowned and then brightened. "Pau?"

"Do you mean your friend Paul, dear?"

She nodded vigorously. "Yes. Marry Pau?" It was a question, not an answer.

"Yes. Would you like to marry Paul?"

"Marry Pau!" This time there was no doubt. A huge grin made her eyes crinkle, and she clapped her hands. "Marry Pau! Good!"

"Well, I guess that answers that!" Jamey exclaimed. "That's not a promise, Martha, but we're thinking about it."

Off Martha went, almost skipping down the hall, chanting, "Marry Pau! Marry Pau!"

⌘

The wedding was to be a simple affair in June, held in the backyard rather than formally at the church, which Katerina thought might overwhelm Martha. All her sisters had to be informed, of course, and in each case, disbelief was followed by suspicion and then by reluctant acceptance. For the older girls, Paul Davidson was a stranger, and one who would have to earn their trust. Still, they all assembled on the appointed weekend.

Lillian arrived in an open two-seated carriage pulled by a frisky white horse. The driver was a dapper young man in a distinctive get-up. He wore a dress shirt with a high stiff collar, but he had his sleeves rolled to the elbows. He sported a bright plaid bow tie and matching suspenders. He drove with the reins and whip in one hand and the other wrapped protectively around a beagle sitting on the seat next to him. Lillian clung to the seat on the other side of the dog.

In the yard, the young man leaped to the ground, hand extended toward Jamey. "Frederick Cummings, at your service, sir. I'm your newest son-in-law, at least the newest before this weekend." Behind him, Lillian alighted from the carriage without assistance, coming to stand slightly behind the young man. Jamey and Katerina gawked at the couple in silence for a long moment. Then Katerina shook her head in denial. "You can't be married. Not without our knowledge or permission."

"I didn't need your permission, Mother. I'm over twenty-one. Besides, we had the blessing of our church elders, and only they know what is God's will for us."

"But—"

Jamey reached out to stop his wife's protest. "What's done is done, I suppose. But I shan't tell you that we are happy about it."

"We are happy about it. That's what counts," Lillian replied, her chin jutting out in defiance.

Jamey responded with nothing more than a raised eyebrow to express his displeasure. "Well, you shall have to come in and introduce the rest of the family. What's to be done with that dog?"

"Bentley?" Cummings looked down, smiling at the beagle. "Bentley's a house dog, aren't you, boy? He'll stay with us."

"Not in my house, he won't." Katerina had been pushed to her limit. "I have eight daughters to take care of and a wedding to get ready for. I have never allowed a dog in my house, and I'm not about to start now."

Lillian tugged at her husband's arm. "Please, Frederick. Don't make a scene. Tie him to the carriage for now. Later, we can take him over to stay with my Aunt Becca. She loves animals. She'll be glad to have him."

It did not take the Grenvilles long to notice various oddities in Mr. Cummings's behavior. He was fastidiously clean, washing his hands at every opportunity, or at least dusting them off with a handkerchief whenever he touched something. He straightened objects, lining up books with the edge of the table or arranging three pencils in descending order of size. At dinner, he used his napkin to polish his silverware before he could begin to eat. Katerina glared at him, but he didn't notice.

Dinner itself did not go well, either. Katerina made a point of passing him the platter of fried chicken, only to be told that, no thank you, he was a vegetarian.

"Well, you'll still make out well. This is a working farm. If there's one thing we have, it's vegetables." But the potatoes were awash in chicken gravy and the beans seasoned with bacon fat. Frederick poked at his food, pushing it around his plate in an effort to find a morsel he deemed fit to eat. The rest of the family dived into their mother's cooking. The chicken platter was soon empty. "Someone send that platter down this way, and I'll get the rest of the chicken from the kitchen. Poor Lillian didn't even get a chance at it before you hooligans emptied it."

"It's all right, Mother," Lillian said. "I found the tail and that will do for me."

Frederick made a warning sound at her, and she turned with just a touch of hostility, emboldened, perhaps, by finding herself back in the family circle. "For heaven's sakes, Frederick, it's only the tail—a single bite. It won't kill me to eat that bit of meat."

"As if it's meat at all," Nora sniffed. "I declare, Lillian, I don't know how you stand eating that tail end of fat and gristle."

"It's good, what there is of it. And there's enough of it, such as it is." Lillian recited the phrase she had been using since childhood, sending her sisters into fits of giggles but leaving Frederick mystified and more than a little miffed at finding himself on the wrong side of the joke.

To change the subject, Jamey asked about Ruby's absence. "Surely she's not going to miss a chance for a party?"

"No, she'll be here," Lillian said, "but not until later tonight. I'm afraid she's planning a grand entrance of her own."

"Oh, no! What's she up to now?"

"Not my story to tell," Lillian murmured.

⁂

And a grand entrance it was—Ruby swooped into the house, trailing a long cape and holding a bundle in her arms. Behind her came a little man in a leather jacket, carrying four suitcases, one in each hand and the other two tucked into his armpits. As the family looked on in shock, the bundle emitted a loud, shrieking wail.

"Is that a—a baby?"

"Yes, Mother dear, meet your newest granddaughter, Miss Frankie Sheffield." She thrust the crying baby at her mother and turned to help with the luggage. "This is Herbert Sheffield, by the way, but don't get any ideas. He's not Frankie's father. He's just loaning us his name to keep us looking honest. Herbert's a tinker by trade—lives in his wagon and travels around fixing things for people. You'll find the wagon in the yard, if any of you have a pot that needs mending."

"Ruby! Quit flouncing around and find this gentleman somewhere to sit. He looks exhausted, and I can see why." Katerina was staring at the child in her arms. She was used to babies, of course, but this one was most unexpected.

"I think you have some explaining to do, daughter," Jamey said. "If Frankie—what kind of a name is Frankie, by the way?—if Frankie is not Mr. Sheffield's child, where is the father?"

"More important, who is he?" Nora asked.

"Beats me! Her baptismal name will be Frances—that is, if I can find someone willing to baptize a bastard child belonging to a barmaid. As for her father, I never did get his name. He's a shoe salesman. He passed through New Castle about a year ago and left only this little calling card." Ruby's shell of bravado was beginning to crack around the edges. "Is there anything else you'd like to know about my wild and dangerous life in the big city?"

"That's quite enough for the moment, Ruby. Let's all try to remember that this is Martha's big weekend. You all know that she is easily upset by raised voices, so let's be civilized and loving in our personal dealings. Time enough later for recriminations."

⟨≈⟩

Martha's wedding went more smoothly than anyone could have hoped. The minister handled the vows carefully, giving Martha only two or three words at a time so that she could repeat them. She beamed with pleasure when she succeeded. Lillian's preacher and Ruby's tinker finally picked up on the family dynamic and managed not to make further trouble. There was a slight hitch at the reception when

Martha announced that it was time for bed. She cheerfully said, "Night, Pau!" and headed for the ladder to the girls' loft. But no one giggled, and her mother was able to explain gently that she was to go home with Paul, not send him off by himself.

"I still don't know whether this was a good idea," Jamey confided to Becca, but even Becca was so taken with the picture of Martha as a bride that she simply shushed him. "Give them a chance. They'll work it out for themselves."

When all the guests had left for home, the Grenville house seemed uncomfortably quiet. Katerina puttered around her kitchen for a long time, unwilling to let her world sink back into its everyday worries. Then, as was her habit, she whispered the catch phrase that had sustained her through all the years of Jamey's illness. "*Jeden Tag seine eigene Plage hat.* One day at a time, my girl. Sufficient unto the day are the troubles therein."

Chapter 15

The Dreams Girls Dream

Pittsburgh, Pennsylvania
Summer 1905

Meanwhile, Gloria was having a crisis of her own. She was facing her last year of schooling, without a beau in sight and no real direction for her life. Unwilling to trouble her mother, who already had a basketful of worries of her own, Gloria began spending more and more time with her Aunt Becca.

"When did you know you wanted to become a writer?" she asked.

"Not for a long time. And I never believed I could do it until recently. Don't worry, Gloria. A path will open for you when the time is right."

On another day, Gloria asked a more intimate question. "It's none of my business, I know, so if you don't want to answer, you can tell me to hush up and go home. But I've always wondered why you never married. Didn't you ever fall in love?"

"There was a boy, once," Becca said softly, "but it didn't work out."

"Oh, no! What happened?"

"I've never talked about it. It's just a silly story about a couple of children."

"Please tell me."

"Well, we were very young. I was only twelve, and Josh was fourteen. It was 1862, and the Civil War was in full swing. My family had moved to our farm in Aiken, South Carolina, to escape the dangers of Charleston, and I had lost all my childhood friends. I met Josh McKay at church, and he was awfully nice to me, despite the fact that he must have thought of me as a little kid. He introduced me to some of his friends, walked with me through the downtown streets when my family came into town to shop, and sat with me at church suppers. He said I was easy to talk to. That was because I hung on every word he spoke, of course. And he talked to me about how frustrated he was that everyone told him he was too young to go to war. Both his older brothers were in the army, and he felt useless.

"That winter, his family got word that their oldest son had been killed at the battle of Fredericksburg and that the middle son had also been wounded. His mother begged her wounded son to quit and come home, but he refused, his letters telling the family that his unit was then on the move, headed to Pennsylvania for a little place called Gettysburg. Josh decided it was his duty to go and find his brother and help him stay alive. I told him he was too young and that his mother and father needed him, but I really meant that I needed him. Nothing I said made any difference. He ran off and made his way all the way to Pennsylvania. I had one letter from him. He said he had found his brother and was marching with his regiment. And that was the last I ever heard from him.

"Then one Sunday in late July, his parents came to church all dressed in black. Both their remaining sons had been killed at Gettysburg, they said. No one knew why I went home and took to my bed. They thought I was sick, and I was—sick with grief. We were young—too young to have been involved in what you might call a romance. But I somehow decided he was the love of my life and I would never find another man to take his place. So now I have a cat and a comfortable, if solitary, life."

"How sad! Did you ever learn what happened to him? You must have wondered . . ."

Becca shook her head. "No. It was such a long, long time ago. I seldom even think about it now. And I'm content as a single woman. Let's talk about you instead. You have an eighteenth birthday coming up soon, which calls for a special present. What can I get you? Something pretty to catch a young man's eye, perhaps?"

"Nothing like that, but there is something I would like, if . . ." She hesitated.

"Tell me."

"Didn't I hear you tell Mother that you have to make a trip to Pittsburgh this summer—some business to take care of concerning your next book?"

"Yes, that's right. There's something from there that you want?"

"No. I want to go along with you."

"Gracious, Gloria! Why? I didn't even know you knew anyone there."

"I don't, not yet, but I want to apply for a job in Pittsburgh's big department store—Kaufmann's, at the corner of Fifth Avenue and Smithfield."

"A job?"

"Yes. Mother has always told us that it is as easy to fall in love with a rich man as it is a poor one. But there aren't any rich men around here, as far as I can see. So I plan to go where the rich men are. And what better place to find them than an eight-story department store selling objects of the highest quality and style? If I can just get there, I can talk to the other shopgirls and find out exactly what it takes to get hired. And then I'll do whatever they recommend. But first, I need that trip. Please say you'll take me with you."

"Only if your parents approve."

"Why wouldn't they? Working in an elegant department store certainly sounds better than a snake-charmer church or a tinker's wagon or a barroom."

⸙

Becca and Gloria took the early morning train to Pittsburgh on a warm July day. A hansom cab dropped Gloria at the front door of Kaufmann's Department Store just before its ten o'clock opening. "Remember, Gloria, you are not to leave the store. You'll be able to get something to eat in the store restaurant, and go to the ladies' lounge if you get tired and need to rest. I'll meet you here under the big clock at five o'clock sharp."

"Aunt Becca, I'm a big girl now. I can handle myself just fine. You go on and take care of your book business. We'll have time to share our discoveries at dinner."

And true to her promise, Gloria had her day all planned out. She lingered for a while on the first floor, wandering seemingly aimlessly from one cosmetics counter to another, fingering the buttery-soft gloves on offer in ladies' accessories, trying on a hat here and there, and whenever possible, smiling at the shopgirls who tracked her every move. Then she summoned the courage to board the iron cage of the elevator and travel to the top floors. She chatted with the woman running the elevator to hide her nervousness and to pump her for information on which floors did the most business.

In her pocket, Gloria had a small notebook, in which she kept track of what kinds of merchandise were available in each department. She investigated furniture, housewares, and linens. She pretended to be interested in baby furniture and children's clothing. The salesmen in the menswear department looked at her so suspiciously that she did not linger. But in ladies' ready-to-wear, she indulged in an orgy of trying on the latest styles, making quick friends of the girls who proffered their suggestions of which outfits might look best on her.

At lunch, she visited the store's dining room and sampled the kinds of offerings she would never find back in Ellwood City. She had a watercress salad, assorted tea sandwiches with the crusts cut off, and a tomato aspic that made her eyes water from the horseradish flavoring. A chocolate tart and a cup of strong black tea convinced her that life in the city was indeed worth living.

She spent most of her afternoon talking with the girls her own age who worked in various departments. In each instance, her questions were the same: How did you get your job? Who is the most influential person to contact about working here? What are your hours? What restrictions do they place on what you wear and how you behave? Where do the shopgirls live? And all the while she was observing their dresses, their hairstyles, and their mannerisms. It was almost four o'clock when she met Miriam, who was rearranging the soap display just inside the front entrance.

"Do you enjoy working here?" she asked.

"Oh, I love it! It's hard work, standing all day long, but I meet so many interesting people. I see them all as they come through the door—our city socialites, actresses, local politicians. That was the mayor who just walked in, by the way. But why do you ask? Are you looking for a job?"

"Oh, I am! I'm trying to learn as much as I can about the store, so that I can sound knowledgeable if I ever get a chance to apply."

"Well, I can help you there. I happen to be walking out with one of the powers-that-be, and he's headed this way now. Would you like an introduction?"

"Yes!" Gloria could hardly breathe. "My name's Gloria Grenville, and I'm from Ellwood City."

Miriam greeted the dapper gentleman who approached the counter with a dazzling smile and then introduced her new friend. "This is Miss Grenville, visiting us for a day, Mr. Simmons. I do believe we could persuade her to join us here at Kaufmann's, if you know of an opening."

"How do you do, Miss Grenville? I'm Charles Simmons, floor manager here. Are you enjoying our little shop?"

"Very much, sir. I feel as if I've entered a palace—the mirrors, the flowers, the chandeliers—and your offerings are the stuff that dreams are made of."

He smiled indulgently and looked her over, his glances frankly taking in her blond curls and trim figure. "Have you any experience?"

"There are no department stores in Ellwood City, I'm afraid. But I'm a hard worker, strong, and good at math, too."

"So you're not from Pittsburgh?"

"No. I'm visiting the city with my aunt, who is a rather famous writer of children's books. She is spending the day with her publisher, so I thought I would take this chance to get to know more about your store."

"And are you free to start work immediately?"

Gloria caught her breath. "Ah, yes, yes, certainly. I would need to find somewhere to live, but . . ."

"Oh, we can help you there," Miriam said. "Quite a few of us share quarters in a boardinghouse just down the street. Mr. Kaufmann provides us with lodgings and meals as part of our salary, if we so desire."

"That sounds wonderful."

"Well, then, we've been looking for a shopgirl to work in sixth-floor housewares. You'll have to become familiar with silverware and china patterns as well as cooking implements, but you'll meet a great many young brides from our most prominent families. Do you think you could handle that?"

"Yes, I'm certain I could."

"Well, then, why don't you come back in the morning? Take the elevator up to the top floor and ask for Samuel Kaufmann, the hiring manager. He will get you set up with all the necessary arrangements."

Gloria was clutching her chest, sure that her hammering heart could be heard by everyone around. "Th-thank you," she stammered. "I didn't expect . . ."

"You'll do fine. You have the look of one of our girls."

Gloria was still trembling when Becca arrived to meet her. "I have a job, Aunt Becca. I start tomorrow. And Mama is going to kill me!"

"Well, she will certainly kill me if I come home without you. Fortunately, the family is expecting us to spend another day or so in Pittsburgh. So let's see what tomorrow brings. Perhaps when you talk with the hiring manager, you can ask for the time to go home and get your things. That's not unreasonable."

Rebecca's Journal

March 1906

And so began Gloria's career as a shopgirl. As I suspected, the store had no intention of putting her to work the very next day. She had, in fact, two weeks to go home and get herself ready to move to Pittsburgh. The biggest challenge, she found, was piecing together a wardrobe, since the store required all their shopgirls to wear black dresses or black skirts with white blouses. There was, of course, no money in the Grenville household for new clothes, but luckily, she had seven sisters, who scoured their own clothing chests for suitable attire.

She soon fit right in with the other girls at the boardinghouse. "I have seven sisters," she laughed. "I'm used to sharing my living space." She learned to dress her hair in the latest Gibson Girl style and tailored her wardrobe to suit the store's demanding requirements. She saved as much of her salary *as she could and practiced charming her customers with her knowledge of her wares. Soon she was promoted from sixth-floor housewares to the main floor, where new customers were treated to demonstrations of the finest in soaps, parasols, jewelry, and gloves. Then she moved to ladies' fashions, where she was put to work modeling new styles for gentlemen who wanted to see how their wives or mistresses might look in the outfits they were considering. It was only a matter of time before she started to catch the eyes of several young blades who were eager to take her dancing or dining. All has been going just as she and her mother planned . . . and just as I feared.*

I have tried not to criticize my brother's wife. I understand that we have different backgrounds and different goals in life, but when it comes to the way she guides her daughters, I am often forced to bite my tongue. For as long as I have known Katerina, she has talked about the need to marry off her daughters. She convinced them all that they needed to find husbands as soon as they were old enough to wed. And she and the girls have been none too selective in their choice of mates. Look at their matches.

Nora married a schoolteacher who has many good qualities to his credit. Henry Southerland works hard, he is intelligent, he is kind, financially stable, and devout. But he's also dull. I've noticed that when they visit the family, he seldom says a word, not even to Nora. If there is any love or passion— or even friendship—between them, they keep it well-hidden.

Millie's husband, Joseph Sweitzer, has more personality, and he and Millie seem to be very happy with one another.

But he is also remarkably lacking in ambition. His little family lives in what amounts to a shack along the side of the road. The house has not a single modern convenience—no piping to bring water in, a two-hole outhouse set much too close to the surrounding woods, no lighting except for candles, and a wood-burning stove to do the double duty of cooking and heating.

Lillian's husband, Frederick Cummings, is so odd as to be frightening. He is, at best, a complete religious fanatic, given to handling poisonous snakes and speaking in tongues. I also fear that he suffers from such severe mental disturbances as to be dangerous to those around him. He has various nervous tics and several mannerisms that he repeats over and over again. He completely dominates Lillian's every move. I watch her closely when she comes for a visit, afraid I am going to see bruises or other signs of physical abuse, but if they are there, she keeps them concealed. I probably should not blame Katerina for this choice. She had nothing to do with Lillian's decision to marry the man, but she did not do anything to stop the match, either.

Then there's Ruby's situation. She's certainly not the first young girl to find herself pregnant by a traveling salesman, but her decision to attach herself to an itinerant tinker just to use his name strikes me as cold and calculating. It's something Katerina might have advised: One must have a man, no matter what the cost.

And now they have married off Martha to Paul Davidson. He appears to be a perfectly polite young man, but I can't help but be suspicious of him. His proposal came as something of a business deal. He offered help on the farm in exchange for a wife, no matter that she has been severely handicapped from birth. What does he want from her? Just companionship, he says, but he has thereby wormed his way into controlling much of the family's financial affairs.

All of which brings me back to young Gloria, now alone in a big city and openly in the market for a rich husband, as her mother has so carefully taught her. And I worry that she will allow herself to be bought as a commodity, an attractive decoration for a rich man's arm, but only so long as she is young enough and pretty enough to please him. And behind her will come two more young girls, Fiona and Sally, to be bent to their mother's plan to see all her daughters married and safely protected under the wing of a strong man.

Oh, I know! I am the family spinster. Who would listen to my advice about marriage? But I look at this new century through different eyes and see enormous challenges ahead for women. The drive to give women political and economic power is vigorous and has been ever since the abolitionist movement during the War between the States. In some places, women already have the right to vote; it must come to the rest of us in due course. In this new twentieth century, women can have careers. We are allowed—even encouraged—to be educated, talented, and independent.

Katerina surely understands that. After all, she herself has been preparing to work as a practical nurse ever since Jamey's illness became known. Dr. Higgins and his wife have been diligent in teaching her how to handle a patient. She has studied the lists of medicines that the doctor has provided her, and she's become quite proficient in concocting her own potions and soothing ointments to relieve whatever ills may plague. She speaks of nursing as a career and sometimes observes that she could be earning good money doing for others what she does for her own family.

But while she sees her own potential for self-sufficiency, Katerina is still raising nineteenth-century girls, all of them ill-prepared for what the twentieth century holds in store. She encourages the older girls in their total dependence upon their husbands—though she, of all people, should understand how dangerous that is. And when Ruby and Gloria talk about their jobs, she belittles their efforts, assuming that, in due time, they will be able to quit working and find a good man to support them. I worry about what lies ahead for Fiona and Sally. Will she help them become strong women, or will she encourage them to live their lives as she wishes she were still able to do?

Chapter 16

If Wishes Were Horses, Beggars Would Ride

North Sewickley, Pennsylvania
1906–1908

On April 18, 1906, the San Francisco earthquake struck. Becca first read the descriptions in a Pittsburgh newspaper, and she was immediately thrust back into her memories of the Charleston quake. Each time she read of a person suddenly buried under the fall of a brick wall, or of herds of cattle being swallowed up by a gaping crack in the earth, she remembered her own terror. She could still hear the shrieking of the earth as it was torn apart, the sounds of glass shattering, the oddities of stationary objects suddenly moving of their own volition across a room. In her mind, she pictured the streets filled with rubble, the families frantically calling for lost loved ones, and the tilted buildings, the smell of broken gas lines, and the gushes of water released from broken water mains.

"I can scarcely bear to read the newspaper accounts," she commented to Jamey. "Every word reminds me of what I experienced in Charleston. There is the horror of seeing everything you thought you knew suddenly turned upside down or sideways. I watched an entire fireplace disappear in our parlor. It simply sank, leaving behind a gaping hole in the floor. And the constant fear—for days and weeks you couldn't sit down or go to bed without the knowledge that, at any second, a wall or a roof might come crashing down and crush you on the spot."

"What I fear even more than the destruction," she remarked a bit later, "is what I hear from my friends who remained in Charleston. They say that, even now, the fear of more disasters permeates the city. Everyone looks for someone else to blame, and the result is that society as a whole is filled with hatred and fear. The daughter of one of Father's abolitionist friends writes that there is a widespread rumor that God was punishing 'Uppity' Negroes after Reconstruction. And that somehow justifies random attacks on black people, just because they are available. This country doesn't need any more reason for its citizens to distrust one another."

"I'm more worried about the financial implications," Jamey responded. "All you see in the papers these days are stories about massive rebuilding projects in San

Francisco—how they are planning to rebuild it as the most beautiful city in the world. I'm hearing about speculators borrowing huge amounts of money to invest in the city with its new design. Add that to the other policies of the Teddy Roosevelt administration, like expenditures on the creation of national parks, and you have a government digging itself into a huge financial hole."

"Aren't spending, expansion, and investment good for the country?" Becca asked.

"Only if the money is there in the first place. These people might as well be playing with paper money. You don't happen to have any old Confederate bills lying around, do you? Someone would probably be willing to spend them."

❧

The financial crisis Jamey had been worrying about reared its head early in 1907, and by October and November, there was a massive run on regional banks, as several brokerage firms, including the Knickerbocker Trust, went broke. Jamey now refused to discuss the crisis, but he was distracted, pale, and frightened. In 1908, the local bank foreclosed on the Grenville farm. A sheriff's deputy nailed the notification to the door early one morning.

"What mortgage?" Katerina demanded, and Jamey was forced to admit that he had borrowed funds against the farm years ago, hiding it from her. He had seen it as a simple, quick bank loan to tide them over a bad spot at the turn of the century. He had been paying on it periodically ever since and also secretly selling off pieces of land to raise the payments.

"How could you? How dare you!" Katerina demanded. "This is my land. My parents' land. My inheritance, not yours. How could you just gamble it away?"

"Kat, I wasn't trying to steal it from you, but legally it is mine because I'm your husband. I was trying to save it for you. I am ill, and I know I cannot work the farm the way I used to. I wanted us to keep the land—to be able to live here and raise the girls—until . . ."

"Until you die? And then what did you think would happen to us?"

"I hoped to pay it off before then. I thought that Becca's purchase of her cottage would surely be enough to carry us over. And it would have been, too, if it had not been for last fall's bank crisis. Now there has even been a run on our local bank, and they are unable to return their depositors' money. The federal agents have locked the bank doors and recalled all outstanding loans. That's not my fault."

"Isn't it?" Katerina glared at him and then turned her back to hide the angry tears coursing down her cheeks. She ripped the foreclosure papers from the door and read them silently for several long, painful minutes.

"So here it is," she said at last. "Our only choice. We have sixty days to try to sell the land and pay off the loan. If we can do that, we actually get to keep any amount we get above and beyond the loan amount. But if it is not sold within that period, the sheriff intends to show up and move our possessions out onto the road. Then the government takes the entire farm and does whatever they want with it. No matter what, we're out of this house within sixty days. And where will we go then?"

"I don't know, Kat. I just don't know. Selling the farm will affect Paul Davidson as well, because he'll lose access to land he has been farming. We'd better talk to him. If he would be willing to buy it from us . . ."

"*Wenn das Wörtchen wenn nicht wär, wär mein Vater Millionär.*" There was no smile on her face as she spoke.

"I don't know what that means—one of your German proverbs, I assume?"

"'If the word "if" did not exist, my father would be a millionaire.' My mother used it whenever someone was engaging in pipe dreams. The English equivalent, my foolish husband, is 'If wishes were horses, beggars would ride.'"

⁂

"I want to call a family meeting," Katerina announced a few days later.

"No! I won't let you do that. I can't bear to have to tell my daughters that I have lost their ancestral home." Jamey pounded his fist on the table and tried to shout, but he produced nothing but a wracking cough that left him gasping for breath.

"You're not in any condition to make demands, Jamey. You're ill, and the girls have to understand that. Not one of them has the money to purchase the farm, I know, but perhaps if everyone chips in . . ."

"No. It's my problem. I won't let them drive their own families into financial ruin to save me."

"You always told me, Jamey, that the Grenvilles settled all crises around a dinner table. It's time for us to do the same."

"I refuse to sit there in front of them all and do that."

"Then you can take yourself off to your sickbed and leave me to it. I intend to have them all here by the weekend."

"Please, let me talk to Paul first. Maybe he will have another idea."

"Try that if you must, but I intend to be in on the conversation. Ask him to come here."

That night, Katerina sat in front of her dressing table and stared into the cracked mirror. What happened to my dreams—that marrying Jamey would solve the problems of a lifetime? And how did I get so old? She wondered. Straggly gray hair pulled back into an ugly bun, wire spectacles on the end of my nose, deep lines from nose to chin, twisted fingers, a disappearing waistline, and a stooped back. I look like a hundred-year-old crone, and I'm barely out of my fifties. Where will I find the strength to pull us out of this crisis?

Paul Davidson arrived the next afternoon with Martha in tow, as usual. She kissed her mother with a smile and went off to find her sisters. Fiona and Sally were on the porch, playing with a litter of kittens, and Martha settled happily among them. Paul looked at his in-laws and shook his head. "I don't like what I see on your faces," he said.

"We don't have good news, Paul," Jamey responded. "We have just been served with a notice that the farm is being foreclosed. We have sixty days to sell it off. I didn't want to do that without filling you in on the situation, because I know the outcome will affect you as well."

"It certainly will! I want to hear the details." For the rest of the afternoon, the three of them hashed over all the facts and figures. But there were no easy answers. At last, Paul threw up his hands and strode away from the table.

"If I could see any way to purchase the land from you, I would do so, but I can't. I don't dare risk my own financial state, especially now that Martha is . . ." He shook his head and moved to the window, watching as the three sisters, like children of a similar age, played dress-up with a couple of very tolerant cats.

Katerina felt every muscle in her body tighten in alarm. "Martha is . . . what? What were you going to say? Is she ill?"

"No, not exactly. She's expecting a baby."

"No." Katerina's lips drew into one tight line. "No. She's not. She can't be. She cannot bear a child."

"I didn't know she had to ask your permission."

"It's impossible. Mentally, she's a child herself. What were you thinking, Paul?"

"I wasn't thinking of her as a child. She's my wife, and she is carrying my child. You needn't worry. The baby will have two parents. I'll be there to help her."

"Ein Kleinkind Sie nicht eine Mutter machen."

"You know I don't speak German."

"It means that having a baby will not turn her into a mother. No! I will not allow it!"

"I'm afraid there is nothing you can do about it."

"There are ways . . ."

"No! Now I'm the one saying no. You will not take this child away. It is my child, and Martha is my wife. That was our agreement. Now you will have to live with the consequences of that choice." He threw up his hands and stomped to the door before turning to them once more. "You invited me here because you have a serious problem. Don't use the coming of this baby as an excuse to forget about the foreclosure. Jamey, if you still want my help, I will talk to a couple of friends tomorrow. I'll see if I can find you a buyer. But the two of you must stay out of my marriage."

Chapter 17

A House Needs a Family
to Make It a Home

Three days later, Paul Davidson returned alone to talk to the Grenvilles. "I think I have a solution to your problem," he said. "I want you to hear me out before you react."

Jamey nodded. "If you can solve this dilemma, I'm more than willing to listen."

Katerina looked skeptical, but she, too, nodded in agreement.

"All right, then. A fellow named Michael Volenti is willing to purchase your farm, sight unseen, based solely on its location."

"Volenti? An Italian?"

"I said, hear me out. He's not a farmer but a business-man. And he doesn't want to live here. He's only interested in claiming the mineral rights to your land."

"But why—"

Paul held up a hand to stop the question. "Mineral rights. The right to mine the land and claim whatever resources lie beneath the surface. He's been following the news of oil discoveries in Texas and noticing how the price of land escalated once the first wells struck oil. He says—and from what I can find out, he's correct—that lands rich in coal often also have deeply buried oil and gas deposits. So he looks at our local coal mines and sees dollar signs."

"He's a goddamned speculator!"

"Jamey! Language!" Katerina cautioned.

"You agreed to listen. Yes, he's a speculator. That's what he does."

"Speculators are to blame for the financial crisis we're facing now," Jamey said. "They took advantage of the San Francisco earthquake to propose their own pipe dreams of the future, and the banks were foolish enough to listen to them. There are millions of dollars worth of unsecured loans out there, and the market cannot absorb them. So people worry about their own life savings being invested in get-rich-quick schemes, and they try to withdraw their money from the banks. Then, when the banks do not have sufficient funds, they are forced to close their doors, and the feds step in to collect whatever secured loans are floating around out there. You can't tell me about speculators. I'm one of their victims!"

His agitation led to another long coughing spell, and Paul waited quietly for the spasms to pass. "You mustn't shoot me, Mr. Grenville. I'm only the messenger. And I don't mean to upset you. I understand your objection to speculators in general. They are mere gamblers, usually betting with someone else's money. But in this case, you would be profiting from his plans, and you needn't care where the money is coming from. It's going into your pocket, not being taken out of it."

"Making me one of the people I hate?"

"I wouldn't look at it that way. As I see it, you're simply going to be getting back what is rightfully yours. Volenti is willing to pay top dollar for your farm—the full amount you owe on the loan plus five hundred dollars for your trouble."

"But we'd still have to move?" Katerina asked.

"Yes, it's my understanding that he intends to send his people in to clear the land of all structures . . ."

"Tear down the house, you mean?"

"Yes, but that's only because . . ."

"I don't care why he does it. It seems a terrible waste to me."

"Perhaps so, if you're looking at the farm as agricultural land. He wants it cleared to make it ready for any industrial use he may find for it. That's quite a different matter. I should also mention that he has agreed to let me continue cultivating the fields I'm now using, until such time as he is ready to use the land himself. I, in turn, will continue to split the income from those fields with you. You win again."

"Your plan still leaves us homeless."

"But with money in your pocket to find a new place to live. And I've solved that one for you as well."

"Lord Bountiful these days, aren't you?" Katerina could not disguise the sarcasm dripping from her words.

"I'd rather you think of me as a loving family member, but be that as it may. Are you familiar with the Nasmith property up on the ridge, right at the edge of Ellwood City?"

"No. Oh, wait, you mean that cabin that sits up there all alone, silhouetted against the sky? Only a single tree around it?"

"That's the one. Silas Nasmith owns the Ellwood lumber-yard. He built that cabin for his wife because she wanted to enjoy the view from up there. But then she died in childbirth, and he couldn't bear to live in the cabin without her. He sent their surviving baby off to grandparents in Philadelphia for care and schooling, and Nasmith himself moved into a rooming house in Ellwood City. He's unwilling to sell the house, in case the son wants to claim it some day. And there's no market for selling the house, anyway. So it's been sitting empty."

"How does that help us?"

"He would like to have a caretaker for the property. It's generally in good shape—a sturdy roof, two well-drawing chimneys, a big front porch, a good water supply, a place for a kitchen garden, and a few small outbuildings to house a chicken coop or stalls for a cow or a horse. He's willing to rent it to you for five dollars a month, provided you take care of the property for him."

"How many rooms?"

"A large parlor and dining area in the front, a kitchen and bedroom in the back extension, and a roomy loft above that can be divided into two sleeping areas."

"Not nearly as big as this house."

"No, but then you have only the two littlest girls living at home. You should have plenty of room, particularly when . . ."

"When I die, you were going to say, weren't you?" Jamey glared at him. "I'll be getting out of everyone's way soon enough."

"Jamey, you mustn't talk like that." Katerina laid a protective hand on his, but he shook her off.

"And if we don't take these offers?"

"Then, at the end of next month, federal agents will show up at your front door to move your possessions to the side of the road. They'll probably raze the buildings just as Volenti is planning to do. And the Nasmith cabin will continue to sit empty. The only difference will be that you will no longer have a roof over your heads."

"We don't have a choice, do we?"

"I'm giving you the best option I could come up with. But I can't make you take it."

Jamey and Katerina stared at one another, almost identical tight-lipped grimaces on their faces. "We'll take it," Katerina said at last. "Make it happen, Paul."

※

In the end, it took only a few minutes. Paul drove the Grenvilles into town in his carriage. They met in the old bank manager's office and signed papers they hardly bothered to read. Money changed hands. One bank order went from Mr. Volenti to the federal agent charged with closing the books on the loan. A second smaller bank order went to Jamey, who exchanged it on the spot for cash. Then he handed several of the bills to Mr. Nasmith, who turned over the key to the cabin. And they were done.

Katerina did her best to turn moving day into an adventure. She had asked her daughter Nora for assistance, and Nora had taken it from there, rounding up her sisters, with husbands and children in tow. Even Ruby showed up, although without her tinker friend. The only one missing was Gloria, who could not get days off from her shopgirl job. The daughters went straight to the Nasmith cabin. Armed with brooms, rags, and buckets full of lye soap and vinegar, they tackled several years' accumulation of windblown dust and trash. Spiders were rooted out without mercy. Windows were scrubbed with vinegar and newspaper. The children—Nora's Eva, Millie's Homer and Glenda, and Ruby's Frankie—went to work on the yard, raking leaves and gathering twigs. By the time the men arrived with the first wagonload of furnishings, the little cabin was ready for them to move it right in, except for one last family ritual.

"Wait here," Katerina told her sons-in-law. "I have four things that need to be taken into the house first."

"We'll get everything, Mother Grenville," Joseph said.

"No, you don't understand. This is a ceremony—an important one. First, I take in a broom. That's to sweep out any bad luck and to make sure that our home is always free from hidden dangers. Then I bring a loaf of bread, which promises that the family will always have our daily needs met. Next comes a cup of sugar, to add love and sweetness to our lives. And finally, there's a shaker of salt, to give our lives here flavor and fun." Katerina gathered her small basket and made a show of stepping into the cottage and arranging the ceremonial items on the shelf in the kitchen. "Now, with God's blessing, we are ready to move in!"

Becca had prepared a lunchtime feast at her Magnolia Cottage, since the cast-iron stove from the farm would have to be moved to the new cabin. Now she arrived, bearing salads, fresh bread, and a half of a baked ham for the hungry movers. Jugs of lemonade and sweet tea in honor of the Grenville's southern origins accompanied a huge chocolate cake Becca had prepared the night before. Katerina dithered from one chore to another, worrying unnecessarily about small things to keep her mind off the bigger problems.

Jamey spent his day on the front porch, wrapped in a blanket, supervising the whole process and feeling useless.

As for the girls, they were not as upset as their parents expected them to be. Especially for the older ones, the original Grenville farmhouse was in their past. Their focus was now on their own families. Nora did a bit of tut-tutting about the relative lack of room in the new house, but Millie thought to herself that it was bigger than her own place. Lillian worked hard at the cleaning, although her new husband Frederick did rather more pontificating than actual lifting. Even Martha, once given a specific job of eradicating spiders, pitched in willingly. All of them were happy to be acting as a family once more.

The younger girls, however, were experiencing some mixed emotions. Fiona, at age thirteen, could not decide whether to feel superior or put-upon when she was given adult-sized chores instead of being asked to work with the younger children. And Sally, at age ten, was simply overwhelmed by the changes taking place around her. After lunch, the two had been told to return to the farm with the men and help bring the animals to their new home. The last wagonload contained nothing but the cast-iron stove, leaving room for the girls to hitch a ride along with it. Fiona was in charge of several crates of chickens, while Sally held her cat under one arm and grasped the cow's lead rope with the other.

"You'd better put that cat down and hang on with one hand," Fiona advised. "If Bossy takes it into her head to stop and graze for a while, she's liable to pull you right off the back of the wagon."

"I don't dare put Cathagoras down," Sally said. "She doesn't understand where we're going, and if she gets away, she'll never find us again."

"So what? She's just a cat. There are always cats around."

Sally's eyes filled with tears. "No, she's my special friend. I need Cathagoras so I have somebody to talk to."

"That's such a dumb name for a cat. Why not call her Fluffy or Boots?" Fiona giggled as she realized she had found a new way to tease her little sister.

"It's not dumb! Cathagoras is named after a famous Greek . . .uh, a Greek person."

"That's Pythagoras, and he was a mathematician, not a cat."

"No, Pythagoras is a name for a boy, and Cathagoras is a girl."

"Oh, Sally, you're such a . . . a child."

Quiet reigned for a while, and then Sally spoke up again. "Fiona, aren't you scared?"

"Scared? About what?"

"About going to live someplace new?"

"No, silly, it's not all that far away. We'll still go to the same one-room schoolhouse and attend the same church. Mama and Papa will still be there. What's to be scared of?"

"What if . . . if Papa dies? I heard Paul and Frederick talking about him. They said everything will be different when that happens."

"Fathers don't die when their children aren't even grown. Papa's just sick. He's not going to die, so quit being a worrywart." But inside, Fiona was not so sure.

Chapter 18

Having a Baby
Does Not a Mother Make

North Sewickley, Pennsylvania
1908-1909

As the year drew to a close, the Grenville sisters and their families adjusted to their new reality. The Nasmith cabin was comfortable but not large enough to allow for a real family gathering at holiday time.

"Why don't I start playing hostess for Christmas dinner?" Nora suggested. "If we meet in Ellwood, you folks and Aunt Becca and the Davidsons are close enough to run back and forth, and the New Castle relatives can be housed here—Lillian and her husband with us, and Ruby and her daughter at Millie's. Little Frankie will love staying with her cousins. And if Gloria manages to get home, which does not sound promising, we can make room for her, too."

"That should work. I don't think we can expect to see Gloria. She says their store will stay open until almost midnight on Christmas Eve for last-minute shoppers. And they open extra early on Boxing Day for a giant sales event. It doesn't sound like much of a festive Christmas to me, but she says it's worth it for all the overtime pay she gets. And there's evidently a new man on the horizon, as well. I'm afraid she has taken my advice on finding a rich man all too seriously." Katerina looked thoughtful for a moment and then shook her head. "Never mind. I wish her well."

By the time Jamey and Katerina arrived at Nora's house on Christmas morning, the festivities were in full swing. Wonderful smells of roasting meats and coffee penetrated the cold. Ruby was playing Christmas carols on Nora's new piano, and the children were eyeing their bulging stockings with barely contained excitement.

"Christmas is one day in the year when we all eat well and don't worry about eating wisely," Nora announced. "Here's a platter of cookies and muffins, and the hot chocolate is ready in the kitchen."

The younger children squealed over the apples, oranges, and nuts they found in their stockings and secretly were thankful that no one had ended up with lumps of coal. Under the tree were piles of gaily wrapped packages—one toy for each child and a good supply of hand-knit scarves, socks, and mittens for everyone. Katerina had brought her daughters small packages—each containing an heirloom brooch or a pair of earrings passed down from their McDevlin ancestors. Henry Southerland disclosed an unknown talent for whittling small animals out of wood to delight the younger children. Joseph Sweitzer had brought beautiful semi-precious stones he had found in the coal mine, and Lillian gave everyone a small picture frame containing a hand-embroidered Bible verse.

But the greatest excitement of the morning came when Becca brought out a stack of her newest children's book, *Herbert the Hedgehog Finds a Friend*, each copy signed with a dedication to a family member who had helped inspire her career.

Even Ruby was impressed. "Aunt Becca! A hedgehog? How wonderful! And look how cute he is, all rolled up in a ball. Do you remember when I told you that you needed to learn to draw fuzzy?"

"I do, indeed, my dear critic. You forced me to greater efforts—and there he is!"

Martha wrapped her new scarf around her neck and patted it. Then she spotted little Eva's new doll and reached out to touch it gently. "Baby doll," she said.

Eva clutched the doll possessively. "Mine."

Nora frowned a warning at both of them and distracted everyone by producing a tray of dried fruits. "These came from one of Henry's students," she announced. "The dates are really quite wonderful, but the figs and apricots are good, too."

In the midst of all the laughter and chatter, Lillian pulled her mother to one side. "What's wrong with Martha? Is she ill? She looks . . . uh, puffy or something . . . not like herself."

"She's fine, Lillian. Don't worry about her."

"I don't believe you. I can always tell when you're hiding something. You smile, but the smile doesn't reach your eyes."

"She's not ill . . . she's . . . pregnant."

"No! She can't be! She can't have a child." Unexpectedly, tears welled in Lillian's eyes. "That's not fair! She won't even be able to care for a baby, and I've tried so hard to . . . Why would God give her a child and not me?"

"Oh, my dear, I'm sorry. But you mustn't be jealous. We can't presume to understand why things happen the way they do. There's a purpose in everything, even when we can't see it."

"I don't believe that. It just sounds like one of Frederick's platitudes. I'm sick of everyone telling me that things are God's will, as if everyone but me has a direct connection to the mind of God. If that's true, God makes some pretty stupid mistakes."

"Don't blaspheme, dear," Katerina said automatically.

"But what will they do? Martha is incapable of caring for a child, and . . ."

"I know, I know. Believe me, your father and I have hashed this over and over again. We talked to Dr. Higgins, and he has persuaded Paul to hire a live-in housekeeper.

He's found a reliable widow lady, old Mrs. Perkins, and she will be able to help."

"When is the baby due?"

"We don't know." Katerina rolled her eyes toward the Davidsons. "They don't even know. Martha didn't keep track of such things. But it's bound to be soon, now. We've known about it since summer."

"And you didn't tell anyone?"

"What good would that have done, except give all of you something more to worry about? We'll handle this as it comes. Now, why don't you see if you can help Nora in the kitchen? She won't let me get near her newfangled stove."

⸎

The baby arrived with little fanfare on a blustery February night—a strapping eight-pound boy that Paul named Carlton Elijah. Martha had no difficulty with the delivery. She complained for a while about a stomachache, but since she had no idea what was actually happening to her body, she remained calm and untroubled. Katerina, on the other hand, was a frantic bundle of nerves, remembering the near disaster of Martha's birth and being frightened both for her daughter and the baby.

Luckily for all of them, the formidable Mrs. Perkins was already on hand. She swept the baby away for a thorough cleaning and swaddling before bringing him back into the room and thrusting him into his father's arms. "There you

191

are, sir. Your fine-looking son. He's all yours now, to raise as you see fit, remembering that you will live the rest of your life at the mercy of the man you turn this boy into."

Despite herself, Katerina smiled. "She's right, you know, Paul. More and more now, I'm careful about how I treat my daughters, because I know they'll be the ones taking care of me when I'm an old lady."

One by one, the Grenville girls came home to greet their new nephew and to wonder that their poor little sister could produce such a healthy and bright-eyed baby boy. It was Lillian, however, who arrived with a full suitcase. "I'm here to stay for as long as you'll have me," she told Paul. "Frederick agreed that I have a responsibility toward my sister's child, and I'm the only one of the girls without real commitments of my own. Mrs. Perkins seems wonderful and fully competent, but you can't expect her to be on duty twenty-four hours a day. I'm here to fill in the gaps."

"You've quite changed your tune, haven't you?" Katerina remarked the first time she had Lillian alone. "What happened?"

"Prayer. Long talks with Frederick. And a dream in which a voice said to me, 'You are meant to be a mother to a child who needs you.' This child needs me, so here I am."

Together, Lillian and Matilda Perkins worked out a schedule that allowed Martha ample time with her son but made sure she was never alone with him. It worked well, until one fateful day in September.

Carlton was now a healthy seven-month-old baby. He had more than doubled his birth weight, and he boasted a strong set of vocal cords. On this particular morning, he was irritated about something. Both Lillian and Mrs. Perkins had checked him to be sure he was clean, dry, and fed. Still he fussed, his whimpers going from mild protest to violent screams. Attempts to distract him by handing him a small object to examine did nothing; he demonstrated his growing strength by hurling the items across the room.

"Yesterday, he was fascinated by the new litter of kittens in the barn," Lillian said. "I think I'll go and get one of them. Maybe a little soft fur will soothe him."

"Or give him something else to throw. I think you're just trying to give your ears a break," Mrs. Perkins said, laughing, "but go ahead. Maybe it will work. Besides, Martha will be coming down any minute now, and all three of us do not need to be here."

When Martha arrived, Mrs. Perkins settled her into the rocking chair and handed her the screaming child. "Here. He's your son. Rock him for a while and see if that helps. I'm going to fill this tub with warm water. Perhaps a warm bath will put him down for a much-needed nap."

Bath water, of course, had to be heated on the stove, so filling the tub in the corner of the kitchen took a while. While the women walked and rocked and sang silly songs to him, Carlton wailed. Then came a knock at the door. "You keep rocking," Mrs. Perkins said. "I'll get the door."

The visitor was Katerina, bringing a gift of the last tomatoes from her garden. "Bad timing?" she asked, as the shrieks assailed her ears.

"No, no, it's definitely time for an experienced grandmother to try her hand. We've determined that he's not sick or wet or hungry. He's just mad about something. Martha's rocking him, but it hasn't . . ."

But even as she spoke, the cries stopped in mid-shriek. Startled, the women froze for a moment, eyes wide. Then they were running toward the back of the house. Martha was kneeling next to the bathtub—holding the now-quiet baby under the water. She turned toward them with a smile on her face. "Doll-baby no cry," she said.

Katerina yanked her daughter away from the tub, while Mrs. Perkins reached in and lifted the child from the water. Grasping him by his heels, she held him upside down and pounded on his back until the water poured from his mouth. And at last, another angry cry burst from his lungs.

When Lillian entered the back door, a small white kitten in her arms, she faced a scene of total chaos. The floor ran with water from the overturned tub. Martha crouched across the room, her arms wrapped around herself as she sobbed, "Mama hurt me." Both Katerina and Mrs. Perkins were shaking and crying, and a very wet baby shrieked at the top of his lungs. The kitten took one look, leaped from Lillian's arms, and dashed toward the barn. For a moment, Lillian wanted to join him.

"*Gott im Himmel!*" she exclaimed. "What has happened?"

It took several minutes for emotions to settle down long enough to let the story come out. By then, Paul had arrived, looking for lunch, and the tales had to be told again.

"The baby's all right?" he asked.

"Yes, yes. He's fine, except for having his feathers ruffled. He'll probably hate taking baths for a while, but he wasn't submerged long enough to cause any real damage."

"But a couple of minutes longer, and . . ."

"This is what we've always feared," Katerina said. "I know my daughter, and I know she would never intentionally hurt this child. The problem is that she cannot understand the consequences of her actions. To her, he's just another baby doll. She's been throwing dolls around all her life without hurting them. She doesn't know that a child is different. And I don't care what you say about how much she has improved, Paul. There are limits to her understanding that she will never overcome."

"So there were three of you right here, helping out, and she still almost murdered her son."

"That's too harsh, Paul. It wasn't a murderous intent. But yes, she almost killed him."

"What do we do?"

"I don't know. I'm too shaken to think."

"Well, I can tell you what I am going to do," Mrs. Perkins said. "You people have been good to me, but I cannot take responsibility for protecting this child from his own mother. I wish you luck in finding a solution, but I quit."

"I'll take him." The quiet voice was Lillian's, offering what she knew could be the only sure solution.

"You'll . . . what?"

"I'll take him as my own child, just as the voice in my dream told me to do. I will take him home with me and raise him as my own. You all can see him as often as you like, but until he is in school and old enough to protect himself, he will live with Frederick and me."

Chapter 19

Death Is a Thief
Who Comes in the Night

The Nasmith Cabin
1910

The shock of the near drowning seemed to have weakened Jamey's will to fight his disease. More and more now, he retreated into his memories of the past, repeatedly telling Katerina that he felt responsible for the way his daughters had turned out. Katerina tried to argue with him for a while, insisting that the girls were doing better than he was giving them credit for. Still, he fussed about the poverty into which Millie's coal miner had led his family. He compared Nora's husband to his own father, casting them both as dewy-eyed dreamers, hiding behind their books while the world around them collapsed. He worried about Frederick's fanatical devotion to his religion and Ruby's total lack of religious conviction. He became convinced that Gloria was being led into a life of sin in the big city, although he concluded she might be better off away from the pernicious influence of her sisters. And Martha? He couldn't even talk about her.

In his more maudlin moments, he would call Fiona and Sally to his side, making them promise to be everything their sisters had not managed to become. The constant lectures irritated fifteen-year-old Fiona, but they frightened Sally. Both girls were learning to stay away from the house as much as possible.

Katerina was bone-tired. To give her some respite, Becca tried to help take care of Jamey by sitting with him and reminiscing about their Grenville relatives. Becca's unfailing good cheer sometimes helped to lift his spirits for a while. They could laugh together about family pranks, the things they had hated about the old Dubois plantation house, and the difficulties of life on the Aiken farm. When he fussed about his own family going off in all directions, she reminded him of that remarkable afternoon when all their family members—even the disaffected Johnny—had joined hands and marched out to stand in defiance of General Sherman's advance through their property.

"Your girls have Grenville blood in their veins and Grenville courage in their hearts. You can trust them not to wander too far from the paths on which you have set them."

"You're an optimist, Becca. Always have been." Jamey stopped for a moment as his persistent cough overtook him. Then, when he could breathe again, he continued, "I agree that they are strong, but I remind you that some of their blood comes from the hard-nosed but impractical Scotch-Irish McDevlins. I love Katerina, but more and more, I see that she is focused on this idea that the girls need to be rich."

"She's just worried about them, the same as you are."

"Maybe so, but when I'm gone, I fear . . ."

"You're not going anywhere, dear heart," Becca said, patting his hand.

"Oh, yes, I am. I can't live if I can't breathe, and it's becoming more difficult every day. So what happens to Fiona and Sally when I'm gone?"

"They'll still have Katerina and me to love them and look after them."

"Katerina will have them both married off to the first man who waves a few dollar bills under their noses. And what will you do about it?"

"I'll be there to advise them to hold out for love."

"The way you did?"

"That's a bit cruel, Jamey. Yes, I held out for love and never found it. But look where I am today. With a husband and a family to raise, I probably would never have tried my hand at writing or drawing. Much as you might wish to do so, you can't choose a life path for someone else. The girls will find their own way, just as I did."

"Promise me they will be all right."

"I cannot do that, Jamey. But I promise to do whatever I can to protect and guide them."

❧

As the last weeks of the year counted down, both Becca and Katerina were forced to admit that Jamey was dying. His coughs had so wracked his throat that he now had difficulty swallowing. At most meals, he found it easier not to eat at all. His weight dwindled, the bones of his face starting to stand out in a macabre foreshadowing of a skull. His every breath now was labored, and his lungs whistled as he tried to draw the next breath. He was too weak to get out of bed, even to sit in a chair. He lost interest in his previous debates and now simply slept or stared out the window.

Katerina struggled to find the words to notify her daughters that they needed to visit their father for one last time.

My dearest daughters,
I heartily wish that I did not have to write this letter to each of you. However, the time has come for all of us to help your father prepare himself for his passing. His consumption has reached a stage when there can be no further hope for improvement. Dr. Higgins says that death could come at any moment.

It would ease your father's mind to know that each of you is well. I urge you to come home as quickly as possible. If there are things you wish to say to him, gratitude to express, love to share, this will be your last opportunity. You may feel free to bring your entire family if it is possible to do so, but if you can only come by yourself, then please do so.
Your loving and grieving mother,
Katerina

❦

Nora and Millie were the first two to arrive, since they lived no more than a couple of miles away. "We're here to spell you, Mother. We can take turns sitting with Father so that you can get some needed rest," Nora explained. "We have agreed that there is no need to have the young grandchildren running around underfoot at this time, unless, of course, Father asks to see them."

"Thank you, my dears. I have always relied on you too much, I know. It's the price you pay for being the oldest. But I am comforted by your presence, and I feel sure your father will be, too."

"How aware is he, Mother? Does he know who is in the room?"

"Sometimes I am not sure, but it seems to comfort him to hear someone talking to him. So do talk to him and believe that he is listening, even if he is too weak to respond."

Lillian, too, arrived alone. "Some of the ladies from our church are watching Carlton during the day," she explained. "I did not want to take any chance of causing a scene with Paul and Martha if he came with me."

"That's wise, I agree."

Ruby breezed in without warning one night, bringing little Frankie and a large amount of baggage with her. "I'm home for good," she announced. "If the rest of you girls need to take care of your families, you can rely on me to handle things here."

"As if we have ever been able to rely on her for anything!" Lillian muttered under her breath.

"Where's your tinker escort?" Nora asked.

"Heaven only knows. He hasn't been seen in New Castle for months now. Maybe he's found a new lady friend. Or maybe he's dead. I don't know, and it really doesn't matter much, either way. I needed his name, but now that everyone knows me as Mrs. Sheffield, I don't have any more need for him. Frankie and I get along just fine on our own. Don't we, darling?" She chucked her daughter under the chin, and the little girl drew away in irritation.

Katerina winced in displeasure. "This will always be your home, Ruby, and you will always be welcome, but please don't discuss your independent living arrangements in front of your father. He was worried enough about you when he thought you had a common-law husband supporting you."

"You should have just told him that I'm a survivor. Somehow, I always manage to come out on top. And little Frankie will be another, won't you, love?"

Lillian was shaking her head in righteous disapproval, but before she could ignite a real argument, everyone was distracted by a knock at the door. Gloria stood shivering in a short fur jacket and flimsy dancing shoes. "It never used to be this cold!" she said when they opened the door.

"Of course it did. You didn't notice because you were dressed for the weather. Have you been walking through the snow in those shoes?" Ever the mother, Katerina pulled her to a chair in front of the fire and hurried to find her a towel.

"Where did you come from?" Nora asked.

"My erstwhile boyfriend, Mr. Tomlinson, drove me up from Pittsburgh in his new Ford Model T, but when he saw the icy condition of the road up to the house, he was afraid to risk it. He dropped me off at the bottom of the hill and went off to town to find himself a hotel room."

"And who is Mr. Tomlinson?" Millie asked. "Is this someone we need to meet?"

"I doubt it." Gloria's eyes began to well with tears. "He's a customer who invited me out to dinner a few times. When he heard that my father was dying, he insisted on driving me here, but then . . ."

"Then what?"

"When he saw the house, he said he had been expecting to see a prosperous horse farm or something, not a . . .

a hovel. He asked me whether my family had ever heard of paint, or at least whitewash. And that's when he dumped me along the side of the road. I doubt that you—or any of us, for that matter—will ever see him again. He looked positively terrified at the idea that I might be . . . poor."

"Good riddance!" Ruby remarked to no one in particular.

"It doesn't matter now. I'm here. Is Father still . . ."

"Alive? Yes, but he's sleeping now, for which we are grateful. You can see him first thing in the morning, when both you and he are more alert."

⌘

But morning brought little change. Jamey opened his eyes briefly and then shut them against the light. Dr. Higgins arrived to listen to his chest and shake his head in resignation. "Nothing more to be done," he said. "His system is shutting down. Gather around him, if you will, and share any of your last messages, but then I advise letting him pass in peace."

Lips compressed in a tight line, Katerina led each of the girls, in order of their ages, to his bedside. She gave each one a few moments alone and then encouraged them to indulge their grief out of Jamey's hearing. Nora was as stolid as her mother, unconsciously mimicking her mother's lip line. "Rest in peace, Papa," she murmured.

Martha, on the other hand, shuffled in, looking curious. "Hi, Papa. Get up and play with me. I have new doll-baby." She turned to her mother for an explanation. "Won't talk," she said.

"No, dear, he can't talk any more. He's going to sleep soon. Say good-bye."

"Bye-bye, Papa!"

In their turns, Millie, Lillian, Ruby, and Gloria came quietly into the room, leaning over their father to brush his cheeks with a kiss and whisper a few private messages.

Then it was time for the two youngest girls. Fiona looked suitably solemn but not particularly grief-stricken. "Don't worry about us, Papa. We're going to be fine," she assured him.

Sally, on the other hand, started to cry the moment she entered the room. "Don't die, Papa," she begged. "I need you." When Katerina led her from the room, Sally went straight to Fiona and kicked her in the shins. "You promised me he wasn't going to die," she snarled. "I'll never believe anything you say, ever again."

While Nora took the cart and went to summon Becca, Katerina had her own last farewells. "Go in peace, my darling. Your work here is done. The girls and I will support one another and take care of each other, just as you would want us to. Let go. You've suffered enough."

Becca came to the doorway, seeking her own last moments. Katerina stepped away from the bed but did not leave the room. Becca bent over the still figure in front of her. "I don't think I ever thanked you, Jamey, for saving me after the earthquake. You brought me here and gave me a whole new life. I will be forever grateful to you. And in case you ever wondered, I have always loved you, even when you were an annoying brat and I felt obligated to box your ears. You're my baby brother, and nothing, not even death itself, can change that."

She motioned Katerina to join her at the bedside, and the two most important women in Jamey's life held his hands until, with one shattering breath, he was gone.

Rebecca's Journal

December 1910

*A*nd so began another new phase of my life. At first, I simply could not comprehend the loss of my brother. He had been my anchor to the Grenville family, my childhood nemesis turned into my closest friend, my savior at a time when my world had been turned upside down. I had spent the last twenty-five years living alone but near enough to Jamey to count on him always being there—to shovel a path through the snow, fix a leaky pipe, or lift a heavy load. He and his family of daughters had given my life meaning and purpose. Now I felt cut off, isolated, and stranded in these woods.

My current cat, a tuxedo Tom named Jeeves because he looked like a butler, worried about me. Could a cat understand what had happened? Maybe not, but he knew I was distracted and unhappy. When his usual tactics of chasing his *tail or running headlong through the cottage failed to elicit my laugh, he began to head-butt me, rearing up on his hind paws to reach my hand or my lap, mewing deep in his throat as if to ask, "What's wrong?" I scratched his ears and smoothed his fur, but he seemed to sense that my response was halfhearted. On cold winter nights, he curled next to me in bed, gently kneading my shoulder and sniffing at my cheeks if there were tears. I began to talk to him, as if he could understand. And yes, maybe he did.*

After all, whom else did I have to talk to these days? Oh, I tried to see Katerina as often as I could, but, of course, she was deep in her own grief. She had lost much of her sparkle. So long as Jamey was alive, she had remained optimistic and upbeat. She had pushed us all to live in the present moment, enjoying what we had rather than worrying about the future. But now? Now she still lived in the present, but she seemed to see it as a trap from which she could never escape. The girls did their best to cheer her, but they failed miserably to break through her shell. When one said, "I understand, Mother," her answer was, "No, you don't." If they tried to share their own feelings with her, she pushed them away. If they tried to take some pleasure in happy memories, she left the room. If they talked about the future, she refused to listen. In her sadness, she could only imagine a world completely and perpetually sorrowful.

For my part, I soon learned that silence was her only comfort. She tolerated my visits if I brewed her a cup of tea and sat with her as she sipped. But she would not talk to me about anything beyond the most inconsequential matters. Did she eat?

Did she sleep? I suspected she did not, but she simply answered such questions with a shrug. She tended to those chores that mattered. She milked the cow, slopped the pigs, and looked after the chickens. At mealtimes, she managed to put together something for the younger girls to eat. But dust accumulated on the tabletops, and houseplants withered and died. She wore the same dress, day after day, and only bothered to comb her hair when her bun came completely unraveled, allowing greasy strands to dangle in her face.

To be truthful, I had days when I was as bad as Katerina—days when I cared about nothing, and I didn't bother to wash my face and forgot to eat. But I struggled to return to normalcy, for the girls' sake, if for no other reason. I tended my dying garden and fed the small birds and animals that shared my woodland. I worked on my books. And eventually, as the days began to grow longer, so, too, did my spirit begin to sing once more.

Chapter 20

Growing Old Is Mandatory; Growing Up Is Optional

North Sewickley, Pennsylvania
Spring 1912

It had taken well over the traditional twelve months of mourning for the family to recover from the shock of Jamey's death. But by the spring of 1912, the Grenville women were learning to cope with their new circumstances, each in her own way.

Katerina had always been the barometer by which her daughters measured their own well-being, and they were well aware of the depths of her grieving. During those first few months, Katerina had refused all of Dr. Higgins's requests for her nursing assistance. When he told her about a patient who could benefit from her help, she simply shook her head. "I can't. I can't bear the thought of another sick room."

"But Mrs. Grenville, you have worked so hard to become qualified as a practical nurse, surely you're not going to give it up," Dr. Higgins urged.

"The memories are too painful, Doctor. I can't do it."

But in February, Mrs. Hazen, who lived just down the road from their old farmhouse, grew ill, and Becca joined the doctor in pleading with Katerina to do what she could to help. "You know Elvira Hazen well. You and she have been neighbors all your lives. And you know what a debt we owe her for helping to make Magnolia Cottage my home all those years ago. The least you can do, Katerina, is to visit her and see whether she is in immediate need of anything. I can't imagine that Micah Hazen is much good at managing their household on his own. The poor woman is probably starved for a good bowl of soup as well as a little cheery conversation with a friend."

"I'm not much good at being cheerful," Katerina grumbled, "but I can probably manage the soup."

And so it happened that Katerina made her way across the fields one sunny morning, bearing a container of rich chicken soup. And what she found at the Hazen house broke through the shell she had built around herself. Elvira had suffered a small stroke and was left with limited use of her right arm and leg. She also had trouble speaking. And because her husband could not understand what she needed, he had seriously neglected her beyond the rudiments of feeding her and keeping her clean. Katerina took one look at the poor woman's sad, pleading eyes and went straight to work. She started with preparing a bath and giving her a good scrubbing from head to toe. The smile she received in return was a little lopsided, but it left little doubt about how grateful Elvira was to have another woman there at last.

By the time Mr. Hazen returned that evening, Elvira was dressed and sitting in her parlor. Her nails had been pared and her hair styled. The floors had been swept and the windows opened to let in some fresh air. A jar on the table contained a bouquet of freshly cut forsythia blossoms, and a pot of soup was bubbling on the stove. Katerina tried to shrug off what she had done. "I just stopped by to see if I could cheer Elvira up a little," she said.

Mr. Hazen shook his head. "You've done much more than that. Dr. Higgins told me you were the best practical nurse around these parts, but he said you had given up nursing. If you're ready to go back to work, Mrs. Grenville, we will be grateful to have your help." And with that, Katerina realized that she could still find a purpose in life.

As she began to smile more often, to hum again as she went about her daily chores, and to take a renewed interest in her daughters, so they, too, felt more hopeful about their own futures. The youngest girls were, of course, growing up. Fiona was nearly sixteen and Sally was thirteen. Katerina encouraged them to spend more time with their friends and to enjoy their last years of schooling. "I still expect you to do your chores around here," their mother told them, "but it's time for both of you to start thinking about what you want to do with your lives. Don't waste these years worrying about me or what's going on at home. We're all going to be fine."

❧

Becca, too, reached out to the youngest Grenville sisters, offering them what Jamey had always called a "a place to turn to when they felt like running away from home." The two girls often visited on Saturdays, and Becca tried to offer a sympathetic ear while avoiding any suggestion of lecturing. Sometimes, however, the temptation was too great. On one particularly rainy Saturday, the three of them were gathered around her kitchen table, sharing a batch of oatmeal raisin cookies.

"What's happening at your house today?" Becca asked.

"Well, Mother and Ruby have embarked on spring housecleaning, and we had only two choices—either pitch in or get out from underfoot. From what I observed after breakfast, little Frankie was already giving them more help than they could handle, so we decided it was time to visit you."

"Funny—I always rather liked spring-cleaning time. Lots of good conversations get inspired by scrub brushes and soapsuds."

"Not at our house," Sally said. "When Mother is attacking dirt, she also attacks anybody else who is within earshot, and I've already had quite enough lectures for this week."

"I only wish Mother would quit pushing us to think more about our futures. I don't need any reminders. I'm worried enough already. What else is there to think about?" Fiona's lower lip jutted out in what was becoming a characteristic expression.

"Mother's just afraid nobody will ever be willing to marry you," Sally said, suppressing a grin.

"Hah!" Fiona shot back. "You're the one she should be worried about. With those big feet and skinny legs, you're not going to be much of a catch."

"Nobody thinks I'm too skinny except you, Fiona, and that's only because you're so fat."

"I'm not fat. I'm just developing a curvaceous figure, and you're jealous because you know you'll never be as beautiful as I am!"

"Girls! Stop it! You're both lovely, but that's not what your mother is worried about. She's learned an important lesson these past few years, and now she wants to make sure you don't ever face the same problems she has endured."

"Such as . . .?"

"Such as needing to support yourselves, not being strong and independent enough, unable to stand on your own two feet . . ."

"Well, Sally won't have any problem there! Look at the size of those feet!"

"Fiona, enough. Seriously, girls, have you given thought to what you will do after you finish high school?"

"A career, you mean? A job like Gloria's position as a shop-girl or Ruby's stint as a barmaid? No, thanks. All I've ever wanted is to be a wife and mother, with a whole passel of children—a big family like the one we grew up in before . . ." Fiona stopped, not wanting to remind them of her father's death. "Like ours, but closer in age to one another," she amended.

"Have a husband in mind, do you, or haven't you considered that?"

"I'm looking around. Oh, and I also want to move somewhere new. I'm tired of these dumb mountains and the rocky soil and the worn-out houses and dilapidated barns. There's a fellow at school who has traveled to Ohio, and he says that there the fields are flat and fertile, and where there are hills, they are gentle slopes, not treacherous outcroppings of rock. And there's brand-new land available where you can start from scratch and build whatever kind of house you want."

"Sounds almost too good to be true," Becca quipped, tongue firmly planted in cheek. "And what about you, Sally? I saw your eyes light up at the mention of Ohio. Are you planning an escape, too?"

"Not to another farm! And definitely not to a passel of children and a demanding husband! I want to be famous— a singer, an actress, a writer—but not something like children's books. I mean, that's fine for you, Aunt Becca, but I'd like to write poetry or maybe pithy articles for a famous magazine. As for Ohio—well, its cities, like Cleveland or Cincinnati, are much more attractive than smoky old Pittsburgh."

"So you're both planning on moving on? That's commendable, but it will take some preparation, you know. That's all your mother is worried about. You're allowed to dream big dreams at your age, but the path to their fruition can be longer than you think."

"Yes, but the dreams have to come first. Otherwise, we wouldn't know how to start getting ready."

"Fair enough. But do me a favor, my dears. Make haste slowly. Big changes are coming in women's lives, and you'll both need to be very well-educated to take advantage of those changes."

Fiona quirked an eyebrow at Becca. "Changes? Like what?"

"Like women's suffrage—the right to vote, to share in government, to act independently in a court of law."

"Are you becoming a suffragette, Aunt Becca?" Sally asked. "There was a picture in last Sunday's paper of several men beating up a woman for trying to exercise her right to vote in a local election. You wouldn't want any of us to get involved in something like that, would you?"

"I saw that picture, and I admit it was terrible. But what I saw was a strong woman doing what needs to be done, regardless of the cost."

"Well, I said I wanted to be a famous woman, but that's not how I want my picture to get into the papers."

"Nor I," Fiona agreed. "Can we quit talking about this now, please? Growing up is scary enough without all the adults in our lives making it more complicated."

❧

Ruby and little Frankie were still living at home, and Katerina confronted Ruby about her plans. "I've been grateful to have your help since your father died. I admit your competence and efficiency have surprised me. But things are back on an even keel now. If you want to move back to New Castle, I'll understand."

Ruby bit her lip and looked away. "Are you telling me nicely that it's time I pack up and go home?"

"No, never. This is still your home, and you will always be welcome. But I thought you might be missing your old job and your friends there."

"Actually, I've been surprised myself at how contented I have been living here. I know I always bragged about my great life in the big city, but I don't miss it. And I'd rather not have Frankie grow up having to tell her friends that she lives in one little room above a tavern. I've already managed to deprive her of knowing what it's like to have a father. I want her to be surrounded by a loving family, not a bunch of itinerant peddlers and local drunks. And life in the country is . . . I don't know how to describe it, exactly, but I can breathe here."

"Then let's agree on our arrangement, shall we? If you keep on managing the day-to-day things around the house, I can spend more of my time with my nursing jobs. You do the cooking and tidying up, along with keeping an eye on your sisters, and I'll go out and earn enough to support us all." Katerina laughed at herself. "I never thought I'd hear myself saying something like that! Imagine me, at my age, having a real job, while someone else runs my household for me."

"I think it's rather wonderful. But are you sure you trust me to keep an eye on the girls?"

"Who better? You always got into more mischief that the rest of your sisters combined. Fiona and Sally will have a very hard time putting anything over on you."

"That's what is called a backhanded compliment, isn't it?" Now Ruby was laughing as well. "I'll accept it gladly. It's good to see you smiling again, Mama."

❧

At the end of April came the belated news that the *Titanic* had sunk in the Atlantic. For days, the local papers were filled with survivor stories and eyewitness accounts of the high-seas drama that had resulted in the deaths of over 1,200 people.

"Look at these headlines!" Katerina spread the newspaper out on the table.

Titanic Sinks; 1,294 Drowned
Greatest Atlantic Liner Destroyed by Huge Iceberg
Appalling Disaster Happens 500 Miles from Cape Race
Women Alone Are Saved

"So many lives lost! And just think of how many people are mourning each one of them. It makes me almost ashamed that I have been so hurt and bitter about Jamey's death, as if I were the first to suffer such a loss," Katerina commented to Becca.

"No, my dear. You must not feel ashamed. Every death is the worst death for someone. But what you may be feeling now is a certain camaraderie, a kinship with those who have experienced the same depths of grief. That's natural, I think. And a tragedy such as this does tend to place our own feelings in perspective."

"Nevertheless, I'm seeing it as something of a sign, a reminder that I need to get over feeling sorry for myself. Perhaps it's time we officially declare our period of mourning over. I know Jamey would not want us to spend the rest of our lives in suffering and sadness because of him. He would want us to be happy with each other. And grateful for the family members who are still with us," she added, reaching out to squeeze Becca's hand.

"Perhaps we could do something special for the girls, a sisters' reunion this summer, where we only allow happy memories," Becca suggested.

"Oh, I'd love that! Perhaps we could plan it for the Fourth of July— our own Independence Day, as well as our country's. And you know what else I'd like to do? I'd like to have a family portrait made of all of us together, while we still can be."

"That's a wonderful idea, Kat. Why don't you do it? You and the girls could all wear white dresses to show that the mourning period is over. They will treasure a picture like that for years to come."

"I said 'we,' Becca. I was including you, of course."

"I'll be here for the party but not for the picture, Kat. That should just be the nine of you. I would give anything now if I could have a picture of my parents and my brothers and sisters all together as a family."

"I understand. I'm going to send a note to each of the girls right away, asking them to plan on coming home for that weekend and to bring an appropriate white dress to wear in the photograph."

Chapter 21

Off with the Old;
On with the New

Ellwood City, Pennsylvania
July 4, 1912

The Grenville sisters welcomed the suggestion of a Fourth of July reunion and family portrait. No matter how much they squabbled, sisters were still sisters, and they relished the chance to spend some time together. Logistics were easy enough. Millie, Martha, and Nora lived close enough to the Nasmith cabin to allow easy travel back and forth. Lillian would have to come from New Castle, but Nora offered to have the family stay with her. Gloria wrote from Pittsburgh that she would be there and would like to bring along a new beau to meet the family. She would move into the loft with Fiona and Sally, while her guest, Thomas

Maloney, would take a room at the Ellwood City Hotel. They would arrive via his new Model T, which also meant he would have transportation to and from his lodging.

The three oldest sisters immediately began planning for new white dresses to extend their wardrobes. Katerina was already working on dresses for herself and the two youngest girls. Paul Davidson promised to make sure Martha was suitably attired, and Ruby refused her mother's offer of a new dress, saying that she already owned something suitable. The local photographer assured Katerina that he could stage the background of the picture so that the dresses stood out and made a strong statement about the freshness of their lives.

Becca remained adamant that she did not want to be included in the portraits, but she pitched in wholeheartedly when it came to planning the weekend activities. The Fourth of July fell on a Thursday, which gave the family an extra free day to travel. They would come together in time for an evening picnic supper and then watch from the top of their hill as the veterans' organization in Ellwood put on a short display of cannon fire and other pyrotechnics.

<hr />

The family had assembled by late on Thursday afternoon. Katerina emerged from the kitchen to announce that she could use some help setting up the trestle tables in the yard. The sons-in-law—Henry Southerland, Joseph Sweitzer, and Paul Davidson—all jumped up to help. Only Frederick Cummings, sitting off in a corner reading his Bible, pretended at first not to hear. Then, his attention attracted by the others, he asked, "You fellows have that well in hand?" A snort of disgust came from Paul, and the others simply shook their heads.

The newcomer, Thomas Maloney, stood up to join them. "Sounds like this is a job for four fellows. You go on with your reading, Reverend. We'll handle it." Gloria gave her friend a smile of approval, while Lillian winced to see her husband once again avoid any task that involved actual labor.

In the kitchen, Becca gave Gloria a quick hug. "I think I like your friend Mr. Maloney. He seems quite pleasant." Then, as a roar of laughter came from the yard, she added, "And he seems to be getting along well with the other men."

"He is a nice man, Aunt Becca. He's always ready to help, and he doesn't mind getting his hands dirty, even if he is a stockbroker by profession."

The picnic supper that evening also went well. Katerina had made a point of fixing several vegetarian dishes, so that there would not be a repeat of the mealtime fiasco during which Lillian's new husband had failed to find anything he could eat. While the rest of the family stuffed themselves with thin shavings of country ham and larded biscuits, Katerina urged Frederick to try the beans—baked with molasses but no bacon—and the bowl of potato salad, full of fresh vegetables from her garden. He responded by taking huge helpings but made no comment to show his gratitude for her concern.

Later that evening, when the local veterans had finished setting off their fireworks and firing their cannons, Henry Southerland made a small gesture of dismissal. "I'm glad that's over," he said. "I'm afraid I shall never understand the soldier's fascination with gunpowder. I should think that once they've seen what damage it can do, they would want to avoid it all the more."

He turned to Mr. Maloney. "What are they saying in the big city about the current turmoil in Europe? Is there another war coming, do you think?"

"Well, the politicos I know are a bit concerned about this whole business of large countries drawing up sides and allying themselves with others who hate the same folks they do. It's rather like the neighborhood bullies drawing a line across the schoolyard and daring their rivals to cross it. A threat of violence almost always is meant to invite the very warfare it purports to avoid."

"I'm afraid I'm not very familiar with European politics," Becca commented. "Can somebody explain to me what's been going on?"

"My Henry's the historian," Nora said, "but I don't understand it either."

"I like Mr. Maloney's image of the schoolyard bullies," Henry answered. "To grossly oversimplify things, there was an agreement in 1882 among Austria-Hungary, Italy, and Germany to stand together against anyone who threatened any one of them. That's what the politicians call the Triple Alliance. In 1907, Britain, France, and Russia formed a similar agreement called the Triple Entente, directed primarily at Germany. So there are your two sides lined up against one another."

"Exactly," said Mr. Maloney. "Now this year, we've seen a new set of alliances combining Serbia, Greece, Morocco, and Bulgaria into a Balkan League. They stand opposed to the Ottoman Empire of Turkey, Macedonia, and Albania. And there are other interrelated rivalries, like that between Italy and Turkey, or the most recent, between Austria and Serbia."

Becca was shaking her head at the whole story. "So one little dispute between places we've never heard of could pull all these major powers into war with one another because of their threats or promises?"

"That's right. It's a possibility the great Otto von Bismarck predicted in 1878 when he said that 'some damn thing in the Balkans' could ignite a worldwide war. Begging your pardon for the language, ma'am."

"I'm glad we didn't have this discussion before the fireworks," Becca quipped. "I'd have been scared to death as soon as the first gun went off."

"I don't want to hear any more war talk tonight," Paul Davidson said, "but I'd be curious to know, Mr. Maloney, where you think the economy is headed."

"Oh, I'm much more hopeful about that topic!" he said, smiling. "I think we're heading into a period of unprecedented growth, based on manufactured goods rather than agriculture for the first time in this country's history."

"That doesn't sound like good news for a farmer like me," Paul answered.

"It can be, if you recognize what's coming and take steps to benefit from the changes. Farm land can be sold and new jobs found not very far away."

"Such as?"

"Well, take Ohio, for example. Canton's only about seventy miles from here. And there, a fellow named Timkin has opened a plant manufacturing steel ball bearings that let wheels and engines turn easier and faster. At the same time, the Goodyear plant in Akron—just another twenty miles or so—is creating stronger and more durable rubber tires. Both are about to revolutionize the world of transportation."

"You're talking about the automobile?"

"Yes, but also trains and airplanes. Our world is on the move—literally, on the move—and the economy is going to move with it."

Fiona and Sally had been sitting near Becca, only listening with half an ear to the political discussions. But the mention of Ohio had piqued their interest. Fiona nudged Becca and whispered, "We told you Ohio is the place to go!"

"Lucky guess," Becca whispered back. "Don't try to convince me you were talking about going to work in a rubber plant."

"No, but all those new workers are going to have money and need to be entertained," Sally laughed.

"Hush!"

Then another voice emerged from the gathering darkness. "I guess we're making the right decision, then." The speaker was Lillian, and all heads turned toward her.

"Decision? What decision is that?" Katerina was more than a little alarmed whenever Lillian made one of her announcements.

"Well, we weren't going to tell you for a while, but this seems like the perfect time, doesn't it, Frederick?"

"It's your family. It's up to you," he said with a shrug.

"All right, then. Frederick has been called."

Lillian stopped and looked around, as if she expected some strong reaction. Instead, she saw only puzzled faces.

With a sigh, she explained further. "He has been called by God to become the pastor of the Church of the Lord's Truth in Canton, Ohio. The formal invitation came only this week."

"God sends formal invitations now?" Ruby's tone was openly sarcastic.

"It came from the elders of the church, naturally, but we know that God has spoken to them. They have almost fifty members of their congregation, and they are inviting Frederick to lead them, particularly as they start a series of revival meetings to gain converts. They will provide us with a house, and he will be receiving a regular salary, so that he can give up the awful business of being a butcher."

"You know, I've always wondered about that, Frederick," Joseph Sweitzer said. "How can you make a living selling meat but refuse to eat it at your own table?"

"If you saw meat the way I do, day after day, you wouldn't eat it either," Frederick replied.

"I thought it was a religious belief."

"No, it's a personal preference, all right?"

"Sorry."

An uncomfortable silence descended on the group. Then Paul Davidson spoke again, his voice choked with anger. "And what about my son? What about Carlton?"

"He goes with us, of course. He's only three and not ready to be put back into his mother's care."

"But we won't see him."

"You don't see him now. What difference does it make where we live?"

"I don't want him taken out of the state. Is this why you didn't bring him to the reunion with you?"

"No, we just felt he was too young to enjoy it. He is in the care of the women from our church."

"His mother and I . . ."

"His mother has not even asked how he is. She doesn't remember he exists. And that's why he is still with us. It is for his own protection."

And on that note, the gathering broke up.

❧

Friday was given over to preparations for the family portrait. Mr. Jernigan had recommended that they pose outside on the porch, which would provide ample room for them to line up or group together on two levels. Although Becca was sure that a little dirt wouldn't show up in the final picture, Katerina insisted that the yard and porch be scrubbed and trimmed into perfection. The sisters and their families pitched in to give the house and yard a quick makeover before the photographer arrived. Then, with a flurry of face washing and primping, the eight sisters and their mother went to get ready for their sitting, after which the men of the family would take charge of an outdoor corn and sausage roast.

Katerina was fervently hoping that the disagreement that had ended the previous evening would be forgotten, and indeed, no one had mentioned it the next day. But there was more trouble to come. As the Grenville daughters came down from the loft, one by one, they twirled to show off their new white dresses. The two youngest girls had shorter skirts than their adult sisters, but the styles of the dresses were similar. All had elbow-length sleeves, rounded necklines, and tightly cinched waists.

Gloria caused a few raised eyebrows when she appeared in a dress belted with a bright red sash and further adorned by a long golden medallion. Katerina thought briefly about asking her to remove the embellishments but decided, in the name of family harmony, to avoid the issue. That decision held only until Ruby made one of her grand entrances. Her dress had a flowered bodice and a striped skirt, with an overlay of a white apron.

"Ruby! What on earth are you wearing?" Katerina cried out before she could stop herself. "Where is your white dress?"

"This is a white dress, Mother. The background color is white. It is just a bit more ornate than the others."

"It's striped and flowered and ruffled, to boot. It ruins the whole idea this portrait is meant to convey!"

"And what idea is that? That we have gotten over the worst of our grief? That we are formally through with mourning? This dress does that as well as any other."

"But I wanted us all to look alike."

"Why? Because you want us to all be alike? That's not ever going to happen. I'm the black sheep of this family. I'll never be like the rest of you, and I won't pretend to be. Take me the way I am, or leave me out of the picture. I really don't care."

Katerina's eyes brimmed with tears—the tears she had never shed over her husband's body, perhaps. But then she shook herself and straightened her spine. "Have it your way, then. But if you are determined to remain the black sheep of the family, you will take your position at the end of our group, not the center of it."

Chapter 22

Love Makes
the World Go 'Round

On Saturday morning, Ellwood City held an Independence Day parade, which had been postponed from Thursday so that all could participate. At its conclusion was a community picnic, which most family members attended. Mr. Jernigan promised to return later that afternoon with the first print of his pictures. And Katerina planned to bring the weekend to a close with one of her famous chicken dinners. Then the sisters could attend church together on Sunday morning before the travelers started for home. At least, that was the original plan.

At the end of the parade, Becca sought a shady spot to rest her feet, and Gloria soon joined her on the park bench. "The same people and the same displays are in that parade, year after year, but it always feels new," Gloria commented. "I'm glad we could be here to see it again."

"We seem to be missing a few family members, however. Nora tells me that Lillian and Frederick left for New Castle very early this morning, explaining that Frederick has a revival sermon to deliver tonight—one he had conveniently forgotten to mention. And I haven't seen Paul and Martha. I suppose he's still angry that the family did not object to Lillian's announcement."

"The Sweitzers aren't around, either. Millie told me that, since Joseph got himself hired at the mill, he pulls all the long weekend shifts. But she and the children will be at the house this afternoon."

"Where's your young man?" Becca looked around, as if she expected him to pop up from somewhere.

Gloria's response was an indulgent laugh. "Henry has him over at the sand pits, teaching him to pitch horseshoes."

"He doesn't know how?"

"I don't think he'd even seen a horseshoe until this weekend. Thomas is very much a child of the city. But he seems to be enjoying himself out here."

"He and Henry have really hit off a friendship, haven't they? I haven't heard Henry laugh and talk so much in all the time we've known him."

"Kindred souls when it comes to history!"

"Well, whatever it is that they have in common, I find it refreshing. I really like your fellow, Gloria."

"You keep saying that—that he's somehow my 'fellow,' but I'm not sure of that. I think it's premature. But I do like him, a lot, and I'm pleased that you do, too."

"I see a fine man—bright, energetic, compassionate, and more interested in others than in himself. That's a rarity these days. How did you meet him?"

"Actually, it was on the train when I was returning to Pittsburgh after Father's funeral. He helped me with my valise, and then he noticed my mourning clothes and offered condolences. I thought he was very nice, and we had an enjoyable conversation that lasted all the way to the train station. But I thought that was the end of it—strangers who pass on a train. Several days later, though, he came into Kaufman's and headed straight for my ladies' accessories department. I helped him choose a pair of fine kidskin gloves for his mother's birthday, and he asked me to have dinner with him that evening."

"Sounds to me as though he is really interested in you."

"I think so, too. He took me to the Schenley Hotel, which features the finest dining room in Pittsburgh. It was full of dangling chandeliers, marble floors, and Louis XV furnishings, with a menu printed in French. When he suggested escargots as a first course, I must have looked completely puzzled, so he started to explain. Silly me, I cringed at the word 'snails,' and he shifted easily to order a paté instead. Then we had chateaubriand for two, which came on a single platter. That meant he had to carve the beef and fill my plate, which really impressed me. And we finished with something smooth and cold that arrived at the table decorated with cascading curls of flaming orange peels. I was practically speechless the entire evening, thinking that I was totally out of place in those elegant surroundings.

"Once again, I figured I had acted like an ignorant country bumpkin, and I never expected to see him again, but the next week he came back with an invitation to go ice skating, which, thankfully, I knew how to do. Since then, I've learned a lot about the city from touring the sights with him and hearing him recite its charms. He's a man of many interests and varied tastes, unpretentious and comfortable in all kinds of company. He makes me happy, Aunt Becca."

"I'm delighted for you, my dear. Treat him well. He sounds like your perfect match."

"Well, I'm trying not to rush things, but I keep wondering what will happen if the world really does go to war, as he and Henry were suggesting the other night. I don't want to lose him, like you . . ." She stopped and blushed, teetering on the edge of an embarrassing comparison.

"It's all right to say it. I lost the man I loved, and you don't want to end up like me, living in a little cottage with only a cat for company."

"I didn't mean . . ."

"I understand what you meant, and I'm cheering you on. In truth, I'm probably not the best person to give you advice, but I'm going to do it anyhow. Think about what you like best about Thomas—his openness, his enthusi-asm, his kindness, his willingness to let you see how he feels about you. Then repay him in kind, rather than playing hard to get. You can remain a lady while still letting him know how much you like him."

On impulse, Gloria reached out and hugged her aunt. "I'm so glad you're part of our family! You'll be the one who will understand when Mother finds out . . ."

"Uh-oh! Finds out what? What haven't you told us, Gloria?"

"You remember one of her favorite sayings: We can marry anybody we want, so long as he's not a Democrat, a Catholic, or a redhead."

"Yes, I've heard her say it often. And I always bristle a bit when she does so. Of course, she doesn't know it, but my Joshua had a head of curly red hair and big freckles, too. I thought he was beautiful."

"Well, Thomas definitely doesn't have red hair."

"But . . ."

"He does support a lot of the Democratic programs, like labor unions and the right to strike."

"And . . ."

"And he's a Catholic, which Mother will discover in the morning when she finds out he's attending his own mass in Ellwood instead of coming with the rest of us to the Presbyterian church."

"Oh, Gloria, you're setting yourself up for trouble, aren't you?"

"No. His religion doesn't bother me, and Mother really doesn't have anything to say about whom I marry any more. I'm much too old to need her permission."

"But I think you'll always need her approval."

"Then I hope you'll help me win her over."

❧

As promised, Mr. Jernigan brought the proof copies of his photos out to the house in mid-afternoon. Katerina pinned them to the wall so that everyone could study them. The formal pose showed the nine women lined up like spoons, their left sides to the camera. In a more casual shot, they clustered on the front steps, three sitting in front and the others facing forward behind them. Katerina and Becca were the first to study the results of the photo session.

"I think I hate photographs," Katerina declared. "Cameras don't lie, but it would often be better if they did."

"The pictures really came out quite well, Kat. You will cherish these for years."

"No, don't try to be diplomatic. I'm looking at all of us here and seeing our personalities on display as clearly as if we were wearing big signs around our necks."

"I admit, I don't like the formal line-up as well as the other one. I know convention says one should not smile in a photograph, but I've never understood why. You wanted these pictures to show that the long months of mourning were over, but everyone still looks too serious."

"It's more than looking serious. We all look like we've been sucking on lemons. I suppose those sour expressions are the result of my blow-up at Ruby for showing up in that horrible dress. But there are other things wrong with the pictures, too. I deliberately made Fiona and Sally's dresses shorter, because they are still young girls. But captured this way in a photograph, it just looks like they are sprouting so fast that they've outgrown their own skirts."

"They are growing up fast, I give you that. Look at them. They are easily the tallest. I suppose Mr. Jernigan did the arranging deliberately to put the two shortest girls on the ends and the tallest in the middle. But I see what you mean about the skirt lengths."

"And the facial expressions! Take us one at a time: Martha is a complete blank. She neither knows nor cares what's going on around her. I, on the other hand, am clearly biting my tongue to keep from screaming at someone. Nora? Nora looks tired. I think she is tired most of the time, and that makes me worry about her health. Then there's Lillian—the unhappy, confused, browbeaten wife of a miserable prig!"

"Kat! Really!"

"Well, she is. At best she looks stupid. Then there's Sally, she of the perpetual pout, and Fiona, she who is so smug about her own charms that she sometimes makes me want to slap her. Millie's the sweetest of the lot, but here, even she appears to be wondering how she ended up in this group. Gloria is serene. I suppose having a rich man in love with you will do that, although I wouldn't know from experience. And, of course, Ruby, the perennial bone in my craw, doing whatever she can to upset things and then thoroughly enjoying the show."

"All right. I admit the line-up looks like it could be added to the post office wall, where they show mug shots of miscreants. But the informal grouping is much more pleasant."

"Only because some of us are laughing at the rest of us. Something else in that picture bothers me, too. Ruby has her head cocked in that smart-alecky way she has of sneering at us. And if you look on the other side, you'll see that Sally is doing the same thing. Heaven help us if Sally turns out to be as troublesome as Ruby has been!"

"They are still your daughters, Katerina, and I know you love each one of them."

"*Ich liebe dich immer.* Love them? Yes. I can't help that. *Aber ich weiß nicht immer Sie mögen.* But nobody says I have to like them. And this has been a weekend when I really don't like any of them. Too bad this was the moment I picked to preserve their images."

"You'll still have copies made for us all, won't you?"

"Maybe I'll have them framed and give them as Christmas presents—the grown-up equivalent of coal in their stockings." No matter how she was feeling, however, Katerina was still a mother, and she headed off to the kitchen to start dinner. Fried chicken and mashed potatoes

would go a long way in smoothing over the small wounds
of the past few days.

❧

But the weekend was not quite finished twisting Becca's
heart. After dinner, Gloria and Thomas went for a walk
and then returned to settle on the front steps as darkness
fell. "Aunt Becca!" Gloria called. "Come join us for a few
minutes, won't you?"

She complied, wondering if she was about to hear news
of a marriage proposal. It turned out to be something quite
different.

"Miss Grenville," Thomas began, "I hope you don't mind
that Gloria has told me the story of your young love and the
loss of Joshua McKay at the Battle of Gettysburg. I was quite
moved by the story. It reminds me of how the past continually
travels with us and throws its shadows over our lives."

Becca stared at him silently, not understanding what
was expected of her.

"Thomas has an idea—a suggestion of a way to bring
that experience to a satisfactory close," Gloria added.

"It was all a very long time ago. It's over and done with."

"Yes, but you don't know how he died, do you?"

"No, his parents never said, and I couldn't ask anyone,
either—not without upsetting my parents and making our
friendship sound like something it wasn't."

"Has it occurred to you that next July will be the fifti-eth anniversary of Gettysburg?"

"Will it? Yes, I guess it will. But, heavens! That simply makes me feel old and even sillier to still be sitting around, talking about a childhood crush."

"The anniversary is an important milestone for many people, and while it hasn't been publicized much yet, there are plans underway for a huge celebration . . . or rather, a com-memoration of what happened there," Thomas explained. "I've been privileged to sit in on some of the planning, be-cause my family's brokerage firm will be financing part of it. Anyone who was touched by the battle in some way will be invited to return to Gettysburg for the occasion. Old regi-ments will reassemble the last of their veterans and camp on the same grounds they held in 1863. There will be re-enact-ments and lectures, dioramas and artistic impressions, models and new monuments. And best of all, the records of all who were there are being reassembled and catalogued, so that sur-vivors can learn where their loved ones fought and fell."

Becca took a deep breath but could not find the right words.

"We've been talking about it, and we think you should be there. Gloria will go with you, if you like. And I can ar-range for the docents to look up Mr. McKay's information ahead of time, so that someone can give you a guided tour."

Becca shook her head. "I don't know what to say. It's an interesting idea, and I will think about it. But I don't know whether . . ." Her voice trailed off. "We'll see."

Rebecca's Journal

December 31, 1912

*I'm almost embarrassed to admit—even here—that I've
spent the last six months dithering about Mr. Maloney's
suggestion that I travel to Gettysburg this coming summer.
One part of me shivers a little every time I think about it.
The trip offers one last chance to understand what went on in
that battle. To know what my Joshua must have seen and felt.
To learn how he died. Did he fall instantly? Or did he suffer
for hours or days before succumbing to a wound? Or perhaps
he wasn't wounded at all. Perhaps he fell ill and died of some
horrible disease. And where was he buried? Is there a plot with
his name on it? Or was he shoved into a mass grave? There's
so much I don't know, and it's no wonder the not knowing
still haunts my dreams now and then, although I would never
admit that to Gloria or her young man. And I do want to find
the answers to my questions.*

But while I catch my breath in anticipation, there's another side of me that protests—a nagging voice in my head that keeps asking other kinds of questions. How will you ever manage to find things out once you get there? How will you know where to go? What if the town is so crowded you can't find a place to stay? What if you lose your valise? Or your money? Who will be there to help you? What if there's an accident? You could fall and break a bone. Or hit your head. Or fall ill. Thieves could pick your pocket. You could get lost or waylaid. The idea is much too dangerous. You're too old to be going off like that on your own.

Back and forth. Back and forth. Of course I'll go. Nonsense. I'll just forget the whole thing. I want to go. But I'm afraid. I've argued both cases with myself so many times that I've lost track of which side is winning. And here I am, at the end of the year. The new year, 1913, looms ahead of me. What will it bring? I'm no clearer tonight than I was on the Fourth of July.

Something happened today, however, something to trigger a small memory, and I can't shake the image. I was out for a brisk walk this afternoon when I saw a cat—not one of mine, just a stray—run across the road in front of a car. And suddenly I was remembering a day several years ago. I was walking along that same road with Jamey and Katerina and their two youngest girls. Sally was about seven, I think, and Fiona no more than ten. There was a squirrel sitting in the middle of the road, and a new Model T was coming toward us. Time scrunched to a standstill as we watched—helpless to change what was about to happen. The squirrel froze, and the car's tire flattened him as easily as a hot iron might smooth a piece of clothing. The girls screamed and tears flowed. Sally, always the more dramatic of the two, shouted, "I hate automobiles!"

And Jamey seized the moment to teach the girls a lesson. "It wasn't the car's fault," he said. "That squirrel could have easily run to the side of the road. But what did he do? Nothing. He just sat there. Squirrels are like that. They can't make up their minds. It doesn't make any difference what may be bearing down on them—an automobile, a man on horseback, a mule pulling a farm wagon. A silly squirrel will sit there. I once even saw one lift its hind leg and scratch its ear. And then BOOM! It's too late. The roads are littered with flattened squirrels that couldn't make up their minds. Don't you girls be one of them! Most of the time it doesn't matter what you decide when danger threatens. All that matters is that you do something."

I'd forgotten all about that incident until today, but I heard Jamey's voice clearly in my own head, saying, "Quit being a squirrel, Becca. Either go or don't go, but make up your mind. Either forget about that young man, or go investigate his story and find a way to say your farewells."

And so it's decision time. If I go, I may fail to find what I'm looking for. But if I don't go, I'll never know if success was possible. Making that trip on my own will take courage. But refusing to do it will be giving in to fear. And I know what my dear brother would say: "Fail if you must, Rebecca, but never give in to fear. When in doubt, do something."

Katerina will say I'm being foolish. I don't think she really believes that I was ever a young girl in love. She sees only one side of me—the spinster, the loner, the poor woman who never wanted to marry. But I know better. It's time to start planning my trip.

Chapter 23

Old Soldiers Never Die

Gettysburg, Pennsylvania
July 3, 1913

ecca Grenville's train ride to Gettysburg proved uneventful. Tom had provided a first-class ticket, so she
was separated from the cars packed with the returning veterans. She was aware of them, of course. At every stop, new
bands of men pushed their way aboard, all of them showing
the ravages of old age but as eager as schoolboys for the trip.
The track itself was sometimes bumpy and the sway of the
carriage disorienting, but the scenery was beautiful. Becca
found that she could relax once the train was underway. All
the decisions had been made. Now control of the journey
was out of her hands, and she found that oddly comforting.
With nothing to think about for several hours, she closed
her eyes and let happy memories wash over her.

The conductor approached her as the train slowed outside of Gettysburg. "We're stopping here at a special platform built to accommodate the veterans arriving at their campsites. You'll see the sea of tents they have provided for them. But you just stay seated. We'll go on into the main station once the men have been unloaded."

Becca stared out her window, almost unable to take in the scene unfolding before her. For as far as she could see in any direction, the ground was covered in orderly rows of long white tents, each large enough to hold ten or twelve men. Above many of them fluttered ragged battle flags. The platform and the surrounding paths swarmed with old men, many of them sporting their former uniforms. All along the platform, men were welcoming each other with bear hugs and handshakes, even if they wore opposing uniforms. Somewhere in the distance, she could hear the blare of trumpets and the steady beating of drums. Smoke curled lazily above the campfires being tended amidst the tents. And everywhere, there was an almost palpable air of excitement. Without fully realizing what she was doing, Becca grinned with delight at each small reunion she witnessed.

So it was with an easy heart that she stepped off the train in Gettysburg itself, ready now to face whatever surprises the town and its celebrations might have in store. A short one-block walk from the station brought her to the Gettysburg Hotel, an imposing four-story structure on the town square. The desk clerk had a frazzled look about him, as customers clamored for room keys, sought information on meal times, and asked directions to various battle sites. But he brightened when she gave him her name.

"Miss Rebecca Grenville? Oh, yes, you're Mr. Maloney's aunt, I understand. He's one of our owners, and he's asked that we take very good care of you."

"Oh, no—" she started to say. Tom Maloney was not her nephew, as least not yet, since he was showing no urgency about marrying her niece Gloria. Then she realized that instead of correcting the statement, she ought to be flattered and grateful for the care that had prepared a way for her. Smiling, she amended her words to say, "Thank you. I'm sure I will enjoy my stay."

"He also left a message for you. He'll be joining you for breakfast in the morning. We've reserved a lovely first-floor room for you. George, here, will take your bag and show you the way."

The young porter directed her across the lobby sitting area to an ornate door with a small brass number on it. "This is your room, ma'am." He held the door to let her step inside ahead of him. He carefully placed her satchel on the quilted counterpane that covered the iron bedstead. "There's a washroom attached right over here," he explained, opening another door to reveal a water closet and washstand. "And this door leads to a porch for sitting a spell. Don't be leaving the door into your room open, though. Mehitabelle likes to sun herself out here, and she'll try to get inside, if she gets a chance."

"Mehitabelle?"

"The house cat."

"I see. I'll be careful. Will she settle for sitting on my lap?"

"If she likes you. That's up to her."

Becca smiled again at his refreshing honesty. The young fellow knew his cats! "I'll try to make friends. Thank you for your help."

"Is there anything else you need, ma'am?"

"Well, you could point me toward the registration center. I'd like to find out if there are any South Carolina troops in attendance."

"It's too late to be going there now. They'll be closing up shop soon. Best save that for the morning. Besides, supper is almost ready. You'll hear the bell when they open the dining room."

With some surprise, Becca realized that she was famished. "Supper sounds like a wonderful idea. Thank you again."

Supper was, indeed, ready. Becca made her way to the dining room, where a motherly woman in an apron handed her a plate. "Evenin', ma'am, and welcome to Gettysburg. Find yourself a place anywhere you see an empty chair. We'll be passing the food just as fast as our ladies in the kitchen can dish it up."

Becca hesitated, her eyes widening as she surveyed the crowded dining room. People jostled for space, and the serving women raised their voices to be heard above the general clamor.

"Mashed potatoes coming through!"

"Who needs another biscuit?"

"More chicken here!"

The woman at the door laughed at her surprised expression. "Yes'm, it's a madhouse. The hotel usually offers a quiet and elegant dining experience, but with this many people in town, all they could do was bring in every available housewife and hope that we could cook fast enough to keep everybody fed. So don't be shy. Get in there and help yourself to whatever anybody passes your way."

Again Becca found herself grinning at the novelty of the experience. Bowls of chicken and dumplings, green beans, fried squash, brown gravy, and sliced tomatoes all tempted her to overfill her plate. Sliced country ham, smothered pork chops, fried chicken, and ears of corn followed. After her long day on the train, everything tasted wonderful. The gentleman next to her poured her a glass of lemonade, and a friendly woman across the table leaned forward to offer some advice.

"We were here last night. Be sure to save room for dessert. They make wonderful pies and chocolate cakes."

"There's nothing like country cooking, is there?" Becca replied. The last remnants of her fears about the trip faded away as she settled into the homey atmosphere.

In the morning, she had barely found a seat at one of the community tables when Tom arrived, greeting her with a warm hug and the usual questions about her trip.

"It was smooth and uneventful, Thomas, and my room is lovely, too. I could get used to those electric lights. But I wasn't expecting to see you here. Surely you haven't made the journey simply on my account?"

"Well, not completely. Our investment firm holds shares in this hotel, and this is perhaps the biggest week the business will ever experience. Someone needed to keep an eye on how the staff is coping, so I volunteered—killing the proverbial two birds with one stone, you might say."

"I'm grateful. The crowds out there on the street are a little intimidating. A familiar face is most welcome."

"I have the use of a small car, so after breakfast, we'll set out to find whatever you need to see. But first, let me fix you a plate of eggs and sausages. You'll need lots of energy before this day is over."

Fueled by the hearty breakfast, Becca was ready to find some answers to her questions. Tom confirmed her impression that the returning veterans would be signing in to locate the tents designated for their units. "The folks managing the camp are headquartered over at Gettysburg College, so that's where we will start."

Although it was still early, the narrow streets of Gettysburg bustled with foot traffic as well as vehicles and horse-drawn carriages. Among the visitors and sightseers dressed in everyday clothes, bands of grizzled soldiers wearing their old uniforms practiced their marching and greeted one another with hugs and backslaps.

"What a mass of humanity," she commented. "How many people . . .?"

"The responses indicated some 50,000 veterans would be coming, and some officials expect at least that many more civilian visitors. It's a tremendous load to put on this little town of less than 5,000 residents. Almost every house is offering their spare rooms, and churches and schools are prepared to house the overflow as well. That's why I took the liberty of reserving early a room for you in a comfortable hotel."

❧

At the makeshift headquarters of the encampment, Becca managed to catch the attention of a kindly woman behind a desk littered with handwritten account books.

"Can you tell me how to go about finding the friends of two soldiers who fought here?" she asked.

"Union or Confederate?"

"Confederate."

"Do you know their regiment?"

"7th Regiment, South Carolina Volunteers."

"Name and rank?"

"Oh, dear, the older one was a private, I suppose. His name was Job McKay."

The woman busied herself for some time, flipping pages in one of the registers and then turning to a bank of drawers filled with cards. "No one by that name in our records, ma'am, but we don't know much about the enlisted troops. Most of our records are for the officers. There were some 170,000 men who fought in the battle of Gettysburg, you realize. We have records for less than half of them."

"I understand. I knew it was a long shot. But I was hoping to get some idea of how he died."

"Well, I can tell you that the South Carolina troops were in McLaw's Division, Kershaw's Brigade. Most of them saw action on July 2, around Rose's Farm, the Peach Orchard, and the Wheatfield, so most of the South Carolina veterans are housed—or tented, as the case may be—in that area. But beyond that, I don't . . ."

"Is there a map? I don't know any of these place names."

"I'd recommend that you try to find someone to guide you around the battleground. Most of our volunteer guides are checking in right over there," the woman said, pointing to another desk swarming with people. "Any of them who are available will be hanging around that desk." She gave Becca an apologetic shrug and a smile before turning to the next person in line.

"'Scuse me, ma'am. Sorry to eavesdrop, but maybe I can be of assistance. Sergeant Hiram R. Jones, 7th SCV, at your service, ma'am."

Becca whirled around to find herself face-to-face with a bewhiskered old soldier dressed in the faded and tattered butternut-gray uniform of the Confederate Army. Above the right breast pocket she could faintly make out the stenciled name "H.R. Jones" and the regimental designation "7 SCV."

"You are . . . really . . . a veteran from South Carolina?"

"Yes, ma'am. Joined up in Abbeville in 1861, fought in every battle up till . . . well, till I couldn't fight no more."

"Abbeville! I lived in Aiken during the war. Did you by any chance know my friend Job McKay from there? He was in the 7th Regiment, Company E, I believe."

"McKay? Let me think. McKay. I do remember a fellow from over that way. Carrot top, was he?"

"Yes! He and his brothers all had bright red hair—and freckles, a whole band of them across their noses."

"Yes, ma'am. I remember him now. And he had a funny name, too. Uriah, I think it was. He tried going by his initials, but that just led to more jokes. You know—he'd introduce himself as U. R. McKay, and somebody would say, 'No, I'm not McKay, you are.'"

"Ah! He went by his formal name when he signed up? No wonder that lady couldn't find his records! The family always called him Job. They said he had to have the patience of Job to put up with all the teasing about his name."

"Sure. I remember him now, but . . . didn't he get himself killed here?"

"That's what I was told, but no one talked about the details. I was hoping I could find . . . could learn what happened . . . could come to understand . . ."

"I don't know anyone can really understand what happens in wartime, ma'am, but I can tell you a little about the battle we were in. Care to go for a bit of a walk, do you? Mind, it's probably several miles from here."

Tom had been standing a respectful distance behind her, letting her conduct her own investigation. Now she turned to find him and took his arm to make the introductions. "We have a car," she explained. "If you could ride along with us . . ."

"Sure thing. We can travel west on Fairfield Road till we get to the general area of the Confederate camps. Then we'll take the Millerstown Road over to Rose's Farm, where our boys faced the enemy."

Chapter 24

Only the Dead
Have Seen the End of War

The Peach Orchard and the Wheatfield
July 3, 1913

As they drove, the old sergeant studied Becca carefully. "Were you Job's girl?" he asked.

"Oh, no. I wasn't that old. In 1863, I was only thirteen. But I was new in Aiken, didn't know anyone, and Job's little brother befriended me at church. Joshua was, maybe, fifteen—too young, anyhow, to go off to war. But he was feeling very lonely, with his two older brothers off in the army, so we sort of gravitated together. He became my best friend—my only friend, actually. And then his family got the bad news about their oldest son, and Joshua ran off to find his remaining brother."

"Did he ever write to you?"

"Once." She shrugged. "He said he was catching up to Job's unit. Then the next thing we heard, both McKay boys had died at Gettysburg. His parents left town, and I never knew . . ." Her voice trailed off, and she turned quickly to stare out the window.

"Josh McKay. Of course! Who could forget that spunky kid? He came running up to us on the road somewhere around Hagerstown, and we knew right away who he was related to, what with that red hair and freckles. Colonel Aiken wasn't happy to have a youngster among us, but his brother pleaded to let him stay. They finally reached an agreement. The boy would do what he could to help around our encampments, and Job would see to it that he stayed out of any fighting and didn't get in anyone's way. Worked pretty well, at least for a while."

"So you knew him? You know what happened to him?"

"Ah, yes, ma'am, but I'm not sure you . . ."

Becca straightened her back and glared at the old soldier. "Sergeant, I'm much too old to be shocked by anything you have to tell me. I want to hear the whole story, so let's get on with it."

"Fair enough. Our regiment was marching up to Gettysburg from Hagerstown when we spotted a big black building built of fieldstones. It had a sign out front with a black horse painted on it above the word 'Tavern.' Colonel Aiken pointed to a large open field a short distance down the road and announced that we would be camping there.

Everybody cheered. Then he explained that he had been assigned to take possession of the tavern to use as a field hospital if we got into a fight."

Becca raised an eyebrow at him. "Really? A tavern?"

"Why not? Its stone walls were practically bullet-proof, it was roomy and situated at a crossroads for good access, and it was almost sure to have a ready supply of medicinal alcohol. If you turn left here, we'll come to it in a few minutes. This whole overgrown area you see on your left is where we set up our camp. We weren't allowed to patronize the tavern that night, but a small cavalry troop frightened the owner off, took control of the building, and did their best to parcel out kegs of beer for each regiment. Before we go to see the tavern, though, let me take you to view our battlefield.

"We learned that there had been fighting in Gettysburg that day, but we were not supposed to join in until the next afternoon. So we got settled, slept some, and then started getting ready for an attack on July 2nd. The 7th was assigned to McLaw's Division, Kershaw's Brigade, and we were part of a very long line assigned to take control of Seminary Ridge and then move east toward the town. We were in position by two o'clock, standing shoulder to shoulder in a single line that stretched for almost fifteen miles. We didn't actually start to move until about five-thirty, though."

"Why so late?"

"Well, it was very hot that day—triple digits, they said—so it helped to fight after the sun started to set.

Besides, it just takes a long time to get a fifteen-mile-long line organized."

"And this Seminary Ridge—where is it?"

"You're right on top of it, actually. It's just a bit of high ground that stretches north-south from near here up to the Lutheran Seminary north of town and to the Devil's Den to the south."

"How did it feel to stand there, knowing you were headed into a major battle?"

"Well, we didn't know it was going to be a major battle. And, first, you also need to understand the meaning of that line. When you are waiting for the fighting to start, the world takes on a different aspect, somehow. You quit seeing fields and distant hills, barns, houses, trees. Your vision shrinks, until all you are aware of is the ground beneath your feet and the men standing on either side of you. You are literally touching them, shoulder to shoulder, hip to hip, and you move as a single body. You know that your life depends on them and that their lives depend on you. You become united by a bond of comradeship—love, really— that makes you brave and unafraid. There's no feeling that quite matches it."

"You haven't said anything about love of country, or believing in your cause, or . . ."

"That's because those things don't matter much in the heat of battle. All you care about is staying alive and keeping your comrades alive. So you do whatever it takes, which includes killing your enemies. You don't have time to think about why you are fighting or about the loved ones you left behind, either. People who have never gone to war don't—can't—understand that."

Becca's expression began to crumble, but she once again straightened her posture and said, "All right. Go on. What happened?"

"Well, we were marching across here, headed down the ridge and straight for a line of Union cannons that had only a small infantry line protecting them. They were waiting over there beyond the road. The hope was that we could keep the artillerymen from firing those cannons by picking them off every time they moved. We were in a wooded area and trying to get beyond it, so we could fire our guns without the bullets bouncing off the trees. Then we ended up in Farmer Rose's peach orchard, which wasn't much better. When we broke free of the orchard, we found ourselves in a real fight, but we were only a few hundred yards away from capturing that artillery line. There's a stone wall right over there that gave us some protection, but beyond it was an open, level clover field, and our color guard fell as soon as we emerged from behind the wall.

"Still, it looked like we were winning for a while. We managed to drive the enemy infantry back for almost half a mile. And then came what General Kershaw later described as the fatal blunder. We were still marching shoulder to shoulder, closing ranks whenever one of our number was hit. Then here came a young officer on horseback, crying out the order, "Wheel right!" So that's what we did." He grimaced at the memory and fell silent for a moment.

"I don't understand what that means. What happens when you . . . wheel right?"

"The line breaks. The first soldier turns to his right ninety degrees. The men next to him—three or four, depending on how wide the field is—move up to stand beside him, and they march on in that new direction. Then the next man turns to form a new row. And so on. Now instead of a single unified line, you have men marching in a wide column. And instead of facing those cannons, we were now facing sideways from them. So we couldn't fire at the artillery men, while they had a clear shot at our whole flank."

"The order was the fatal blunder?"

"Yep. We later learned that it was meant for a small group of men who were marching in the wrong direction. But the young signal corpsman heard it, thought it was a general order, and passed it all down the line. We didn't know. We just did what we were told. The Yankees blew us away, mowed us down like they were taking target practice. When we moved out of the range of one cannon, we marched directly into the next line of fire. In our one regiment, we had eighteen killed outright and many more mortally wounded. Another sixteen lost an arm or a leg. And some were knocked unconscious by the blasts. A hundred or more suffered lesser wounds, which is what happened to me. I had a hole in my left shoulder and a gash in my left leg, but I was still upright, at least for a while. Most weren't.

"We finally made it to the wheat field on the other side, where an earlier battle had driven the Yankees out, but by then it was getting dark. The order came to lie down and spend the night right where we were in order to hold the ground, which meant trying to sleep amidst dead bodies."

"Nobody removed those who had been killed?"

"No point in doing that. Eventually, they would be buried where they had fallen, some of them under those same peach trees. But the immediate need was getting the wounded carried to the rear and to the field hospital for medical attention. If you'll drive us a little further west down the next road, Mr. Maloney, I'll show you the tavern. It's still there."

It was a bigger building than Becca had expected, nearly three stories high, its walls solid and almost unbroken with windows. It loomed over the crossroads, still displaying the "Black Horse" sign to invite travelers to stop. Trees sheltered it in the back and partially concealed the smaller house and farm buildings that surrounded it.

"I see why someone would think the crossroads made a good location for a hospital."

"Yes, true, but by the time we got our men moved all the way back here, it was full to bursting. We had to take our wounded boys across the road and lay them out in the shelter of those trees you see. Just beyond, there's the Marsh Creek, which is actually more of a river than a creek. It's deep and fast flowing, though, so it was a good source of drinking water, and the trees offered some protection from the hot sun. Nevertheless, it was hard on the wounded to lie there, waiting to be moved into the tavern for treatment."

"And Job?"

"Job was one of the most seriously wounded. Poor fellow. He had been promoted to corporal that very day but hadn't had the time or opportunity to sew on his new insignia before he fell. He had a deep wound in his abdomen and had lost a lot of blood. Little Josh was right there when we carried him in, and I found myself yelling at the boy for trying to use his shirt as a bandage for his brother's wound. I told him it would get cold after nightfall, and he would need his own shirt. But Josh said his brother needed it more."

The sergeant stopped talking, a faraway look in his eyes.

"That sounds like something my Josh would do. Please. What happened then?"

"I don't know that you need to hear the rest, ma'am."

"I do. Go on."

"In the morning, Job was still alive and calling for water. Josh took his canteen down to the creek to refill it. On the way back, he got stopped by two renegade Yankees, fellows not in uniform but definitely looking for trouble. They asked the boy if he was a Yank or a Rebel, and Josh pulled his shoulders back, declared himself to be a South Carolina soldier and proud of it. So they . . . they shot him."

"No!" Becca could not control her cry.

"Sorry, ma'am. Job saw the whole exchange and struggled to pull himself upright. Then he fell backward, dead from the effort."

"So the Yankees killed both of them." Her voice was bitter. "And what happened to their bodies?"

"We buried them, ma'am, in a real cemetery. It's right over there." The old soldier pointed back across the road, where, not far from the tavern, a stone wall surrounded a small group of tombstones. "That was a private family graveyard, but we buried our dead there, too. Josh and Job are together, in the upper northeast corner. It's kind of overgrown, but you can walk there if you like."

"Yes, I need to do that."

"You two go ahead, then. She'll need some help across the uneven ground, Mr. Maloney. I'll wait for you here. I've already seen all I need of that cemetery."

Becca stood in the graveyard for several minutes, head bowed, as she tried to absorb all the old soldier had told her. Then she turned, taking a deep breath. "That's it. That's what I came for. We can go back now. Thank you for making it possible, Thomas."

As they made their way back, Becca's glance passed over a headstone she had not noticed before. On it was inscribed "Sgt. Hiram R. Jones, 7th SCV, d. July 6, 1863." She grasped Tom's arm in shock. "Wait! Look at this! That's our sergeant."

"Where is he, by the way? We left him standing by the car, but he's nowhere in sight."

"He's gone! You don't think . . ."

"That he was a Gettysburg ghost? Maybe. Or maybe he was just an impersonator. Whoever he was, he brought you the answers you needed. Ready to go home?"

"Yes, indeed, and with a much deeper understanding of what that war was all about."

Rebecca's Journal

July 1913

*A*s is ever the case, no matter how rewarding a trip may have been, I am always happiest when I return home. I was pleased this time to discover that I am still capable of making my own way, even if those around me regard me as a little old lady. None of the catastrophes I feared came to pass. I didn't lose anything or get lost or suffer an illness or injury. I accomplished what I set out to do, and I don't think I caused anyone else to be too inconvenienced by my presence. But returning to my little cottage and the company of my loyal cat warmed my heart.

I note, however, that travel tends to be disorienting. It was not just the differences in location and geography; I also experienced a confusion of time periods. I suppose that was partially because so many people in Gettysburg were dressed in their Civil War attire—clothing that I recognized from long ago.

Long-forgotten emotions and memories seemed fresh again, and I carried many of them home with me. Now it's hard to separate the two eras—the war years of my childhood and the current war talk that dominates our own news.

Curiously, I have also had two separate and contradictory reactions to the time I spent at Gettysburg. I went there thinking only of my own personal connections to the battle, hoping to learn more about what happened to Josh as a way of putting an end to my grief. And to a great extent, that's exactly what happened. I met soldier-veterans from both sides of the fray, and they all assured me that there was no question of good versus evil, right versus wrong, on that battlefield. To a man, they insisted that each soldier who fought did so out of a sense of duty to country and a love for his fellow soldiers. And that, they said, is what allows us to think of all those lost lives as "good deaths." I came to understand that Joshua himself would have looked at his death as good and proper, because it came in response to his willingness to give his all for the country and the brother he loved. I came home freed at last from the bitterness I had always felt when I thought of someone killing that young boy.

But at the same time, I gained a deep and abiding hatred of war in all its forms. If what the veterans told me was true . . . if those who fight do so out of honest convictions . . . if there is no right side and wrong side . . . If there is no good and evil, then there is no excuse for war. Ever. Anywhere. For any reason. When I think of all the wars that have been fought over time and all the lives that have been sacrificed for a "righteous cause," I despair of mankind, even as I understand and forgive the individual man who goes willingly to his death in war.

Chapter 25

If You Love Them, Let Them Go

Magnolia Cottage
October 1913

"I still say, I may have to love my children, but I don't have to like them!" Katerina made the announcement as soon as Becca opened her cottage door. "I hope you're not busy, because I really need a friendly face and some pleasant conversation this morning."

"I can provide that, and more. How about a cup of tea? It's a bit chilly for a walk this morning, isn't it?"

"No, I needed some cool air when I got this hot under the collar."

"What in the world has happened, Kat?"

"I'm just fed up! My whole family seems intent on moving out to Ohio, and I'm so sick of listening to them that I'm ready to help pack their bags!"

Becca shook her head in sympathy and added some fresh cookies to a plate. Her sister-in-law obviously needed a little sweetening. "All right. Start from the beginning. Which one are you most angry at?"

"That's easy—Ruby, as is ever the case. I swear that girl is lucky I have let her live this long. Have you heard that she has become a slavish follower of Mary Baker Eddy?"

"Eddy? I don't even know who that is."

"Mrs. Eddy hears God speaking to her. She has founded her own church in response to His personal instructions. It's called Church of Christ, Scientist, and her followers call themselves Christian Scientists. There's nothing very scientific about them, if you ask me!"

"But religion can never be purely scientific. Religion demands belief in the unknowable."

"Good point! But these people equate God's Word with fact. According to Ruby, they believe that all illness is an illusion and the only cures come from faith through prayer. So the Bible and prayer take the place of doctors and medicine and whatever scientists other than Jesus Christ think they have discovered about diseases."

"I'm speechless. This is really what they believe?"

"Well, that's the way Ruby explains it to me. I don't know how accurate she is."

"But Ruby believes all this now?"

"Not only does she believe it, she preaches it to anyone who will listen, as well as to those of us who would rather not listen. That's really what disturbs me. She is welcome to believe whatever she likes. But I cannot allow her to impose her beliefs on my actions. She came into the kitchen this morning while I was boiling wild cherry bark that would give some relief to one of my patients who suffers from asthma. She immediately demanded that I pour it out. She wants to go over there in my place and explain to poor Mrs. Brown how to relieve her breathing problems through prayer alone. I also discovered that she had thrown out the cough syrup I had made from lemon, honey, and flax seeds. All medicine is evil, she says, because it keeps people from finding a true cure for their imagined ills."

"Oh, my! And what happens if I break a leg? Do I just pray about it?"

"Ruby would tell you that there are exceptions to the rule. You are allowed to see a doctor for a broken bone. If your eyesight is bad, you can have an eye doctor measure you for spectacles. You can go to a dentist to have a tooth pulled, and a woman is allowed to have help with childbirth. But you can't just turn to taking medicine instead of praying for healing."

"Does that include vaccinations? Because smallpox, now, is . . ."

"No, it allows vaccinations because the law requires them. The explanation behind that is that vaccinations don't work anyhow, so getting one only because the law says you must is permitted, because you don't really believe it will help.

"I have trouble following that logic."

"That's why I have been so angry. And she forces it on her child, too. Poor little Frankie suffers from a stuffy nose at this time of year because of all the goldenrod growing around here. But she won't let her use the nose drops I gave her or the salt and vinegar gargle to ease her sore throat. Poor child just walks around with a runny nose and her mouth hanging open so she can breathe."

"That's so sad. Surely, you can explain to Ruby that . . ."

"There's no use trying to explain anything to Ruby these days. This Eddy woman has written a book with all the answers to everything in it, and Ruby consults it constantly. I tried pointing out to her that I am a trained nurse and that I now earn our living through the practice of medicine, but she just takes that as evidence that I am an ignorant and wrongheaded heathen. I don't know what she thinks about the fact that nursing is what puts the food on her table and the roof over her head. Personally, I suspect that part of the appeal of this new church is that she thinks that she doesn't have to be sympathetic to anyone who doesn't feel well. Ruby has never been good around sick people. This new religion seems to give her permission to ignore them."

"So what were you saying about Ohio? Is this new church located there?"

"No, it's somewhere in New England, I think. But Ruby has gotten the idea in her head that Frederick Cummings and the Church of the Lord's Truth would be supportive of her ideas."

"She's probably right about that, actually. They are faith healers, after all."

"That may be, but she also thinks she can just show up in Canton with Frankie in tow and move into Frederick and Lillian's house. I'm betting Lillian will not be thrilled about that idea. She has always disapproved of her younger sister's behavior."

"Well, Ruby may have to discover that for herself. Who else are you angry with?"

"Paul and Martha, of course. They are definitely moving to Ohio. Paul is getting ready to sell his farm to the same speculator who bought our old place. And he has landed a job working the assembly line at the Goodyear plant in Akron. He says that there is going to be an ever increasing demand for tires, now that Henry Ford is producing a Model T that everyone can afford. So he sees the rubber industry as a source of sure income for years in the future."

"Again, Katerina, he's probably right about that."

"I suppose he is, what with the predictions of a great war getting ready to erupt in Europe. But I wish that life were not changing so fast."

"What was that saying that you used to use against Jamey whenever he started his wishful thinking? 'If wishes were horses, beggars would ride.' That was it. You can't blame your children if they make their decisions based on facts as they are, instead of how you wish they were."

"Maybe not, but I wish—" Katerina stopped herself in mid-sentence and laughed. "All right. You're correct, as usual. That's one of the things I hate about you—you're always right. But I keep thinking that Paul will really miss being outdoors and working the fields. Those rubber plants must be horrid—hot, smelly, dirty. I'd like to send him up there to do the job for a few weeks before he decides to tear up all his roots and move Martha there."

"Ah, Martha's the real problem, of course. But you can't be angry with her, dear. It doesn't sound like she has had any say in this decision."

"No, but then, she never does. And she'll be fine, I suppose. Much as I regret her handicaps, I sometimes envy her the ability to live wholly in the present, as she does. She never looks to the past with regret, because she doesn't remember it. And she doesn't worry about the future, because she doesn't understand that anything exists beyond the present moment. When Lillian took little Carlton into her home for his own protection, Martha forgot all about having a son. She never even asks how he is. Nor does she worry about him. So I suppose she'll be happy enough living in Akron. She won't remember the Pennsylvania hills . . . or us, for that matter.

"The problem, of course, is that I won't be able to forget about her. And I'll worry about her, too. I've already told

Paul that he will have to hire someone to stay with her while he's at work. She was safe enough here on her own for a few hours. If she did go wandering about North Sewickley, everyone would know who she was and where she belonged. But in a strange new city, the dangers are overwhelming."

"Paul loves her, Katerina. He'll be careful, I'm sure."

"I suppose so. But there's something else that worries me. I'm suspicious of the motivation behind this move. I can't believe that Paul is all that concerned about the future of the automobile industry. I think he just wants to be closer to where little Carlton is living, with the goal of eventually stealing him back. And if he tries that, Lillian is going to be devastated."

"The original agreement, as I remember it, was that Lillian would take the boy only until he was old enough to defend himself, so that Martha could not unintentionally harm him. The separation will have to come sooner or later. Perhaps, with Paul and Martha living closer, they'll be able to manage a gradual transition, which might be easier on the boy."

"And on Lillian, do you think? It sounds to me rather like cutting off a dog's tail a little at a time so that it doesn't hurt as bad."

❦

Becca had no answer for that. The two women sipped their tea for a few moments, each of them pondering the difficulties engendered by family ties. At last, Becca sought to change the subject.

"How are the younger girls? I assume they were not included in your blanket statement about not liking some of your children, since they are still in school and out of your hair all day."

"Ah, not so!" Katerina's eyes flashed daggers as she wound herself up for another diatribe. "Fiona is part and parcel of the 'off to Ohio' movement, and what she wants to do, her little sister copies."

"Oh, yes, the two of them gave me an earful last summer. I was hoping they'd forgotten about it by now."

"Not a chance. Fiona is counting the days until she can graduate from high school. Then she is bound and determined to marry that little pipsqueak of a boy she has grown up with."

"Pipsqueak?"

"Oh, you know who I mean—Lester Cole. They've been best friends since they were toddlers, but he's completely unsuitable as a husband. He's half-a-head shorter than she is and skinny as a rail. On top of that, he has one leg shorter than the other, so he limps and looks bowlegged. She outweighs him, too. If they ever did get married, she'd have to be the one to carry him over the threshold!"

Becca laughed at the image despite herself, but then she tried to look stern. "You're being very unkind, Kat. I'm sure he's a perfectly lovely young man."

"Oh, he's nice enough, even if he's not very ambitious. But they make a ridiculous-looking couple. Is it too much to ask that with eight girls, at least one of them could come up with a handsome, wealthy, and cultured son-in-law for me?"

"Patience. Gloria's still working on that one, I think."

"Yes, Mr. Maloney did show promise, but they're not moving forward, so far as I can tell. Fiona, on the other hand, is making wedding plans left and right, despite my disapproval."

"How does Ohio play into all this?"

"Here's the situation: Lester Cole has a bachelor uncle who owns a hardware store in Canton. He wants Lester to come work for him next summer and learn the business, so that he can one day inherit the store. The great plan, as I understand it, is that Lester will head for Canton the day after graduation. He'll go to work to start earning money, and in his spare time he'll find a farmhouse he can rent or buy. As soon as he can get it ready for occupancy, Fiona will go to Canton, they will have Frederick marry them, and then the two of them will set up housekeeping. They seem to think they can combine the best parts of running a hardware store and a farm at the same time, so that they can eventually turn the hardware store into a farm supply store as well. Fiona gets all starry-eyed when she talks about canning her own vegetables and selling her produce at the store. To hear her talk, you'd think they were going to build a merchandising empire around her backyard garden. She's going to join the Grange and . . . oh, you get the idea! It's a gigantic pipe dream, based on completely unrealistic expectations."

"And once again, Lillian and Frederick are part of somebody else's great plan. Do they realize, I wonder, that they are attracting Lillian's sisters, one by one, to join them?"

"I'm sure Frederick, at least, would be horrified by the idea. He has never liked us any better than we have liked him."

"And you, Kat. What will you do if half your daughters are in Ohio and half in Pennsylvania?"

"I don't know. I suppose that's partially the reason behind my anger at all these plans. I feel as if my girls are spinning out of control and away from me."

Becca caught her breath. She suddenly had a strange, faraway look on her face. "I remember my mother once saying almost exactly the same thing. I was still in school, but I knew my older brothers and sisters were disappearing from our lives. Charlotte and Eddie were both married. Johnny was moving to Columbia to work for his old military commander. Mary Sue and Eli were on their way to Beaufort to start a horse ranch, and Robbie and Jamey were headed off to boarding school before college. I was the only child still left at home. And I remember how it made me feel. I wanted to rush to my mother to comfort and protect her. Actually, I think I did. I put my arms around her and said, 'I'm still here, Mama. I'm not going anywhere.' And she answered, 'I know you are, my darling. You'll always be my own little house cat.' And that's what I became. If there was ever a decision that I would never marry, it was made at that moment, when I felt completely responsible for holding my mother's life together."

Katerina stared at her, startled. "I don't want to do that to Sally," she said.

"Then don't. Let all your girls know that you support their life decisions, whatever they may be. And if they all end up in Ohio, we'll have somewhere to visit, you and I!"

Chapter 26

To Each Her Own

The Nasmith Cabin
Christmas 1913

That year, the Grenville family's Christmas celebration was much subdued. Frederick's church responsibilities made it impossible for Lillian to demand that they travel to Pennsylvania. Paul Davidson, just getting settled in Akron, concluded that it would not be good for Martha's adjustment to her new surroundings to go back to Ellwood so soon. And, of course, Gloria's job at the department store required her to be in Pittsburgh late on Christmas Eve and early on Boxing Day, leaving no time for even a quick trip home. Ruby was still living with her mother, but their disagreements continued. She decided to take Frankie and spend the holidays with her new church friends at the Christian Science Reading Room in Ellwood. Even Fiona had plans to be elsewhere: Lester's parents had invited their prospective daughter-in-law to spend the day with their family, and Katerina had given her reluctant approval.

From long habit, Nora and Millie brought their families to spend the day with their grandmother. Nora's daughter Eva was almost thirteen, and son Clarence was eight. The Sweitzer children, Glenda and Homer, were thirteen and fourteen, and then, of course, there was the new baby, little Edna. Katerina had assumed that Sally would be happy to be surrounded by her nieces and nephews, who were nearly her own age. Sally knew, however, that Millie would expect her to take care of the baby while she enjoyed a day to relax. As she watched Fiona ride off for the day with Lester, Sally felt tears of resentment starting to pool behind her eyelids. Her mother and sisters saw her as one of the children, while Homer, Glenda, and Eva regarded her with the same distrust they shared for all adults. Sally spent most of Christmas Day with a pout on her face and baby Edna propped on her hip, envying Fiona her freedom and wondering how soon she could find herself a beau and break free from the stigma of being the only daughter still at home.

Rebecca, from her own position as something of the outsider in the family, watched the others and realized that she was seeing the beginning of a family's disintegration. With Jamey gone, Katerina was the only focal point that held them all together. Becca wondered how much longer she would be able to do so. The bonds that connected the sisters were constantly tested by their responsibilities to their own husbands and their own children, who were growing up fast. Katerina's determination that each of her daughters must find a husband to support her had had the unfortunate consequence of pushing several of the girls out of the family circle.

The signs were everywhere—fewer presents under the Christmas tree, room for everyone to sit around a single dinner table, no rowdy games in the yard, no choruses of Christmas carols coming from the parlor. Instead of both a turkey and a ham, Katerina had chosen to cook only the ham, and she had cut the number of side dishes, too. There were even fewer cookies in the pantry. The children were happy and oblivious, but the grown-ups shared an unspoken nostalgia for Christmases past.

Their pensive mood was made even worse when Fiona arrived home earlier than expected. She came in the back door with tears streaming down her cheeks. Both Katerina and Becca reached to comfort her, not knowing what was wrong but recognizing the intensity of her grief.

"What's wrong, darling?" her mother asked. "Have you and Lester had a fight?"

"N-n-no, not really, but . . ." She choked on her own words and covered her face.

"Then what has happened?" Becca asked. "Here—have a sip of my elderberry wine to settle yourself."

"L-L-Lester's uncle died . . . the one in Canton . . . The telegram came just as we were having dinner. H-H-He just dropped dead of a heart attack this morning."

"How awful! To die on Christmas morning in the midst of what is supposed to be a celebration."

"It was terrible news. And everybody is in turmoil as the family tries to get ready to travel to Ohio. I did what I could to help Mrs. Cole put the food away and clean the kitchen, and then Lester drove me back here. But . . . but . . . it means that all our plans have gone awry. Mr. Cole says that Lester will probably have to stay up there and take over the store immediately. Can I have another sip of that wine, please?"

"Certainly. I suspect you've aged several years this afternoon," Katerina said, looking at her daughter with sympathy. "You mean he'll have to leave school? He won't graduate?"

"Not if he wants to keep the store. There's nobody else to take over—just a couple of part-time clerks and a stock boy."

"But he really doesn't know anything about the store, does he? I mean, that's why he was going there next summer—to learn what it is all about and how it runs."

"But if he doesn't go, they'll just padlock the place and sell it off. It's our whole future, and he's going to have to try and salvage it all by himself."

"There's no other family . . . a cousin or a close friend?"

"No, apparently not. Except for a lawyer. He's the one who sent the telegram, so he may be of some help, but there's no other family. And I'm worried about Lester . . . because he's so scared. He was white as a sheet when he let me out here. He's only eighteen. How will he ever cope with all this?"

"He'll cope because he will have to, my dear. And he'll manage to do so better if he knows that he still has your love and support."

"And the graduation thing isn't all that crucial," Becca added. "He's so close to finishing. The school may be able to look at his record and discover that he has enough credits to get his diploma right now. And even if that doesn't work out, he'll be able to finish at some point, maybe in a night school."

"But how will he manage? He's going to have to open that store tomorrow morning, and he doesn't know the first thing about it—where things are or what they cost. He doesn't know the clerks or the customers. He could let it go broke and lose everything."

"That's not going to happen—not if he has it in him to be the man you think he is. Sometimes all a boy needs is a good solid crisis to turn himself into a grown-up."

"Oh, Mother, you're trying to be helpful, I understand. But you don't know . . ."

"Yes, I do. Let me tell you how I know. I witnessed your father go through a very similar situation when he appeared to be nothing more than an empty-headed playboy." She glanced at Becca, and the two exchanged a slight nod of rare agreement.

"The summer I met Jamey, he was lollygagging around his brother Eddie's farm, pretending to work but hardly ever doing anything constructive. He had avoided going home to Charleston for the summer because he knew his parents were onto his antics and would have made him do something worthwhile. He had no career plans, was barely passing his college courses, and was not interested in anything but having fun and wasting time."

Becca was smiling. "Sounds like the Jamey I knew, I agree."

"He'd never had any responsibility, had he, Becca?"

"No. I remember when we first moved to the Aiken farm during the war. Father gave each of us children a list of chores. Eddie was to take care of the barn, the cows, and the milking. Mary Sue got the stables and all the horses. Robbie was assigned pig duty, and I was in charge of the chickens, the geese, the ducks, and all the egg production. Jamey? At first, he wasn't given anything to do. When the rest of us protested that it wasn't fair, Father put him in charge of the barn cat."

Even Fiona had to smile at that mental picture.

"Then my parents had that terrible accident and died." Katerina swallowed hard as the memories flooded back. "I told him I had to go home to raise my two brothers and take care of our farm, and he offered to escort me on the trip. That's all I thought he intended to do. But when we arrived here and he looked around at what all was facing me, he somehow grew up, right before my eyes. He started asking serious questions and assuming responsibilities. He worked himself to a frazzle, getting the last of the crops to market for me. And then he proposed, offering not just to marry me but to take on all the burdens I had inherited. He wasn't a whole lot older than my brothers, but they accepted him as the authority in their lives. And he soon had the farm running smoothly again. He became a man, as soon as he had adult responsibilities thrust upon him. I'm betting that your Lester will make the same transition."

"But all our plans! He was going to look for a house for us, and . . ."

"And now he will have inherited a house, won't he?"

"Oh." Fiona hesitated for a few moments, realizing how much she didn't know. "Perhaps so, but . . ."

"Fiona, quit trying to argue this situation into impossibility. You have only two responsibilities right now. You need to finish your own education so you can graduate on time. And you'll need to keep Lester's spirits up by writing lots and lots of letters to him. In June, your Aunt Becca and I will take you and Sally to Canton." Katerina hesitated and looked at Becca, hoping she would nod her agreement, which she did.

"We'll help you get the old man's house ready to move in, and we'll also enlist Lillian to plan a really nice wedding. Sally can be your maid of honor, Frederick can perform the ceremony, and you'll have at least some of your sisters in attendance. It's all going to work out, my darling, so long as you believe it will."

❧

Katerina had hopes that her own life would settle down after Christmas as well, but there was one additional surprise waiting in the wings. Shortly after the New Year, a peaceful Saturday was interrupted by the loud "ooga, ooga" sound of an air horn at the back door. She peered out to see a shiny yellow Stutz Bearcat sports coupe driven by someone wearing a wide-brimmed hat, duster, and shaded goggles. Then, from the passenger door stepped an elegant woman who peeled off her own duster to reveal an outfit draped in furs. Katerina gasped to recognize her daughter.

"It's Gloria!" Katerina called over her shoulder to the rest of the family. "And that nice Mr. Maloney, too!" The women and girls poured out of the house to gawk at the car and their sister, as well. Before she could think to curb her tongue, Sally blurted out, "Gloria, what is that thing you have wrapped around your neck?"

"What? This? Why, it's my Christmas gift from Thomas—a three-skin choker scarf. Isn't it beautiful?" She stroked the fur briefly while keeping her left hand tucked into a matching muff.

Sally had always adored this older sister, and she now pushed her way close to throw her arms around her. "I'm so glad to see you," she murmured. Then her attention went straight back to the fur piece. "Look at these darling little fellows! Each one is biting the next one's tail, and all their features are here. The little dangly feet still have claws, and their faces have beady little eyes and leathery noses. What are they, Gloria? Are they minks?"

"They're weasels," Fiona said, just a bit too loudly.

"No, dear. These are stone martens. They are the latest rage in the fashion world."

"They are so cute!" Sally was still petting them.

"They're just dead weasels," Fiona mumbled as she turned away, disgusted with the display of wealth.

But there was more to come. "I'm sorry to drop in on you like this without warning, but we were on our way home, and I thought we should stop and tell you . . ." With more than a little dramatic flair, Gloria hesitated and then pulled her left hand out of its muff. She held it out toward her mother, fingers splayed to draw full attention to a large diamond ring. "We're married!"

There came a collective gasp, and then the questions burst out. "When? Where? Why didn't you tell us?"

"Look at this ring!" Sally was still hanging onto her sister's arm, but now she was focused on the rings that declared that Gloria had indeed found herself a rich husband. "I've never seen a diamond that looked yellow."

"It's called a canary diamond, and they are pretty rare, especially a solitaire this size."

"It's gorgeous! Can I try it on?"

"Sally! Stop it at once. It's bad luck to try on someone else's wedding rings. Leave your sister alone. Let's all move into the house, shall we? It's cold out here."

"At least for those of us who aren't wearing fur." Fiona was still grumbling.

Once everyone was settled around the stove in the kitchen and a pot of coffee was percolating on a back burner, Katerina repeated her questions. "Now, Gloria, I want to hear the whole story. What brought on this sudden . . . elopement?"

Gloria and Thomas smiled at one another before Gloria launched into the explanation. "It just sort of happened. Thomas had to drive up to Niagara Falls to sign off on a hotel deal for one of his clients. He said he wanted another driver to go with him in case he got stuck in snow and needed someone to steer while he pushed the car. So I agreed to ride along, and that was all it was—perfectly innocent, separate rooms and all that. But once we got to the Falls, there was this . . . atmosphere. Everyone we saw was either newly married or about to be married, and we started feeling really out of place. Then we walked by this darling little wedding chapel and peeked in. The woman at the desk said we could get a marriage license down the street at City Hall and then she offered to hold the seven o'clock ceremony open for us while we made our arrangements. She just assumed . . . and we hated to disappoint her . . . so we decided to do it. We'd been talking about getting married, but we hadn't been able to decide how to handle the two-church problem or the fact that Thomas's family all live in New York and wanted a big ceremony there. This was an easy way around all the fuss and bother. So, TA-DAH!"

Chapter 27

Graduation Is Not the End but the Beginning

For several days, Fiona allowed herself to wallow in self-pity. It certainly wasn't fair that Gloria's happy wedding had come on the very heels of news that had crushed her own marriage plans, she complained. School offered little to distract her, particularly since Lester was no longer there. But then Lester's letters began to arrive— one written every night after the store closed for the day and he was alone in a bare-bones rooming house cubicle. He had more reason to be lonely than she did. Yet his messages were generally upbeat. His uncle's staff had been welcoming and helpful. He was learning the business quickly and had already come up with some new ideas to make keeping track of stock easier for his employees.

In one of those letters, he tried to describe the house he had inherited from his uncle. "I'm not sure what you'll think of this big old house, Fiona. It's pretty different from the boxy Pennsylvania houses we're used to. This one has a turret on one side, topped off by a cone-shaped roof that makes it look like a castle. The porch wraps around all four sides, and the railings and roof supports have all kinds of curlicue decorations. The roof is made of slate and is much steeper than on any house I have ever seen. The upper stories have fishtail shingles, while the main story is finished in clapboard siding, and the basement level is made of stone. I don't really understand the design, but it's so much like a fairy tale that it always makes me smile."

His enthusiasm poured over into his descriptions of the interior. The house stood over a basement with a coal chute to keep the fireplaces burning and a root cellar to provide food storage for the winter. On the first floor, the large kitchen opened directly onto a formal dining room, and then a parlor stretched clear across the front of the house. Upstairs were several large bedrooms and a central bath with hot and cold running water. Every room had its own small fireplace and wall-mounted gas fixtures for lighting. The structure was topped with an attic that featured dormer windows, more for looks than for function.

"We're going to need lots of furniture," he wrote. "Uncle Clarence didn't use all the rooms, but I imagine we will do so eventually. You'll have fun fixing the place up," he promised, "and there's a little princess room in that turret that you can have all to yourself—you and the books you love."

Tempted out of her funk by his descriptions of the house that would soon be hers, Fiona began to spend her evenings with the Sears and Roebuck catalog, dog-earing pages that featured furniture items she coveted.

"Is this fellow Lester made of money?" Sally asked one night. "Your dreams keep getting more and more elaborate."

Fiona shrugged. "He says the store is doing well, and we're really very lucky. Most young couples have to save and scrimp to be able to get married. We've had a business and a wonderful house provided for us. And Lester has always had trouble saying no to me. You just wait and see. You're going to be so jealous!"

Katerina had been listening to the conversation from across the room. Now she frowned at Fiona. "*Die Ehe ändert alles.* Marriage changes everything, and you have a very one-sided view of wedded life, my girl. You want things, and you expect your new husband to provide them. I suspect you'll have to learn the hard way that marriage is a two-sided deal. If Lester is as good a businessman as he says he is, he'll be pouring his money back into the store, not into your catalog orders. You can look at pretty pictures all you want, but you'd better be prepared to sew your own curtains."

"Really, Mother, haven't you always told us that it's as easy to fall in love with a rich man as a poor one?"

"Yes, and I still believe that's true. But you didn't fall in love with a rich man. You fell in love with a poor boy from a hardscrabble farm, just like the one you were raised on. Lester may have inherited a business and a house, but he'll have to work hard all his life to keep them. And you? That big old Victorian house he's describing to you will keep you busy every waking hour, what with cleaning it and repairing it. So don't go putting on airs and trying to make your little sister jealous."

"I'm not jealous of Fiona, Mother," Sally laughed. "I want a career, not a husband, and I certainly wouldn't want a husband as scrawny as Lester is."

"That surely sounds like jealousy to me," Fiona shot back.

"Girls! That's more than enough from both of you. If we must talk about Fiona's wedding, suppose we start dealing with the important details, like when we need to go to Ohio."

"Oh, Lester and I have already talked about that. I'll be completely finished with school and graduation exercises on Friday, May 22nd. But Lester expects to be really busy at the store that next week, because Decoration Day will be coming. And then he says the first part of June will be busy, too, because people will have the money to start planting their gardens. So we thought the weekend of June 20th and 21st would be a good time to get married."

"Have you checked with Frederick to see if that weekend fits his church's schedule?"

"No, I just assumed . . ."

" . . . that the world will come to a stop because you want it to?"

"No, but . . ."

"That's the first thing you need to do. Put that catalog away and write to Lillian, asking her when we can come and when her preacher husband can accommodate your wedding plans."

Several days later, Katerina came home from her nursing duties to find Fiona hunched over a letter at the kitchen table. "News?" she asked.

Fiona looked up with a huge grin. "And such good news! Guess what!"

"I can't imagine."

"Remember when Aunt Becca was trying to make me feel better by telling me that Lester might be able to graduate, even if he had to move to Canton? Well, she was right!"

Katerina could not stop herself from grimacing. Of course Rebecca would have been right. She was always right. It was a characteristic Katerina had always resented about her sister-in-law—her proclivity to make snap judgments and the tendency of the girls to take her word as gospel truth.

Katerina forced herself to smile. "Was she? About what this time?"

"Lester got a letter this week, telling him that the teachers had discussed his school record and found that he only needed one more math course to graduate. And then they decided that since he had been running a business for six months—keeping accounts, placing orders, billing customers, taking inventory, paying taxes, and handling a payroll—he probably knew all the math he was ever going to need. So they are letting him graduate on time."

"Oh, Fiona, I'm happy for him—and for you, of course."

"And best of all, his employees have agreed to work extra hours, so he can come home for graduation. And that means we can get married here that same weekend."

"Whoa! Wait a minute. That's a lot to pull off in just one weekend."

"No, it'll be easier than trying to take everyone to Canton so we can get married there."

"Maybe, but it's only three weeks away."

"I know, but Lester has already thought of that. Really, Mother, you're not giving us much credit. We're not children any longer."

Katerina took a deep breath. Patience, she warned herself. "So what's the plan?"

"Well, Lester has a new friend in Canton, a fellow who has agreed to stand up for him at the wedding, and he has a car of his own. He and Lester will drive down here Thursday evening. Graduation and promotion exercises are being held at the church on Friday afternoon, so there will be room for all the families to attend. And after we get our diplomas, his parents are going to throw a picnic supper for both our families to celebrate our graduation."

"That's nice of them. Does that mean all our family? Do they realize you have seven sisters?"

"Oh, of course, Mother. They know all about our family, and everyone will be welcome. Then we'll get married on Saturday, probably early in the afternoon, so that we can have a cake and ice cream reception in the church basement afterward. And then Lester's friend will drive us back to Canton so that we can spend our Sunday honeymoon in our very own house. A weekend will give us plenty of time."

"There's still a lot of planning to do. First, you need to make sure the church and the pastor are free that day."

"Yes, Mother, I'm stopping over there tomorrow right after school. I'm sure Reverend Johnson will be willing to help."

"We'll need flowers for the church, you'll have to have a wedding dress, someone will have to bake that wedding cake and churn the ice cream, and invitations—you have to let all the family know." Katerina was shaking her head and counting on her fingers as she spoke. "Oh, and music. You'll need to check with Esther Goodenough to see if she can play the organ."

Fiona put her arms around her mother in a rare gesture of affection. "Come on, Mother. You've been down this road before. You'll know what all needs to be done, and everybody will pitch in, just as they always do. I'm going to run over right now and tell Aunt Becca the good news. You know she'll help any way she can. It's all going to work out." She did a few dance steps around the kitchen before running out the door. "It has to—because I'm getting married!"

⸎

The next three weeks were forever a blur in Katerina's mind, but, as Fiona had predicted, all the details seemed to take care of themselves. On Friday, May 22nd, Katerina and Becca settled themselves into a church pew to watch the commencement activities bringing the school year to a close. The North Sewickley School was still, in effect, little more than a one-room schoolhouse, although several teachers now shared the space. The youngest children were scheduled to put on a skit about the coming of summer, while the middle grade students had planned a poetry recital. Then the high school chorus would sing a medley of popular songs, one of which would feature a solo by their very own Sally. Proud parents waited for the moment when several children would take a formal walk as they moved from one level of education to the next. The presentation of diplomas would be the final event of the day.

Because the small open space at the front of the church did not allow room for all the students to sit together, the children sat with their parents until it was time for their performances. Sally was perched at the end of the pew next to her mother, and Katerina could not help but notice that she was unusually wiggly—straightening her skirt, touching her hair, leafing thorough a hymnal.

"Are you nervous about your solo?" Katerina asked.

"No, Mother, you know I love performing."

"Then what's wrong? You're as fidgety as a broody hen."

"Nothing's wrong. I'm fine. But . . . who is that across the aisle?"

For the first time, Katerina noticed the tall man seated across from them. He was staring at Sally, it appeared, his bright blue eyes focused on her face. "I don't know. I've never seen him. He's not someone from your school?"

"No, I don't know him either, but he's, oh, so handsome."

Katerina gave her daughter a penetrating look of her own. Noticing a young man at all was very much out of character for Sally. "Well, it's impolite of him to be staring at you, whoever he is. And I don't know that I would call him handsome. That unruly mop of black curls could use a good combing and some pomade to make them behave."

"I think the curls make him look dashing."

"Huh! And that chin. There's an old saying that goes, *'Das Grübchen in Kinn, der Teufel innerhalb.* Dimple in chin, devil within.' I wouldn't trust him for a moment."

"Oh, Mother, you and your wise sayings! Who makes these things up, anyway?"

"Those that are true have come down through the ages, my girl. It would be well for you to pay them some mind."

"I don't care. I like his dimple. Maybe Fiona knows him." She leaned forward to whisper across her mother and aunt. "Fiona, who's the fellow sitting across the aisle from us? Do you know him?"

"Oh, that's Jake, Lester's friend. You'll meet him tonight at the picnic."

Sally's eyes widened, and a small smile spread across her face. Unconsciously, she straightened her back, tipped her head in what she imagined was a come-hither pose, and fluttered her eyelashes at the young man. He grinned in return.

Katerina grasped her daughter's elbow in a vice-like grip. "Stop it this instant. Sit back and watch the program, or I'll make you change seats with me and block your view entirely. Church is not a place for flirting, and you are much too young to be inviting an older man's attention, anyway."

"I just wanted to make him feel welcome."

"Leave that to your sister and her fiancé. He's their friend, not yours."

Chapter 28

*We Always Want
What We Cannot Have*

At the graduation picnic, the mysterious young man immediately made his way to introduce himself to Katerina. "Mrs. Grenville, I'm Jacob Kerrigan from Canton. I'm afraid I may have seemed impertinent during the school exercises. I wasn't trying to be rude. I was simply fascinated by the contrasts between your two girls. Lester had told me all about Fiona, of course, but no one warned me that her younger sister would be so different—or so beautiful."

Katerina observed him without a change in her disapproving expression. "In other words, you were ogling my daughter. You cannot expect me to approve of that, or of you."

"I do apologize. But in fairness, I really was taken by surprise. Lester had told me that Fiona was worried about her little sister's reactions to her marriage. Fiona was afraid that Sarah Jane would feel isolated and left out. So she asked that I pay some special attention to her. I was expecting a homely little waif. That's not what I saw, so I was pleasantly surprised."

"I don't need excuses, Mr. Kerrigan. And everyone calls her Sally, not Sarah Jane."

"So I understand. But nicknames are for friends and family. I am neither, at least not yet. And I promise you, I am not usually so ill-mannered."

"Humpf. I hope not. But I do agree that we have gotten off to a bad start. So let's begin again. I am pleased to meet you, Mr. Kerrigan. How did you get roped into our family gathering this weekend?"

"I'm here to stand up for Lester at the wedding tomorrow. Lester and I met at our rooming house. Both of us were alone, working hard at our new jobs, and not knowing anyone else in Canton. That can make for a lonely life, unless one makes friends quickly. We gravitated toward one another, partially because our work schedules did not coincide. I am free during much of the day to visit Lester's hardware store and explore all the fascinating, odd objects available there. And he was free in the evenings to accompany me occasionally in my work-related investigations. We've become quite good friends, at least in part because of our differences. So when he asked me to stand up for him at his wedding, I was happy to oblige."

"And what, exactly, is it that you do, Mr. Kerrigan?"

"I'm a newspaperman, ma'am. I work the night shift at the *Canton City News*. Most people do not like working at night, but in the news business, that's when all the most interesting events happen."

"I see. I had the impression that you worked with your hands." Her still-disapproving eyes lingered on his fingernails, all rimmed in black.

Embarrassed by her frank staring, he shoved his hands into his pockets, and then, grimacing, pulled them out again. "I must apologize, too, for my grubby appearance. You see, at the paper, when something goes wrong, we all pitch in. Wednesday night, our old printing press decided to spring a leak, and it started to spray printers' ink all over everything. We were right in the middle of running the early edition of the paper, so there was no help for it but to jump in and get that leak stopped. By the time we did so, several of my colleagues and I ended up black from head to toe. Luckily, the ink washes off skin, but once it gets under one's fingernails, it's there for the duration. We saved the paper, though." His grin was so infectious that Katerina caught herself beginning to smile.

"You said you live alone. No family somewhere?"

"No, ma'am. Actually, I'm an orphan, raised by nuns in a local convent after my parents were killed in a house fire.

They ran back into the flames to rescue me, not knowing that neighbors had already pulled me out through a back window. And yes, before you ask, I will always feel guilty about their deaths. But I try to make up for it by leading a good life and making a success of myself."

"A Catholic, then, with a load of good Catholic guilt?"

"Not officially. The nuns raised me and taught me their faith along with my ABCs and my multiplication tables. But my parents were not Catholic, so the nuns did not insist that I convert. To tell the truth, I'm not sure what I am in terms of religion. Does it matter to you?"

"Yes, I'm afraid it does. I've always told my daughters I won't allow them to date a Democrat, a Catholic, or a redhead."

Jacob laughed in spite of himself. "That's quite a combination. I can understand the first two, but why no redheads?"

"I don't want redheaded grandchildren. They get into too much mischief." She shrugged.

"Fair enough, I suppose. I don't intend to date your daughter in any event. But is it all right if I escort her through tomorrow's wedding? After all, as best man and maid of honor, we are sort of required to work together."

"I suppose so, since you're not officially a Catholic."

Sally had been quietly observing their conversation, but she interrupted when she realized her mother had started her usual inquiry about religion. "Mother, you haven't trotted out that old saw about Democrats, Catholics, and redheads, have you?"

"And suppose I have?"

"It's embarrassing, that's all. And it makes it sound as if you think . . ." Her voice trailed off as she realized that anything she said would only make the situation worse.

❦

The wedding came off nicely the next day. Fiona and Lester had an official portrait taken that morning, and then they separated until it was time for the wedding. Sally and Jake, however, spent most of the day together. Jake offered his services and the use of his Model T for running errands, and Sally felt very grown up riding with him and pointing him in the right directions. They helped decorate the church with flowers from neighbors' gardens, fetched the wedding cake from Becca's kitchen, and set up the reception tables in the church basement. They worked hard but so enjoyed one another's company that they scarcely noticed the passage of time. At the last minute, they had to rush to get themselves ready for the ceremony.

As maid of honor, Sally wore her first floor-length gown of royal blue lace. It made her feel grown-up, and, far from being isolated and left out, she radiated her own brand of confidence. Fiona's three nieces, Frankie, Glenda, and Eva, were bridesmaids, wearing matching light blue dresses of dotted Swiss fabric, while Edna, the little flower girl, wore a frilly pink frock. Fiona was a lovely bride, looking less robust than usual in her white gown and veil, while Lester seemed to have grown in stature as well as maturity. Their vows were spoken with heartfelt intensity, and their happiness was almost palpable.

Throughout the ceremony and the following reception, Jacob Kerrigan was as attentive to Sally as Lester was to his new bride. And Becca, as usual, was the first to pick up on the undercurrents.

"Sally seems almost as happy as the bride," Becca observed to Katerina. "Is there something brewing there?"

"No, of course not. Jake has turned out to be a very nice young man, but he's most unsuitable for her. He's an orphan raised by nuns, so there's just no telling what may lurk in his background. And I made sure he understood that this is a one-shot occasion. I doubt we'll ever see him again."

"I'm shocked, Kat. I've never heard you be so dismissive of any man who showed an interest in one of your girls. Surely you've not given up on your dream to have them all safely married."

Katerina understood that Rebecca was laughing at her. "Maybe not, but he's not suitable son-in-law material, no matter what Sally may think this afternoon. He's too slick, too glib at explaining things away, too obsequious around me. I don't trust him, and I'm sure Sally will quickly lose interest as well. Young girls always get emotional at weddings. Then they wake up the next morning, happy that they were not the one taking those binding vows. He'll be gone soon, and *aus den Augen, aus dem Sinn.* Out of sight, out of mind."

❧

She might have been more concerned if she had overheard some of the conversation that kept the two young people whispering to one another.

Jake had been watching the Grenville clan with interest. "I can't imagine what it must have been like for you to live with seven sisters in your household," he commented. "Oh, I was used to having other children around in the orphanage, but it wasn't the same. We didn't really care about one another, and individuals came and went away again without much notice. Your family, however, seems so close. You all love one another. You know all the family goings-on. You understand exactly who is related to whom. And you function like a single unit."

"Well, of course we do. We've grown up together, and at occasions like this one, we all come back together to celebrate, even the sisters who have been married the longest."

"You say that as if it's the most ordinary thing in the world. I assure you, it is not. Most of the families I have come in contact with are broken. In the course of gathering the news, I see family arguments, divorces, physical fights, drunken husbands, abandoned children, abused women, even murders . . ."

"How depressing! I don't think I'd want a job that exposed only the worst side of people."

"You'd get used to it. But that's why I'm so enjoying watching your family. I'm a little jealous that I can't be a part of it."

Sally scrutinized his face, while her breath seemed to catch in her throat. "Do you really mean that?"

"Oh, well, no, not literally. I mean . . ." Jake was floundering for a way to correct the impression he had just given Sally. "I don't have designs upon your family in particular. I'd just like to be a part of one like it, someday."

"You'd be welcome to visit us any time," Sally persisted.

"That probably won't ever happen, but it's nice of you to say."

"Why not? I thought we had become friends."

"Sarah Jane, I hope I haven't given you the idea that I . . ."

"That you . . . what? That you like me? That you find me interesting? That you enjoy my company?"

"I do like you, but, I'm afraid, not in the way you mean it."

"What's wrong with me?"

"Nothing. But there's something very wrong with the idea of us developing a relationship. How old are you?"

"Almost sixteen."

"Almost? When's your birthday?"

"October. Early October."

"So you're fifteen."

"Yes, but . . ."

"And five months from now, you'll only be sixteen. Do you know why they call it 'Sweet Sixteen'?"

"No, but I'm sure you're going to tell me." She was growing angry at the way he seemed to be lecturing her.

"Because it's the last year of childhood, the last year when you remain sweet and innocent. And why do I care how old you are? Because I don't get involved with children. I don't date children. And I don't try to worm my way into their affections."

"You could have fooled me."

"That's not fair. You're reacting out of anger and hurt feelings. Look—I'm twenty-two, an adult. You're still a child, as your current behavior is proving. It would be completely unsuitable for me to have any romantic intentions toward you. Later, someday, if you were, say, seventeen and I were twenty-four, I might well fall in love with you and you with me. But not now. Not yet."

Sally's eyes were flooded with tears that she tried to contain. "Someday? Someday. That's supposed to make me feel better?"

"It's the best I can offer."

"So, go back to Canton and stay there."

"I will. When you turn seventeen, if you still are interested, let me know, and I'll be here in a flash. But not now. Not yet."

Rebecca's Journal

Summertime 1914

othing spectacular happened at Fiona's May wedding
to warn us that our little world was about to undergo
a major transformation. It was a beautiful day, the bride and
groom were beside themselves with happiness, my wedding
cake was a success, and there wasn't a single family quarrel that
I can remember. The newlyweds left early to make the drive
back to Canton in daylight, but the party went on until late
in the evening. We smiled, we hugged, we talked. Eventually,
we sang old songs and held hands while we watched the setting
sun.

Nevertheless, something must have happened. Everything
changed after that night. Perhaps the first thing I noticed was
a change in Sally. She had looked particularly grown up in her
floor-length blue gown, but it was the expression on her face

that marked the greater change. On most days, we had been able to count on Sally to be pouting about something. Even in those famous family portraits the girls had done two years ago, she was the petulant one, looking as if someone had just stepped on her toe. In another of the pictures, she looked as if she were planning to pinch someone else. When I think back to her childhood, she never wore a smile. Maybe that went along with being the youngest, but on this night, she appeared to be genuinely happy. Happy for her sister? Maybe, although the two had never gotten along. Happy to be rid of her sister? More like her, although I saw no gloating here, just contentment and self-assurance.

Even more remarkably, the change appeared to be permanent. She settled into a routine at home of doing whatever she could to be helpful. She begged her mother to show her how to make dinner rolls and flaky piecrusts. She watched Ruby cook and learned how to prepare the stews and casseroles that sustained the family through weekday dinners. When the day's chores were finished, she curled up quietly with a book, losing herself in the pages of the classic tales she had formerly ignored. She made no explanation of what had brought about the change, and the rest of us were too happy with the new Sally to risk disturbing the peace.

Ruby, too, was about to shake things up. She waited until Labor Day, when all her sisters had returned to their homes, to announce that she and Frankie were moving to Akron. I had noticed that she and Paul Davidson were deep in conversation at the wedding reception, but I assumed they were talking about Martha. Instead, it turned out, he had been explaining to her that Akron, with its new rubber industry booming, was experiencing a crisis in service personnel. Restaurants and taverns were in demand, and jobs were plentiful. He had even offered to let Ruby and Frankie move into his house until Ruby found a job and could afford her own living quarters. Katerina was typically suspicious of anything Paul suggested, but once Ruby has made up her mind, there is no arguing with her. She simply packed their things, bought two train tickets, and was gone by the end of the week.

What a difference that made in the little house on the hill! What had been a crowded living arrangement was now a roomy accommodation for Katerina and Sally. Sally fixed up the loft for herself and her old cat Cathagoras, while Katerina had the first-floor bedroom as her own personal space. With fewer mouths to fill, Katerina cut back on her nursing hours, and Sally took over some of the chores that Ruby had performed. Mother and daughter seemed to be enjoying each other more. Katerina also reached out more often to Nora's and Millie's adolescent children, serving as a grandmotherly ear for their young stories.

What about me? Well, I, too, have made some changes. I am, after all, in my sixties now, and long walks around town are getting harder on my old bones. Screwing up my courage, I decided it was time to find a new form of transportation. The Ford Motor Company representative in Ellwood City was offering free driving lessons with the purchase of a Model T. The very idea of sitting behind a steering wheel and trying to control that machine scared me witless. But I also reminded myself of how nice it had been to have an automobile at my disposal to get around Gettysburg. I was terrible at driving at first, and I didn't tell anyone I was taking lessons until I felt comfortable with what all was involved. And then something of a miracle happened. I was driving down one of our local roads with my instructor beside me, and all at once I relaxed my death grip on the wheel. I leaned back, felt the wind in my hair, and discovered that I loved to drive.

At first Katerina was afraid to ride in my new car, but it didn't take her long to learn, as I had, that the convenience far outweighed the fear of disaster. We two old ladies had many adventures during the summer. We visited friends and relatives instead of waiting for them to come see us. We stopped at roadside markets and purchased fresh vegetables, jars of honey, and cute little craft objects. We even traveled to nearby towns, although I drew the line at driving to Pittsburgh. New Castle, however, was close enough and uncrowded enough to be inviting. It was an idyllic period, but one that was not destined to last.

Chapter 29

Deeds, Not Words: Give Women the Vote

New Castle, Pennsylvania
July–August 1914

"Good morning, Katerina. How adventurous do you feel?" Becca Grenville's eyes danced with mischief as she entered the farmhouse kitchen one morning in mid-July.

Katerina held up her hands in mock surrender. "Oh, no, I know that look! You're about to suggest something completely outrageous."

"Not really. Just a little more daring than we usually get. We've driven up to New Castle to shop at the Amish market, but we haven't seen much of the town. How would you like to go up and spend a couple of days there? We could stay at the Leslie Hotel on Washington Street."

"I've never stayed in a hotel."

"Then it's high time you did. The Leslie has lovely rooms and a restaurant called The Branding Iron. I've heard they offer a wonderful roast lamb, cooked on a spit in the window."

"Sounds expensive."

"Not really, but I'll make it my treat."

"There's more to this story than I'm hearing, I think. What's the great attraction in New Castle all of a sudden?"

Becca shrugged. "Well, a famous suffragette named Miss Liliane Stevens Howard is going to be visiting Lawrence County for the next couple of weeks. She's scheduled to speak in New Castle on the 22nd, and I'd really like to hear her."

"A suffragette." Katerina's distaste showed in her face. "One of those mannish women who go around waving signs and yelling about how unfairly the world treats women."

"She's quite attractive, actually, and well-educated, too. She isn't one of those harridans you've read about. She represents the Pennsylvania Women's Suffrage Association, and she is on a recruiting trip for members. She speaks at public and private gatherings, but only where she is invited. She's going to be at the Grocers' Picnic in Cascade Park on Wednesday and then at a members' meeting on Thursday. I promise you, they will both be pleasant and dignified occasions."

Katerina was still shaking her head. "I don't understand why you want to get involved with that group."

"I've long been interested in the cause of gaining voting rights for women. I am, after all, my mother's daughter, and Susan Grenville was already campaigning to have women's suffrage written into the new South Carolina constitution back in 1868. It was a lost cause back then, of course. My father patiently pointed out to her that it was more important to get the newly freed slaves enfranchised. But it has always seemed to me that we women have waited long enough to have our voices heard."

"Be that as it may, I can't possibly go to New Castle in the middle of next week. Sally's home all day because school's out, and I won't leave her here alone."

"She can stay with Nora's family while we're gone. Please, Katerina. I'll feel much more courageous if I have you along to keep me company."

In the end, Katerina agreed to go for one night. They planned to drive up on Wednesday morning and return Thursday evening. It was a lovely day, and the picnic in the park was a pleasant affair. Local grocers provided samples of their wares, hoping to lure more customers. Some offered sizzling bits of sausage cooked on small grills, while others provided fresh fruit, cookies, or lemonade. Musicians took turns during the afternoon serenading the ladies in attendance, but at four o'clock, they turned the bandstand over to Miss Howard.

As Becca had promised, Liliane Howard was a soft-spoken woman whose passionate belief in the rightness of her cause made her a persuasive speaker. She had organized her speech around several accusations that were often made against women's suffrage:

> *Some Say: The majority of women don't want to vote, and women will not vote when they are given the right.*
>
> *We Say: The number who want the vote is always many times greater than the number who don't, and official figures show women DO vote largely wherever they have the right.*
>
> *Some Say: Women have enough to do without voting.*
>
> *We Say: Voting only takes a few minutes and can be done on the way to the market.*
>
> *Some Say: It would double the ignorant vote.*
>
> *We Say: One-third more girls than boys attend high schools, and women are rapidly becoming the more educated class.*

She spoke for almost an hour before inviting those who were interested to come forward and sign up as members of the state organization. Twenty-seven did so, including Becca. As she turned in her signed pledge, she noticed that Miss Howard gave her an appraising look, but she brushed it off, attributing it to her age. As for Katerina, she admitted that the speaker had made some good points but refused to commit herself to further action. "I'm not a joiner, Becca. You know that. I'm one of those who already has enough to do."

When they went down to dinner later that evening, Becca and Katerina happened to meet Miss Howard at the entrance to the hotel dining room. "Thank you for attending my little talk this afternoon," Miss Howard said. "And thank you for joining the Federation."

"We thoroughly enjoyed it. But do you always remember which people in your audience have turned in membership cards?"

"No, not usually. But I do remember when you have a name I recognize—Grenville? There's a well-known author by that name who writes charming books for children."

"Ah . . . yes . . . I . . ." Becca stumbled over her words until Katerina stepped in.

"This is her . . . the author, I mean. Rebecca Marie Grenville."

"Really? You wrote *The Adventures of Mr. Worm?*"

Becca laughed. "I never thought I would hear anyone say that, but yes, I did."

"I adore your books. I've bought several of them for my nieces and nephews. I wonder . . . Would you like to join me for dinner? I'm getting an idea that might work out well for both of us."

Over a fine roast lamb meal, Miss Howard listened as Becca and Katerina recounted the story behind the books—the need for an appealing tale to break through to the mind of a birth-injured child. Then she explained her own proposal.

"Our cause needs a way to reach out to people who aren't interested in political discussions—young women who are too busy raising their children to think about current affairs, or older women who think it's too late to change the world around them. Could you write a book for us? Using ladybugs, perhaps? A little disagreement in the meadow? An argument to persuade the grasshoppers to listen to the ladybugs, even if they are dressed in polka dots?"

Becca wrinkled her brow as she considered the idea. "I suppose I could, but how would you use it?"

"We could sell copies at all our meetings, put it in the hands of anyone who has small children or grandchildren around. When you read a book out loud to a child, you're reading for yourself as well, aren't you? And for others in the room, like the child's father. I really like the idea of a book that appeals to a child but that also carries an important message for the rest of the family. We'd pay you well, of course."

"I'll have to think about it. I don't know how my publishers might react to the idea. There could be contractual reasons why I couldn't do it. I'll certainly consider it, though. In the meantime, is there anything else I can do to help your cause?"

"Since you're staying here in the hotel, I gather you are not from this part of the state."

"No, actually, we live in the next county, just south of Ellwood City."

"Really? Do you know Ellwood well?"

"Pretty well. Why?"

"Because I'm having trouble getting a meeting set up. I was supposed to give a talk there on Friday, but the woman who was in charge has failed to make any arrangements. I'm booked solid next week, but there's an opening on August 4th, if we can find a place to hold the meeting and a group willing to listen."

"I'm sure I can find something for you. Where can I reach you between now and then?"

"I'm staying here at the hotel for the duration. I'll be going out to lectures and Chautauqua classes in the small communities around here every day, but I'll eventually get any message left for me. And any time you are free, I can always use an extra hand to help with signatures and sales of our novelties. I'll leave you a copy of my schedule at the desk, so you know where to find me."

When they returned to their room, Katerina smiled at her sister-in-law indulgently. "You're hooked, aren't you? You're a suffragette."

"It's a good cause, Kat. And it's something I can do."

On the way home, Becca was preoccupied, her mind buzzing with several ideas about how she could help Miss

Howard's cause. "Who do we know in Ellwood?" She was only thinking out loud, but Katerina responded.

"You mean, who do we know in Ellwood besides Nora and Henry?"

"Oh, of course. Henry's so self-effacing, I sometimes forget that he's in a position of some prominence at the high school."

"And he and Nora do move in some social circles in town," Katerina added. "I'm sure Nora will be willing to point you to the local movers and shakers. She's much more socially aware than I am."

"Would you mind if we stopped there on the way home?"

"Of course not. I assume you're not so wrapped up in this brave new movement that you've forgotten that we have to stop to pick up Sally anyway."

Becca glanced at her sister-in-law to gauge her mood. "I don't want to impose my preoccupations on you, Kat. I understand that you're not as enthusiastic about getting women the right to vote as I am."

"I'm not unenthusiastic, my dear. I agree that it's a change that needs to occur. Certainly, with this war brewing in Europe, our male politicians could use some sensible female guidance. But I'm not an activist, as you are. You have been an independent, self-supporting woman your entire life. I've been a homebody, content with my role as wife and mother. And at this stage in my life, I want nothing more than to take shelter in that home that I've worked so hard to put together, watching my children and grandchildren blossom and grow."

"And that's a right you have more than earned. Your children and their children will be your ongoing legacy. I, on the other hand, have no children to grace my memory. My only legacy, if I have one at all, will be in my words and my actions, so I feel duty-bound to make a visible difference in my world."

⁂

Katerina was correct about her daughter's social contacts. As soon as Becca explained to her what she was looking for, Nora picked up her new telephone and cranked a handle to reach the operator.

"Hello, Mrs. Pickens. This is Nora Southerland. Do you have a listing for the new free library? I need to speak to someone who handles their meeting schedule. Yes, Dr. Oldham would be perfect. Can you connect me?"

Within a few minutes, Nora determined that there would be an open meeting of the local Women's Club in the reading room on Tuesday, August 4th, at 7:30 pm. Next, Nora called the president of the club, a Mrs. Cartwright, and learned that they were scheduled to discuss the need for a woman to oversee food inspections for the city. The connection between suffrage and women's concerns about the purity of their food was obvious, and Mrs. Cartwright was delighted to invite Miss Howard to address the club.

"There you are, Aunt Becca. All scheduled. I'm really proud of you for getting involved in this campaign. Let me know if there is anything else you need. I'll be attending the meeting myself, and I hope you'll join us. You, too, Mother."

"Not me, dear. This is Rebecca's project, not mine." Katerina smiled, but with her lips pressed tightly together in an expression that spoke more loudly than her words. Why was it, she wondered, that all her daughters were so eager to support Becca's interests but wanted little to do with her own day-to-day activities?

Once Becca had dropped her sister-in-law and niece off at the farmhouse, Sally prodded her mother for more information. "Are you and Aunt Becca fighting?"

"Of course not. We don't fight."

"Disagreeing, then? It's quite obvious that you are upset about something. Didn't you enjoy your little jaunt to New Castle?"

"There wasn't much to enjoy. We listened to the suffragette's speech all afternoon, and then Becca joined the organization and agreed that we would have dinner with the speaker that evening. The two of them conferred and whispered all through the meal about a cockamamie idea that Rebecca might write one of her bug books about women getting the right to vote. And the next day, we had to attend another meeting, and the much-vaunted Miss Howard simply repeated her speech from the day before. I didn't mind listening once, but twice was a bit much."

"So you're not in favor of women voting?"

"I didn't say that! Honestly, you're just like Rebecca sometimes."

"I hope so. I think she's wonderful."

"Well, 'Miss Wonderful' may be good at writing cute little books, but she's hardly a model for young girls to be following. A single woman carrying a torch for a man dead for fifty years? The lonely sister, always the extra plate at the family table? The childless lady who knows all about raising children? The spinster who knows all about marriage? The family member who has always had everything given to her? What does she know about real life, anyway?"

Chapter 30

In for a Penny;
In for a Pound

Canton, Ohio
Fall 1914

For the rest of the summer and early fall, Katerina and Rebecca saw little of one another. Miss Howard had taken full advantage of Becca's offer to assist her in Lawrence County. By the time she had completed her visits, Becca was committed to the cause of women's suffrage. Howard's formal report summarized the situation in western Pennsylvania:

> *Visited seven towns and six townships; made 72 calls; had 58 interviews; enrolled 222 new members. Plenty of sentiment in New Castle, but little inclination to work. Mrs. E. W. Baer, the current chairman, desires*

to resign due to ill health and lack of time. An active leader is much needed here.

And Miss Howard had found her candidate. She invited Becca first to Harrisburg and then to Philadelphia to meet with the leaders of the Pennsylvania Women's Suffrage Association. Together they approached her publisher with the idea of the women's suffrage ladybugs. He, seeing a chance to widen the market for all of Becca's books, agreed to publish the little volume and then make it available for distribution by the women's association. Almost before she knew it, Becca had become a vital part of the organization, petitioning the state legislature to grant women the vote. She had little time to think about anything else.

Meanwhile, back at the Nasmith cabin, Katerina was embroiled in her own set of crises. The troubles started with a visit from Ruby. She had sent a letter, telling her mother that she and Frankie might be coming for a quick visit but without telling her that she was planning to bring a gentleman with her. So it was something of a surprise when Katerina arrived home from church one Sunday morning to discover an automobile pulled to a stop in the farmyard. The driver was also a surprise. He was a tall, burly fellow with a broad stomach and a perpetual grin beneath his curly red mustache.

"I want you to meet my new boss, Mama," Ruby cried, as she and Frankie crawled out of the passenger side. "This is Mr. O'Malley—Mike O'Malley, owner of Big Mike's Tavern and Corner Grill."

"Pleased to meet'cha, ma'am," he said, extending a meaty palm.

"Uh, how do you do, Mr., uh, O'Malley? Did Ruby say you are her boss?"

"That's right. The little lady wandered in the other day looking for a job, and I snatched her up 'fore anybody else got a good look at her."

"So you're back to being a barmaid?" Katerina gave Ruby a raised-eyebrow glare.

"I'm actually Mike's house manager, not a barmaid," Ruby replied. "I keep an eye on the front of the house, greet customers when they come in, see them seated properly, and supervise the girls who do the serving."

"Yessirree, she keeps the whole place hoppin', she does."

"Well. I shall look forward to hearing more about your . . .um . . . business. Do come in. Have you eaten lunch?"

"Yes, ma'am, but it sure is thirsty out. I could use a . . ."

" . . . a cool glass of water," Ruby finished for him, hoping he was not going to ask for a beer.

"Hello! I'm Ruby's little sister, Sally," said a new voice at the door. "Maybe the gentleman would prefer some lemonade?"

"I would, indeed, little lady," Mike replied. Somehow, he seemed to fill the whole kitchen, as the small party made its way toward the parlor.

Sally gave her mother a knowing look and pushed her toward the front of the house. "I'll get the drinks, Mother. You go on and get acquainted with Mr. O'Malley." She was already guessing the direction the questions would take.

"O'Malley. That's a good Irish name. Ulster or Dublin?"

"Oh, Catholic Dublin, to be sure," Mike answered with a smile. "That's what makes me such a good barkeep, you see. We Catholics carry around a good burden of guilt, but we're always allowed to drink, so we can wash the guilt away with a big tankard or two of Irish beer."

"It helps with our grill business, too," Ruby interjected. "Since Catholics can't eat meat on Fridays, they all come to our Friday night fish fry."

"How convenient for you." Katerina's voice was growing colder by the minute. "Ruby, could I see you in the kitchen for a few minutes, since you seem to have acquired some new culinary skills lately?"

"Don't start on me, Mother," Ruby hissed as soon as they were out of earshot. "I already know what you are thinking. He's a redheaded Irish Catholic. How could I? Well, I'll venture to guess that he votes Democratic, too. Those things just don't bother me. And you shouldn't be judging people on them, either."

"I haven't said one critical word."

"You don't need to. I know how you think."

"Then why deliberately taunt me?"

"That's not what I'm doing. I'm just trying to be honest. I could have hidden him and my relationship with him from you. I thought it would be better to . . ."

"Your relationship? What relationship? He's your boss."

"And also my . . . uh, my landlord, of sorts."

"Your landlord? Oh, my stars! You're living with him?"

"Well, he was worried about my having to walk all the way back to Paul and Martha's house after a late night at the tavern, so he suggested that we share the big apartment above the business. That way, I'm available to . . ."

"Available? I'll bet you are!"

"Available to work when he needs me. And Frankie has her own room, too, so it's better for all of us."

"You're exposing Frankie to this so-called living arrangement? Doesn't that bother you? What kind of example is that setting, for her to see her mother . . ."

"What? To see her mother being treated with kindness and respect? To see her mother earning a good living wage that can take care of both of us? To have a safe place to live and plenty to eat, and to be surrounded by people who love her? Since when are those things bad?"

"To see her mother sharing a room with a man she's not married to. That's worse than bad. It's sinful."

"She doesn't see anything of the sort. I never said anything about sharing a room. The building used to be a rooming house. It has many bedrooms, and I have my own. I don't share with anyone. And I haven't said a word about sex."

"You don't need to. Why else would a man like that take you in?"

"How about, because he's a good and kind man?"

"If he's so good and kind, why doesn't he marry you?"

"We're just getting to know each other. We're becoming good friends. We work well together, and we enjoy each other's company. I hope that someday he will ask me to marry him. But for now, we have a comfortable relationship. I'm happy. And nothing you say is going to change that. I just wanted to be open and honest about it, even if it makes you hate me."

"Oh, Ruby! My darling daughter! You know I love you despite all our differences. I never condemned you because you gave birth to Frankie. I never criticized you when you came home dragging that tinker who was just lending his name to an illegitimate baby. I don't have to like everything you do, but I can't help loving you. And I worry about you."

"If you want us to leave now, we will."

"No. Of course you'll stay as long as you like, although it will be on my terms."

"Which are?"

"Your gentleman friend can have the spare room. Frankie can sleep with Sally, and you will sleep with me."

"I never expected anything else. And we can only stay one night. We have to get back to Akron to open the tavern by supper time tomorrow."

❧

Later in the afternoon, Ruby pulled her mother aside for a private chat. "I have to confess, Mother, that I have an ulterior motive in dropping in on you."

"Of course. You usually do."

"This is important. I need you to come back to Ohio with us."

"Why on earth would I want to do that? I told you girls when you were all so enthusiastic about moving westward that I had no intention of—"

"I know, I know. But we have a real problem. I think Lillian and Carlton are in danger."

"Danger! What kind of nonsense . . . did Paul Davidson put you up to this?"

"Paul knows I'm here, and he agrees that we have a problem, but . . ."

"He's determined to get his son back, isn't he? Without any consideration of whether or not Martha can now handle being a mother to her son."

"There's much more to it than that, Mother. Would you listen to me, please? We've always known that Lillian's husband is a strange little man. From the time of his first visit, when he was afraid to eat your cooking and spent all his time rewashing the silverware, we worried about what kind of influence he was bringing to bear on Lillian."

"Well, yes, but . . ."

"He's much worse now. He's obsessed with the presence of devils in the world. He sees them everywhere, and he's sure they are coming after him and his family. So he goes to extreme lengths to . . ."

"Not literally."

"Yes. He regularly beats seven-year-old Carlton to drive the devils out of him. Sometimes he does it in front of his whole congregation, telling them that the boy has been attacked by devils on the way home from school and that they need to be driven out. And as for Lillian, he has made her a prisoner in her own house. He doesn't allow her to go out, even into the yard, unless he is with her.

"Here's another example. There's a woman who lives on the other side of the fairground at the end of Lillian's street. She sells eggs, and Lillian decided to walk over there once a week or so to buy from her. Frederick put a stop to that almost immediately. He told Lillian that if she wanted fresh eggs, she'd have to raise her own chickens. Then he went out, built a coop in the backyard, and brought home some chickens for her. Of course, the neighbors complained about the noise and the smell, so he moved the chickens into the basement."

"Into the house? But . . ."

"Yeah. And now their whole house smells to high heaven, even though the chickens all died down there months ago."

"He's a bizarre little man, but not dangerous, surely. And Lillian could open the windows and air the place out."

"Not when he's nailed all the windows shut. And, yes, I think he is extremely dangerous. He beats Lillian, too. I see her pulling down her sleeves to hide the bruises, and she limps sometimes. Beyond that, I can see it in her eyes.

She's terrified, but she won't listen to me or to Paul. He and I agree that you may be the only one who can help her."

"And what do you think I can do about all this?"

"She may be willing to talk to you. You can at least help her to understand that she needs to ask for help. Show her how to call the police or signal a neighbor if she's in real trouble. Convince her that Frederick is ill and needs someone to intervene. And, yes, help us get little Carlton out of there before Frederick kills him. Please, Mother."

Katerina closed her eyes, as if she could keep the problem at bay by refusing to see it. Ruby waited, afraid to breathe. At last, Katerina sighed. Her first words came from under her breath, as if she were speaking only to herself. "What have I done? Has Becca been right all along? Have I sent my daughters out into the world without caring about anything except that they have husbands, no matter how bad? And how can I hope to turn things around, now that I seem to have helped one of them ruin her life?"

❧

By Monday morning, Katerina had agreed to go. "*In für einen Pfennig, in für ein Pfund,*" she grumbled. "In for a penny, in for a pound." She even swallowed her pride and asked Rebecca to allow Sally to stay with her while she was gone. On the ride back to Ohio, Ruby continued to spell out the depths of the problem.

"When you get to Canton, be sure to pay attention to the furniture in Lillian's living room. There's a black wooden chair with a face carved into its backrest. Frederick bought it for her when they were first married. But no one ever sits in it. They're not allowed to."

"Why?"

"It's the devil's chair. Frederick insists that it be positioned facing the front window. That's so that, if the devil comes looking for them, he'll look though the window and see that there's already a devil sitting there. So he'll move on without disturbing them."

"Is it really a devil's face?"

"Oh yes, complete with horns and fangs. It's fairly terrifying."

But in the end, the rescue effort was only partially successful. Despite Katerina's pleading, Lillian refused to leave her husband or report him for his cruelty to her and the boy.

"No matter how he treats me," she explained, "I took a vow before God to honor and obey Frederick for as long as we both shall live, and I cannot now abandon him. I know how it must look to outsiders, but he's doing what he believes to be right. He beats us when we stumble in order to protect us from the even more painful fires of hell."

"Lillian, you cannot believe that a seven-year-old child is going to go to hell for coming home with muddy shoes."

"No, I don't, but Frederick says that muddy shoes are just the first step along the road to damnation."

"Nonsense! And you know it's nonsense! Do you love that boy?"

"You know I do, Mother."

"Then, if you cannot save yourself, at least save the child. Let us take him back to his real parents. He's old enough to understand that his mother's thinking can be a little fuzzy. He can avoid her, if necessary. But I promise you that neither Paul or Martha will ever beat Carlton with a whip for being a child."

Katerina stayed in Canton to be sure the little boy had been safely removed from the house and transported to Akron. To protect everyone during the transfer, she suggested that Mike O'Malley be the one to pick up the child. At the last minute, Frederick began to quote Scripture and call down eternal damnation on the heads of everyone involved. But when Mike pulled himself up to his full height and rolled up his sleeves to demonstrate the size of his biceps, the skinny little preacher backed down.

"You see," Ruby quipped when the drama had passed, "sometimes I pick exactly the right man for the job."

"Hang onto him, dear. He may be a redheaded Catholic Democrat, but I have a feeling your sister may need to call upon him again. Stay in touch with Lillian, Ruby, and don't hesitate to turn Mike loose on that miserable excuse for a man, if necessary."

Chapter 31

You Don't Find Love;
Love Finds You

Magnolia Cottage
Fall 1915

While Katerina was busy dealing with the lives of her older daughters, Rebecca was enjoying having some time to get to reacquainted with her youngest niece. Oh, she had known her from infancy, but Sally had always been a private and standoffish child. She pouted and sulked her way through most of her early schooling. In adolescence, her head was in the clouds, imagining a time when she might become a famous movie star or a sultry nightclub singer or a renowned beauty. Not a mirror was safe from her preening, and she oozed disdain for most of the members of her own family. As a result, Rebecca had never felt particularly close to the little girl. If truth be told, she somewhat disliked her.

Something was different about her now, however. After an initial protest at being left in Rebecca's care while more interesting things were happening in Ohio, Sally seemed to settle into a comfortable companionship with her aunt. One night, after they had washed their supper dishes together, she broached a serious discussion.

"Can I ask you a couple of personal questions, Aunt Becca?"

"Of course, dear. I won't promise to answer everything, but ask away."

"When you left for Gettysburg that summer, we all learned the story of your love affair with Josh McKay."

"Whoa! If you're going to pry into my former life, fine, but let's get the story straight from the beginning. It was not a 'love affair.' I was thirteen. Now, what would you like to know about our . . . friendship?"

"I'm sorry. It's just that it sounds so romantic. You were only thirteen, but you already knew that you and he were . . . what?"

"Best friends, I suppose. Soul mates, perhaps."

"All right. But you knew . . . you knew he was special. So when were you sure you were in love with him? Was it from the very beginning?"

"No, I never looked at him and thought that I was in love with him. Not in the way you mean that phrase today, anyhow. But I did allow myself to think in terms of 'when we grow up.' He was so much a part of my life that I couldn't imagine what it would be like not to have him around. And then he was gone, and eventually I had to understand that he wasn't coming back. Maybe then I knew. But first, I had a lot of growing up to do."

"I guess that's my real question. How do you know when you are in love?"

"Ah, if I could answer that question, I'd write a different kind of book and make a fortune."

"You're not being helpful."

"That's because you're looking for easy answers, and there aren't any. In fact, there are probably as many answers as there are people asking the question."

"But there must be some clues, some signs . . ."

"All right. Let's look at the romances in your family. Your mother and father began as casual acquaintances, each sentenced to spending a summer with people they didn't much enjoy. So they teamed up. Then the unthinkable happened, as you know. Your mother's parents were killed in a tragic accident, and she had to grow up on the spot. She was eighteen, suddenly burdened with the full responsibility for a large farm and two little brothers. Then Jamey stepped in and took care of her, took care of her brothers, and took care of the farm. She collapsed in absolute gratitude. As for Jamey, I am well aware that he grew up feeling like the afterthought in the family. None of us made him feel important or necessary. He was just an annoyance. Katerina was the first person who ever needed him. No wonder they fell in love with each other!

"In my case, I had lived through a pretty scary childhood. The war started when I was only eleven. Then my sister's husband was killed in battle, and our house burned to the ground in a terrible citywide fire. We had to move in with my grandmother, who dictated everything we did. And by the time I was twelve, we had moved to a farm, where, instead of having slaves to do our bidding, we had to do everything for ourselves for the first time. There was a skunk in the outhouse, a hawk swooped down and killed my chickens, and my brother lost a leg in the war. I was not only lonely in Aiken—most of the time I was terrified. Josh made me feel safe, and I never wanted to lose that feeling of being protected."

"Do you think you would have married him if he had come safely through the war?"

"Oh, Sally, I don't know. The war took such a terrible toll on all our lives. Some say that we lost an entire generation of young men. Certainly, there were a lot of young women like me, whose potential husbands were killed in battle. But the loss extended further than that. Even those who came home brought with them horrible reminders of the war—physical scars and mental ones, too. My brother Johnny was a good example. He lost a leg at Chickamauga, but he lost more than that. He was never the same emotionally after he was released from his prison hospital. He couldn't connect with anyone except those who had been through the war with him. And he never married. Who knows what might have happened to Josh after the war?"

"I don't want this to sound rude, Aunt Becca, but you were affected, too, weren't you? I mean, you never married, never found a new beau like your sister did."

"No, I didn't. Instead, I learned to stand on my own two feet rather than needing someone else to prop me up. Without Josh, I had to make myself feel safe, and once I did that, I quit looking for someone else who could—" Becca shrugged and shook her head. The discussion had probed about as far as she was willing to go.

"So what you've said is that people fall in love when they find someone who fulfills a need in their own lives."

"Yes, exactly." Becca was relieved to steer the conversation away from her own feelings. "Your sister Nora was the oldest child in the family. She was quiet and studious. Then along came seven more daughters, and instead of a peaceful, bookish life, she was living in a household that was never quiet and always boiling over with some drama or another. Henry offered her books and peace and quiet. Millie, on the other hand, always craved fun. Most of the time at home, there wasn't much time for games or laughter. But Joseph offered her madcap ideas and spontaneous outings to try something new. They still have that adventurous approach to all that they do."

"What about Ruby and Lillian?"

"Ah, I remember when your mother and I fought over letting them go off to New Castle and seek service jobs in wealthy households. Your mother thought it would be a good chance for them to find husbands. I worried that they might not be old enough to make good choices. Ruby was dazzled by the luxuries she saw in her employer's household, so she was easily led astray by the first man who offered her money in exchange for her favors. Lillian saw too many examples of bad behavior in her employer's household. And that made her vulnerable to the sermonizing of her fundamentalist preacher."

"So Ruby ended up abandoned by the fellow who led her astray, while Lillian sought her salvation in a strange religious cult. And Martha—we skipped over her, but she definitely needed Paul to take care of her."

"Indeed she did, and they still seem quite content with each other. She needed a caretaker, and Paul fulfilled his own need to take care of someone else after his sister died."

"You're making it all seem simple, you know. I can even carry the pattern further. Gloria wanted a rich husband, so she set out to find one by going to work in the store where rich people shop, and she evidently succeeded. Fiona never wanted anything other than to be a farm housewife, and Lester offered her exactly that."

"Yes, it sounds simple, I know, but you must remember that we're looking at these examples after the fact. It's easy to look at a finished jigsaw puzzle and see how two pieces fit together. It's harder to find the two that fit when they are mixed in with a bunch of others. The real trick comes with trying to figure out what you want, so that you can find the person that best fits your needs. You can't do that until you're grown up enough to see your own life clearly."

"And that's a warning, I take it."

"Just a caution, perhaps. Now, are you going to tell me why you asked the question?"

"Oh, no reason in particular. I was curious, that's all."

"For the record, I think you're a little young to be worried about such matters. You've still got a year or two of school ahead of you. By the time you graduate—"

"By the time I graduate, this country will be in exactly the same situation it was in when you were a girl."

"Meaning what?"

"Meaning we're going to be at war. Everybody says so. It's all the boys can talk about at school. The sinking of the *Lusitania* was a deliberate provocation to get us into the fight, our teacher says, and no one really believes that Germany is one bit sorry for it. If it happens again—if another ship goes down carrying American citizens—there'll be no way for this country to remain neutral in the Great War."

"Oh, Sally, I hope you're wrong."

"I'm not wrong. It's coming, whether we want it or not. And if another generation of young men is doomed to sacrifice itself on a foreign battlefield, I can't wait around to figure out exactly what I want in a husband. I'd rather make my choice now, while the field is wide open."

Becca allowed the subject to drop, but she couldn't help but notice a small, self-satisfied smile cross Sally's face. It warned of trouble ahead.

❦

Sally celebrated her seventeenth birthday on October 2, 1915. On the next day, she mailed a brief message to Jacob Kerrigan: "I'm now seventeen. Your move."

No answer arrived in the mail, but a week or so later, she returned from school to see a familiar car parked next to their house. She hesitated at the far edge of the yard, checking her outfit, sucking in her stomach, pulling her shoulders back to accentuate her figure, and chewing on her lips to make them red and slightly swollen. Then she strolled into the house, letting her eyes widen in shock and surprise to see Jake sitting at the kitchen table with her mother.

"Why, Mr. Kerrigan! Whatever brings you back to town?"

He was not deceived by her fluttering eyelashes, but he played along. "Ah, yes, Sarah Jane, isn't it? You've grown up since we last met."

"Well, it's been . . . what? A year and a half since Fiona's wedding."

"I suppose it has. To answer your original question, the newspaper has sent me down here to do some investigative reporting about things to do and see in western

Pennsylvania. There's been a crazy interest lately in local legends, and I'm supposed to be looking into some of them."

"Local legends? Like what?" Katerina was looking at him skeptically. "There's nothing special about this area."

"Of course there is. My first subject is the oft-repeated tale that Ellwood City has a mysterious 'Green Man' who lives in the woods and haunts those who cross his path."

"A green man? Nonsense." Katerina was not prepared to listen to foolish ideas from this young man. She still didn't trust that cleft in his chin.

"No, it's not, Mother. I know who they're talking about," Sally interrupted. Then she turned to Jake. "Shall I tell you, or leave you to ferret it out on your own?"

"I'm all ears," Jake said, grinning at her.

"He's actually a boy who suffered a dreadful accident. He climbed up a bridge trellis to see a bird's nest and got caught in some high-voltage wires. He was electrocuted and horribly burned, but he survived. The electricity gave his skin a strange green tinge, and he lost most of his facial features. His nose, eyelids, lips, and ears burned away, leaving him with gaping holes in his head."

"How in the world would you know such a thing?" Katerina glared at her.

"Everybody's been talking about it at school. They say he looks so frightful that he will only go outside at dusk, hoping that no one will see him. When he does meet someone, he screams at them to get them to go away. And they do, of course. Usually they're too scared to wait and find out his story."

"That's positively dreadful! Surely you wouldn't publish a story like that, Mr. Kerrigan."

"On the contrary. It's most interesting from a public safety angle, and our readers would love it. Where can I find him, Sarah Jane?"

"I don't know exactly. I think he lives somewhere over near Koppel. We could go out hunting him some night, though."

"You'll do no such thing, missy!" Katerina was frowning at both of them.

"Your mother's right," Jake said, "but maybe you can help me with some of the other stories."

"I know lots of them. There's Bloody Mary Black. She had an illegitimate baby, and her lover killed both her and the child so his wife wouldn't find out. Now you can summon her ghost by telling her you know where to find her killer. Or there's the ghost of the woman who fell off the Summit Cut Bridge onto the railroad tracks. She's still trying to piece herself back together."

"That's enough, Sally! I'm embarrassed to think you and your friends talk about such things."

"I do have an idea you could help with—one that's not quite so gory," Jake said, intervening before Sally and her mother could carry their quarrel further. "New Castle has the distinction of having the first movie theater the Warner brothers ever opened, and now that the Warners are making a name for themselves in the motion picture industry, people want to know why they started in New Castle. When I came through there this morning, I noticed that their old Cascade Picture Palace is showing *Birth of a Nation* this week. Perhaps, if your mother would allow it, you could go with me to the Saturday matinee. The film is supposed to be a remarkable retelling of the Civil War. It runs for two hours, has a cast of thousands—including some 800 horses—and stars Lillian Gish, who, as it happens, comes from Massillon, Ohio, which is right next door to Canton. The paper would never forgive me if I missed a chance to review her greatest film role."

"How exciting! I've never seen a moving picture show. May I, Mother, please?"

"I suppose so, if you'll promise to have her home before dark, Mr. Kerrigan."

And so it began.

Rebecca's Journal

December 31, 1915

I come to the end of another year, amazed to find myself a political activist. Our initiatives to convince the Pennsylvania state legislature to grant women the right to vote failed miserably in November, but we shall continue the fight for as long as it takes. Meanwhile, the family continues to weave its own tapestry of crises and catastrophes. In November, Sally eloped with her newspaperman from Canton, defying her mother who wanted her to finish school first. Fiona announced a pregnancy. Lillian's husband spent some time in the Massillon State Hospital for the Criminally Insane after he took a horsewhip to one of his parishioners. Fortunately (or not), he proved to be a model prisoner and was sent home after only a couple of weeks. Ruby and her tavern-owning boyfriend are fretting over reports that a constitutional amendment to ban the sale of alcohol is coming ever closer to ratification. When it passes, their livelihood will disappear. Martha has proven herself to be a caring mother for Carlton, although he seems to be having a hard time adjusting to his new surroundings. Frederick's preaching has left him with deep scars, not all of them visible. Fortunately, the other three girls and their families seem to be doing well.

Still, I find it hard to be optimistic about the future. Here we are again, a world embroiled in another cause for warfare. The trouble began, just as Gloria's young man and Otto von Bismarck predicted: some damned fool thing in the Balkans set off a powder keg. At the end of June last year, an obviously deranged young Serbian nationalist named Gavrilo Princip joined a group whose terrorist goals were directed at the Austro-Hungarian monarchy. As the Archduke Franz Ferdinand, heir to the throne of the Austro-Hungarian empire, and his wife, Sophie, drove through the streets of Sarajevo, one of the group tossed a homemade bomb at their car. It rolled harmlessly off the vehicle. Later that same day, Princip saw another opportunity. He stepped out of a crowd and fired his pistol at the couple at point-blank range. Both died on the spot, and that lit the match.

Within a month, Austria-Hungary declared war on Serbia, and its ally, Germany, declared war on France and Russia. The United Kingdom, living up to its treaty with France and Russia, responded by declaring war on Germany. Austria-Hungary then declared war on Russia, and France and the United Kingdom declared war on Austria-Hungary. Soon everyone was jumping into the fray. Little Serbia challenged

Russia, and Austria-Hungary attacked Belgium, which happened to be in the way. Even Japan, allied with the United Kingdom, got into the act, seeing a chance to seize territory in the Pacific from Germany and Austria-Hungary while the European powers were fighting one another.

I read the newspaper battle accounts and weep for lives lost—including those losing their lives today and those who lost their lives in our past wars. All of them are victims of similar traps for the unwary—mistakes, misunderstandings, and isolated incidents that take on a life of their own and drag the world into conflict.

I want to believe President Wilson when he says the United States of America can, and will, remain neutral in the worldwide conflict. But is the neutrality he promises possible? I cannot believe that it will be. War is madness, and that kind of madness is contagious. When I stop to listen, I can almost hear the war coming. We live our lives at a frenetic pace. Henry Ford speeds up his assembly line and promises the world that by next December, he will be able to produce a new car every two hours and thirty minutes. We build bigger and faster steamships to carry people across the oceans. Telegraph messages flash across the Atlantic at dizzying speeds. Mr. Goodyear is working on putting blimps into the air, and airplane manufacturers are figuring out how to equip planes with guns that can be timed to fire between whirling propeller blades. Other manufacturers have already geared up to produce the equipment needed by European armies. Can it be long before that giant conflagration sucks us all into its belly?

And if we go to war, who all will be swept up into that fire? How many men will become soldiers? Millie's son Homer will be dangerously close to age eighteen, and Katerina's brother's son, now in his twenties, will be a prime candidate. Their marriages will protect Fiona's Lester and Sally's Jake from any potential draft, but there's always the chance that they will volunteer anyway. And as I well know, war manages to touch everyone, combatant and civilian alike. I can only pray for our futures.

Chapter 32

The Calm before the Storm

Magnolia Cottage
Summer 1916

"*Y*oo-hoo, Becca? Are you home?" Katerina wiped her wet brow and tried to slow her breathing.

"Who's there? Oh, Kat! Do come in." Becca appeared at the back door of the shotgun cottage, holding the screen open. "I was just getting ready to sit a while in the back garden with a glass of lemonade. It's so much cooler back here in the deep shade of the woods. Come through the cottage and join me while I fetch another glass."

"You won't have to ask twice. I didn't realize how hot it was until I set out."

"Miserable, isn't it? So still. There's not a breath of a breeze to help cool the house. What brings you out in the heat?"

"Nothing. Everything. The farmhouse gets pretty lonely these days, and I could use someone to talk to." She attempted a weak smile, then shrugged. "I always seem to bring you my daughter troubles, don't I?"

"That's what family and friends are for, and I'm both. Worried about Sally, are you?"

"No. Yes. See? My thinking is so muddled I can't answer a simple question without confusing myself."

"So what's she up to now?"

"Her last letter is full of complaints. Nothing makes her happy. Canton is too smoky. She hates the house they're renting, especially when she pictures it in comparison to Fiona's Victorian mansion on a hill. And then, of course, there's Fiona's new baby. Sally's so jealous of her. But worst of all, she's discovered that Jake's been lying to her."

"About what?"

"Well, she was complaining that he has to work nights, leaving her all alone. She told him to ask to become a day-time reporter because they are newlyweds, and a bride can't be expected to sleep alone. He finally got fed up with the nagging and confessed that he's not really a reporter for the paper at all. He's a printer's assistant, and his job only exists after midnight when they do the press run. Now she says she can't trust him any more."

"Oh, dear. She's not thinking about coming home to Mama, is she?"

"No, not yet, but only because then she wouldn't be able to fight with him. What a disagreeable child I've raised!"

"She's young."

"Too young to be married, that's for certain, but I never got the chance to tell her that before she went off on her romantic elopement with a man she didn't really know."

"She'll grow up. The other girls have."

"Sometimes I wonder. Not even Nora . . . Have you seen her lately?"

"As a matter of fact, I haven't. I stopped by her house the other day when I was in Ellwood, but a strange woman came to the door. She introduced herself only as Carrie and said that Nora was sleeping and couldn't be disturbed because she had had a bad night. Is she ill?"

"I don't know. There's certainly something wrong. She's lost a lot of weight, and she looks haggard—almost as old as I am. And she has no energy or strength. When she's awake, she just sits in a chair and stares off into space. Carrie—the woman who answered the door for you—is her best friend from school. Her husband recently died, and Nora offered her a room in their house because she has no children and nowhere else to go. Carrie's now doing almost all the housework and the cooking, while Nora plays the role of invalid. I don't know what to make of it."

"Has she seen a doctor?"

"I don't think so, but she won't talk to me about what's wrong. The last time I tried to discuss it with her, she told me in no uncertain terms to go take care of my own patients and quit meddling in her life."

"That doesn't even sound like Nora."

"I know. That's what worries me. And Henry . . . he always has his head in a cloud somewhere. The house is clean, there's food on the table, and the children aren't making trouble, so he's content. Fortunately, the children are happy and busy with their own young lives, and they've always loved Carrie. So all is well with them. But there's something wrong with my firstborn, and I can't find out what it is."

"Do you want me to—"

"No. Don't try to interfere. That would only make her more irritated. I'm afraid all I can do is wait her out."

Becca again felt out of her depth when the discussion turned to marital woes or problems of childrearing. She had never approved of the importance Katerina put upon finding husbands for her daughters, but she had long since given up trying to express her objections. It was all too easy for Katerina to counter with "How would you know? You've never had a child, never been married." Now, to give herself a little time to think, she busied herself with deadheading some primroses along her garden path.

Katerina watched her for a few minutes. "Wouldn't it be easy if children were like flowers? If you could just plant them where you wanted them to grow, trim them down to size when they grew too big, and dig them up when you finally grew tired of them?"

"Kat, you don't mean that."

"Yes, I do, sometimes, particularly right now when it comes to Sally and Nora. And look at the rest of them. Or rather, look at the lives they are living. Millie usually has a smile on her face, but she hasn't two pennies to rub together. She keeps talking about selling candy at their gas pump, but she can't afford to buy the supplies, even from the wholesaler. Ruby has evaded every attempt to marry her off and is still living in sin and raising an illegitimate child. And Lillian has hitched herself to an insane wife-beater. Did you know that when Frederick was arrested and sent to the state hospital, she lied to the doctors and told them he had never been violent before? That's why they released him so soon. She says she was afraid to make Frederick mad at her. I'd like to pull them all up by their roots and replant them somewhere else."

"Ah, but look at your other rosebuds. Fiona is gloriously happy, Martha is safe, and Gloria has everything her heart desires."

"Three out of eight isn't a very good record."

"Better than some."

"I do better with kittens. I usually find all of them good homes with the neighbors."

"Enough of this, my dear. You must quit blaming yourself for your girls' mistakes. They are ultimately responsible for their own errors of judgment. You've done all you could for them. You and Jamey showed them the benefits of a happy marriage. And when it became necessary, you moved into a career that allowed you to become an independent and self-supporting woman. Moreover, you did it with courage and grace. Those lessons will come out in the end. We have to believe that."

Inwardly, however, Becca was arguing against her
own words. She really wanted to shout at her sister-in-law:
*That's what you get for making all your daughters believe
that marriage was the answer to all their problems!* From
early in their relationship, she had questioned Katerina's
repeated emphasis on the husband hunt. The girls had all
absorbed that lesson from childhood. Katerina's later efforts to become a practical nurse had made relatively little
impression on them, mainly because Katerina herself had
failed to appreciate how great an accomplishment it was.
Or, perhaps, it was because Becca and others had failed to
praise her efforts highly enough.

❧

It was definitely time to change the subject. Becca looked
up through the tree branches and shook her head. "It's getting ready to storm."

"How can you tell? I can't see even a small piece of the
sky from down here under the trees."

"You can feel it. Everything is quiet and still. There's
a heaviness about the air, pressing down on us. There's not
a bit of a breeze stirring, either. And listen—it's too quiet. Not a bird chirping or flitting about. No bees among
the flowers. No butterflies. Not even a housefly buzzing
around. No ants parading across the paving stones. It's as if
the world has stopped."

"And that means it's going to rain?"

"The animals certainly seem to think so. If you look over there, you'll see that Buddy has already settled into his doghouse at a time when he would normally be out chasing rabbits. And here comes Butterball, kitty-tummy close to the ground, scurrying toward the safety of the house. Be a dear, won't you, and open the door for her."

"I thought you didn't allow her in the house during the day."

"Normally I don't. But she likes to be safely under the bed before the thunder starts." As if on cue, a low rumbling sound broke the silence, and Butterball pawed frantically at the door, mewing softly in protest.

"There you go, Butterball," Katerina said. "Maybe your ears are just better than ours."

"Maybe so. She's pretty good at providing an early warning about bad weather. But then, I suppose animals have to be. And it looks like she's right again. I just felt a large drop of water hit my head."

The two women gathered up their glasses and headed inside as the drops of water multiplied and then gushed down on the little cottage. Soon, flashes of lightning and booming thunderclaps filled the air. Katerina stood staring out the window for several minutes, watching puddles form, fill, and overflow into running rivulets.

"So that's what people mean when they talk about the calm before the storm!"

"Yes, it really does happen. And sometimes I think that phrase can also refer to much of what life offers us," Becca

said. "Take this year and all its discontents and disappointments. Nothing much seems to be happening. No real
change or progress in the fighting in Europe. No stunning
new inventions. No action taken on the issue of women's
voting rights, much to my own disappointment. Not even
much political passion stirring over whether or not to give
Woodrow Wilson a second term as president. At the same
time, there's a lot of restlessness going on, people vaguely
dissatisfied with their lives—like Sally, for example. And
others sort of grinding to a halt, as if they are too tired to
keep doing the same old things, day after day."

"Like Nora."

"Perhaps."

"But if we're living through a worldwide period of calm,
what is the storm to come?"

"Well, all signs point to a decision in favor of enter-
ing the war against Germany. No matter which way the
vote goes, I suspect there will be a storm of disagreement
between those who favor isolationism and those who can't
wait to jump into the fight."

"Which result do you favor?"

"I hate war! Everything I learned from the War between the States demands that I object to any interference
in someone else's battles. But who's listening to me? My
sense is that we're going to be headed straight into the war.
The politicians just have to figure out a way to justify it
to the American people. And they won't do that until after the presidential election. That will be not only a choice

between two candidates; it will also be a way to judge the opinion of the voters on a declaration of war."

Katerina sighed. "I'm sometimes ashamed of my feelings about it. I catch myself being terrified by the thought of what might happen to those I love, regardless of how anyone explains the philosophy behind the need to go to war. And sometimes, I'm almost glad that my only son did not live to grow up and be sent off to face enemy bullets. Is that horrible of me?"

"It's the natural instinct of a mother, I should think."

"Or a grandmother? Or an aunt? Gloria's husband was trying to explain to me the principles behind a draft. But all I could hear were his first few words—'all men between the ages of eighteen and forty-five.' Think how many members of our family fall into that category—all seven of my daughters' husbands. Millie's oldest boy. My brother's son. And my other two grandsons, Carlton and Nora's Clarence, won't be far behind."

"I'm sure Tom has also told you that many of those men will be granted exemptions. Some will be unfit for military service, some will be needed in their professional positions at home, and many will be excused because they are the sole support of their households. That takes care of all your sons-in-law, I think."

"Only if they choose to accept their deferrals. I remember the Civil War, just as I'm sure you do. There were many young men who chose to enlist, even when they did not have to."

"Of course. You're right. My brother Johnny was one of them. He was in college, but he refused to accept a student exemption. My sister Charlotte's husband went off to get himself killed in the first year of the war, leaving her behind although she was pregnant with twins. And of course my own friend, Josh, who was much too young but went anyway. I still don't understand the attraction, but when you speak of warfare to most men, they start polishing their weapons and packing their duffels."

Chapter 33

The War to End All Wars

*I*f 1916 had been the calm before the storm, as Becca suspected, the events of 1917 would surely prove her point. In January, Germany resumed its submarine operations in the Atlantic, hoping to break the British blockade. The crisis worsened in March, when it was revealed that an internal note from Germany's foreign minister, Arthur Zimmerman, to their foreign office in Mexico proposed an alliance between Germany and Mexico, directed at the United States. If Mexico declared war on her northern neighbor, thus redirecting the American interest to her own borders rather than to activities in the Atlantic, Germany would offer military and economic support. The great prize to be won if Mexico was victorious would be repossession of much of the land lost during the Mexican-American War, specifically Texas, New Mexico, and Arizona. There was, of course, no way for the war-ravaged Germany to provide the promised military and economic assistance, and the Mexican government was astute enough to refuse the bargain.

The real effect of the Zimmerman Telegram, however, was that President Wilson could no longer make a case for neutrality. It was now obvious that Germany intended to extend its operations into the Atlantic, thus cutting off American support to Britain and France. Wilson had no choice. On the evening of April 2, 1917, he appeared before Congress and asked for a formal declaration of war against Germany—a war that would, in his words, "make the world safe for democracy." The final declaration was signed just two days later.

Issuing the declaration was the easy part. Ahead lay the difficult tasks of building an army, marshaling munitions and food supplies to support that army, and convincing the American people to make the sacrifices it would take to accomplish the effort. The Grenville family, like many Americans at the time, understood little of what was going to be involved. As they had in earlier situations, they turned to Gloria's husband, Tom Maloney, who seemed to understand the financial ramifications. When the family gathered for their usual reunion over Memorial Day, the war effort monopolized their conversations.

"It seems ironic," Becca commented, "that in our own lifetimes, we have seen farmers driven off their land, agricultural acreage turned over to purchasers of mineral rights, farm prices falling below the cost of raising the crops. And now we're being told that in order to support the war effort, every family must become involved, planting victory gardens and cutting back on our own food consumption to feed the army."

"It's true that our country is poorly prepared to feed an army," Henry said. "It's one thing to feed young men on their family farms. But put them with millions of other young men, all thousands of miles away from home, and the logistics of getting food to them become much more complicated."

"They eat the same amount overall, don't they?"

"Yes, perhaps they do, but the difference lies in the preparation, transportation, and preservation of that food."

"Millions of men?" Katerina was shaking her head in denial. "So many lives?"

"That's what it's going to take, Mother Grenville," Tom said.

"And where are they going to come from—these millions of men?"

"They'll be drafted. Congress passed the Selective Service Act just last week." This was a conversation Tom had been dreading, but there was no way to avoid it.

"Don't we already have an army?" Frederick demanded. "I'm a peaceful man, but it seems to me . . ."

"We do have a standing army, Reverend, but it contains only about 100,000 men. And when the president sent out an early call for volunteers to build up its strength, only about 73,000 more stepped forward. We need twenty times that many to match the strength of Germany alone, let alone its allies."

"Have you seen the act itself, Tom? What are the terms, exactly?" Henry's voice was a little shaky as he asked the crucial question, and Nora looked at him with fear in her eyes.

"Surely they wouldn't take you, dear."

Tom cringed. "I'm afraid the terms cover all able-bodied men between the ages of eighteen and forty-five." The statement was met with a collective gasp.

"That doesn't mean you'll be drafted, Henry, although you will have to register. And at first, they'll only be registering those between the ages of twenty-one and thirty-one. They are the primary targets. The others will be added gradually, as needed, starting in 1918. The act also has provisions to exempt certain classes of men from actual military service—farmers and clergymen, for example, and those who are the sole support of their wives and children. So most of you fellows will be excused for one reason or another. You're safe, Reverend." He was fighting to keep himself from adding that they would probably excuse Frederick on grounds of moral or mental instability.

"But between the ages of twenty-one and thirty-one— that's a whole generation of young men!" Millie was looking at her son Homer, who was close to eighteen. "How can they do that?"

"It's a matter of necessity, Millie. And I understand how you must feel. I wish I had better news."

"You need a wife, Homer." Katerina was shaking a finger at her grandson. "Do you have a girlfriend yet?"

"No, ma'am."

"Then you go find yourself one. And fast. You need to court her, marry her, and get her pregnant in the next year. There's not a minute to waste."

The poor young man had by now blushed from forehead to collar. "If they draft me to serve my country, I don't mind going. Really."

"Well, the rest of us would mind losing you. You listen to your grandmother now."

"Katerina!" Becca interrupted before she had time to think about what she was doing. "Stop badgering the boy. You're doing to him exactly what you did to your daughters. Avoiding the war is not a very good reason for getting married."

"Of course, you'd think that. You've never had a husband or a child to worry about."

"Mother, please. This bickering and fussing is making me feel quite unwell. Can we go home, Henry?" Nora was fumbling to push herself out of her chair.

"You're very pale, Nora. What's wrong?"

"Nothing. I'm just tired of this whole discussion. We'll see you at the cemetery tomorrow, where I hope we'll talk about pleasant things, like flowers."

Katerina watched with a small frown as Henry helped Nora into the automobile. "There's definitely something wrong with her, but she still won't admit it," she told Becca.

"I can't decide whether she looks ill or just sad," Becca responded. "But I agree that there's something bothering her. I think perhaps we both need to keep an eye on what's going on over there."

❧

As Tom had outlined, the first national draft occurred on June 5, 1917. The older sons-in-law didn't mind admitting that they were too old for the specified age bracket, and young Homer also sighed with relief. Because he would not turn eighteen until the following August, he would thereby avoid both this draft and the one scheduled for June 5, 1918, as well as his grandmother's demand that he find himself a wife. Lester Cole and Jacob Kerrigan, however, dutifully trudged off to their registration centers to fill out their draft paperwork. The examiners did little but look at them before recording their physical details—height (short, medium, or tall), build (slim, medium, or heavy), eye color, and hair color. Both listed a full-time employer, and both had wives and family for whom they served as sole support. That was all it took to earn them each an exemption.

Katerina was relieved when she learned that her immediate family was safe, but the news from her brother in New

Castle was not as encouraging. Heinrich's son, Wilhelm, was twenty-two and a medical student, and the army desperately needed medical personnel. Wilhelm had not waited for the draft. He immediately signed up for the medical corps, telling his anxious parents that his service was going to provide him with invaluable hands-on experience.

"He's almost the same age as my little James would have been, had he lived," Katerina told Becca. "Wilhelm was being born just as my James was passing. I've always believed that something of James's spirit lived on in him. To know that he will soon be on his way to the battlefields of France frightens me."

"But he's going as a doctor. He won't be on the front lines with people shooting at him."

"Warfare's different now. It's not like the Civil War battles you remember. The enemy has airplanes and mortars and flame-throwers and poison gas. Those things can't distinguish between soldiers and noncombatants. Please don't try to tell me he will be safe. You can't possibly know that."

"All right. But try to remember that our job here at home is to provide support for those troops, not scare them to death with our worries."

"You have an answer for everything, don't you?"

Becca held up her hands in surrender. "Why do you start these conversations if you don't want to hear my opinions?"

"Hoping for a little sympathy, perhaps, a little understanding. But never mind. I'll plant a few more rows of corn in our victory garden and hope they keep him safe."

＊

As is ever the case, people are moved most deeply by that which strikes them directly, and at the beginning of 1918, the world introduced the outbreak of a new and closer calamity. In the early months, people began to sicken from what first appeared to be a new and virulent disease. It struck quickly, without warning, particularly among young and otherwise healthy adults. Symptoms at first resembled the common cold or a simple case of influenza, but this variety had much more in store. Patients rapidly grew worse, their temperatures soaring to as high as 104 degrees. They complained of sore throats, headaches, and painful limbs. Then the disease settled into the respiratory system. Patients coughed until they were exhausted, the effort to clear their lungs often causing severe nosebleeds, bloodshot eyes, and a bloodstained froth at the lips. And in the final struggles, their skin took on a dusky blue cast, as their bodies failed to get enough oxygen. Death could occur within a few days, and sometimes within hours.

In the Grenville family, it was Nora's daughter Eva who succumbed. She was seventeen and had never really been ill. She was strong, with a lively personality and boundless energy—the exact opposite, in fact, of her languishing mother. When she collapsed in pain one March afternoon, her mother helped her into bed but then stood by helplessly, wringing her hands.

It was Henry who went for his mother-in-law's help. "Eva's desperately ill, Mother Grenville, and Nora does not know what to do. Please come."

Katerina grabbed her medical kit and hurried to Henry's waiting car, but by the time they reached Ellwood, Eva was already slipping into the worsening stages of influenza. There was nothing stronger in Kat's medical bag than a bottle of mustard seeds and a jar of Vicks VapoRub. Neither was going to be of much use. While she applied a thick layer of the mentholated salve to Eva's chest, she asked Henry to place a phone call to Dr. Higgins.

The doctor recognized the symptoms immediately. "I'm sorry, Mrs. Grenville, but I'm afraid there's nothing much you can do, except to try to alleviate her symptoms—things like cooling her down. We're facing a national epidemic of a new strain of influenza, and the mortality rates are very high. But there's one long shot. Ask her mother, Mrs. Southerland, for one of her atropine capsules. It might stimulate her heart and lungs."

"Atropine? Belladonna?" Katerina whirled and glared at her daughter. "Get me your heart medicine—now!"

With Henry's help, she managed to coax the girl to swallow the pill. Within minutes, she visibly relaxed, and Katerina had a few minutes to catch her own breath. Her anger, however, was on full display.

"Eleanora Grenville Southerland! Do you mean to tell me that you have been suffering from a heart condition all this time, and you never mentioned it? What on earth were you thinking? I'm your mother, and I have a right to know such things. I could have been helping you, working with you to manage your condition, doing something . . ."

Nora's eyes began to fill. "I didn't want to worry you," she said.

"Worry me? What do you think I've been doing all these months, asking you what's wrong, watching you waste away?"

"There's nothing you could have done, Mother. There's a hole in my heart, and it lets the blood puddle instead of being pumped through my veins. Not even the atropine does much good. I'm dying, and I've been hoping to do it quickly, so as not to be a bother to anyone. You warned me about that often enough as I was growing up. You always said I should not be an inconvenience to anyone else . . . that I had to help take care of the rest of the family because I'm the oldest. So I've been trying to hide . . ."

Katerina squeezed her eyes closed and wished she could also close off her hearing. The reminders of comments made casually to a child were now tearing at her heart. Even worse, she realized that it was too late to correct the damage she had caused. "I'm sorry," she whispered. "So sorry."

The family sat up with Eva all night, but as the hours wore on, it became more and more obvious that their efforts were in vain. She breathed her last ragged gasp shortly before dawn. Nora, awash in her grief and relieved of the need to keep her own health problems a secret, took to her bed.

By the time the family assembled for their usual Decoration Day trip to the North Sewickley Cemetery in May, they found not one but two fresh graves to be tended.

Chapter 34

Dear Mother:
Words from the Front

Somewhere in France
1918

At the beginning of 1918, the newspapers were full of alarming headlines. The British army had been bogged down on the western front in Belgium for months. Their plans for the battle of Ypres had not taken into account the possibility of stormy autumn weather that would continue into the start of the new year. Days and weeks of rain turned battlefields into mud. Cloud cover was so heavy that reconnaissance aircraft could not fly or help aim and direct artillery attacks. Explosive shells that landed in mud puddles fizzled rather than causing massive damage. Infantry troops remained huddled in their trenches, unable to move forward or back. Allied forces were reporting casualties of 275,000 men, with no gain to show for the loss.

Newspapers were also discussing the Russian Revolution, an event little understood at the time among Americans. The February Revolution of the previous year had largely gone unnoticed because it lacked leadership or specific goals. Even after the abdication of Tsar Nicholas II in March, Americans were not too worried, believing that the Triple Entente of Britain, France, and Russia remained united against the greater enemy of Germany. But when Lenin's Bolshevik Revolution took over in November and Trotsky's government signed an armistice with Germany in December, the outcome of the war in Europe seemed less certain than ever.

Still, life at home seemed to go on as usual. Battlefield statistics were too large for most people to visualize. It was one thing to read about a grisly accident or murder in one's own neighborhood. But when a writer talked about a half-million casualties now adding up in Belgium, most readers simply shut down. Whatever was happening was too far away, the suffering was being experienced by people who spoke languages no one understood, and the weapons involved were so advanced as to be incomprehensible. Empathy for the suffering of another requires that one be able to identify with the sufferer. During the early years of the war, such identification was impossible. But with the arrival of a million American troops in Europe, all that changed.

For the Grenvilles, the events of the war had been largely overshadowed by their own double tragedy. Just as she had in the past, Katerina bravely carried on, holding everyone together, no matter how much she might have been hurting inside. Becca saw her façade crumble only once. An eclipse of the sun occurred on June 8, 1918. The path of the total blockage of the sun passed in a line from Minnesota down through Georgia, but people on either side of the line experienced a noticeable darkening in their local area. In southwestern Pennsylvania, about eighty percent of the sun was briefly in complete shadow. The effect was that of deep twilight, except that this twilight was occurring at 3:15 in the afternoon.

Becca and Katerina were sharing a cup of tea when the shadow fell. As the landscape darkened around them, so did a deep silence. Birds, insects, and animals were confused and hunkered down for safety. Finally, Katerina spoke. "I don't see why everyone makes such a big fuss over an eclipse."

"Lillian's Frederick says it's a sign that the world is coming to an end."

"Huh! Doesn't surprise me. But then, I wouldn't really care if it did. My world looks this dark all the time. I've lost a son, a husband, and now a daughter and a granddaughter. My only nephew still lies in harm's way in France, and another son-in-law and a grandson have just been called to register for the draft. Where am I supposed to find any light left in this world?"

Becca felt her own heart twist once more, as she saw the tears sliding over Kat's now much-wrinkled cheeks. There was no answer to that question.

❧

The war itself became more immediate and personal to the Grenville family when Heinrich and Clara McDevlin shared the letters they received from their son, Wilhelm, who was now near the front lines in France. His observations introduced them all to the French people, the locations, and the suffering caused by the war. Even when the place names had been censored, Katerina and her daughters felt they were being given a tour of France:

> *I last wrote you on May 26, 12 days ago. At that time I was at _____, where we were resting. So much has happened since then, and so much has become clear to me that I did not understand before.*
>
> *One day, probably the day after I wrote you, the order came to move. We hiked a few miles, on-trained, and in the same evening, piled off at a station.*
>
> *There I saw what makes me realize how awful war can be. Train after train filled with young and pretty girls passed us. They are the favorite prey of the Germans and have had to leave home in boxcars, where they probably will receive neither food nor water for several hours. Old men and women were sitting*

on the hard floor of cars, with expressionless faces and dry eyes. O, but it is cruel that these old people who have lived and worked all their lives for their little homes and villages should now have to leave it all. They must leave their little gardens and their few cows and chickens, just because the kaiser of Germany cannot control his greed. I tell you it made me hot, and it affected all the others the same.

We marched all night, me on my old horse. I had been very busy the night before, and O, but I was sleepy. Honest to goodness, I fell asleep twice in the saddle, and I don't know how long I slept, but once at least twenty minutes. The fellow next to me noticed it and timed me.

At last we encamped. I slept by the side of a big straw stack. We were up early and soon started. We met many fugitives, drawing carts, cows, oxen, goats, pushing wheelbarrows, handcarts, and baby buggies, carrying food and household articles. We made camp late in the afternoon.

It was really sad the condition in which the houses were. As soon as the people left, the houses were ransacked by the French and roaming Belgians. We were under orders not to touch anything, and not a man did. I had several chances to buy wonderful old things, one a carved tortoiseshell jewel case that was beautifully inlaid with gold, but as I knew I couldn't prove I had bought it, I didn't care to have it in my *possession. The penalty for plundering is death. Our troops touched no man's property, with the exception of food. When we needed that we took it, or when we thought it would aid the Germans. We had a couple of rabbits, chickens, and veal, and also milk from cows which we caught.*

⊸⊷

"What a lovely young man he is," Becca commented as Katerina finished reading the letter aloud. "And how revealing his observations are. I am struck by the differences between this war he is fighting and the one we fought here at home."

"How is it different, Aunt Becca?" Millie asked. She had been visualizing her own son as she listened to Wilhelm's words and wondering if Homer's reactions would be as noble as those of this young cousin.

"Well, it's true that the Civil War drove many people from their homes. That certainly happened to us. The Dubois plantations that should have descended to my mother from her parents were all overrun at one time or another, some by Yankees, some by our own Confederate troops. And, yes, they were sometimes plundered. But the attacks were never directed at people, as these Germans seem to be doing. The Yankees didn't even round up slaves and load them into boxcars to be shipped off to do the bidding of their captors. Civilian lives were always spared, unless they were spies or they perished by accident."

"Interesting, isn't it, that our American boys are so much better-mannered than their German counterparts? They are not even helping themselves to whatever is left behind."

"With the exception of food."

"Yes, but that's understandable. That can be a matter of survival."

"Of course."

"But when I think of the young women being the favorite prey of the Germans—"

"So are we just nicer people, Becca?" Katerina's question seemed to be something of a challenge. Becca took her time answering.

"Actually, I've been thinking that the difference might be explained by the fact that our American boys are still new to the fight. They've only been in Europe for a couple of months, and they haven't seen much warfare. Wilhelm's troops are moving through the countryside and small towns. They haven't been in the trenches yet."

"And that makes a difference? How?"

"I'm not sure, but I'm wondering if men become more brutal in direct proportion to the sophistication and impersonal nature of the weapons used against them."

"I'm not sure I understand." Millie was facing questions like this for the first time, and she was obviously troubled.

"Think of it this way, Millie. Did you ever set a snare for a wild rabbit?"

"Sure. We used to do that all the time in the winter. Father would take us into the woods and we'd set the ropes with a little grain as bait. And then several days later, we'd go back and find a rabbit or two neatly hung up and frozen, just waiting for us to bring them home for dinner."

"Did it bother you?"

"Not really."

"But how would you have felt if your father had handed you a live rabbit and then told you to put your hands around its furry little neck, look into its eyes, and squeeze until you choked it to death?"

"Eww. No. I still can't wring a chicken's neck, either."

"The rabbit's dead, either way."

"Yes, but with a snare, I didn't have to watch it die."

"Exactly. And in this war, the weapons being used are ones that slaughter from a distance. The soldier is separated from the process of the kill, so he gets used to the idea of death without having to experience all the nitty-gritty details. I'll be interested to see if our American boys become more hardened as the war drags on."

An encouraging answer once again came from Wilhelm:

Tonight I am in an old French town. I hope I am not violating any military secrets when I say we are waiting for an attack. I am ready to move either forward or back, as God wills it. I am sitting in a room that belonged, or rather belongs, to a French girl who has been sent to Paris, on account of this new drive. Her mother is staying here in the face of the German invasion, in order that she may take care of her cow, chickens, and rabbits. Myself and another chap have rented this room. We even have a phonograph, which is now playing the "Blue Danube Waltz." I have given the old lady one of my gas masks and showed her how to use it. I can get along with one, and if anything happens to it, I can get one from someone else. There are always poor devils who do not need gas masks or anything else any more.

And now farewell, dear Mother. Do not fear for my safety, for it is all in God's hands, and it all comes out as He wills. If anything ever happens to me, always remember that I enlisted for the sake of you and of my country. Now that I have seen what war means, how horrible it can be, I will give even my life that you may never have to borrow gas masks from some soldier or leave home with only what you can carry. If this is the last war, no suffering, no sacrifices, and no hardship can be too big a price. All we ask is the support of every man in America. Don't be worried, and don't be too hopeful. Just work and wait, and every man here will do his share. When I die, there will be someone else to do my part. "Carry on," as the English say.

And so I close on the eve of what is supposed to be the big German drive. Best regards to all my friends,

and much love for Dad and yourself. I only ask God's blessing upon you, and that you may be spared all this that I see. If I had a hundred lives, I would be ready to lay down every one of them for the good old U. S. A.
Your loving son,
Wilhelm McDevlin
Sergeant, Medical Department
15 F.A.A.E.F., France

The tone of Wilhelm's letters never changed for the worse, although he apparently experienced a great deal of horror as the final months of the war passed. Officially, the signing of the Treaty of Versailles in November marked the end of the war, but the simple logistics of bringing all those American soldiers home meant that their returns were often delayed well into 1919.

As a member of the medical corps, Wilhelm's responsibilities to wounded soldiers meant he needed to remain in France for several months, making sure that the transport ships were adequately equipped to handle men confined to beds or suffering from the loss of limbs. His efforts, however, did not go unrewarded. On December 12, 1918, the local paper published this announcement:

Wilhelm McDevlin, who is serving in France with the Medical Department of the 15th Field Artillery, has been promoted from sergeant to sergeant first class. Sgt. McDevlin has served nearly a year with the colors in France and has seen some of the hottest actions in the war. His regiment is a part of the world famous Second Division, which has achieved a worldwide reputation for valor and gallantry at Chateau Thierry, Soissons, the reduction of the famous St. Michiel salient, the Champagne and Argonne drives. For his work in the Medical Department, Sgt. McDevlin has twice been cited in Divisional Orders, once for his work at Chateau Thierry, the second time for his work near Soissons during the battle of July 18-20. By his latest promotion, Sgt. McDevlin becomes the First Sgt. of the Medical Department of one of the most famous regiments in Europe, the 15th Field Artillery. He is the son of Mr. and Mrs. H. A. McDevlin of 541 Grant Avenue, this city.

Chapter 35

✦

Be Careful
What You Wish For

Ellwood City, Pennsylvania
1920

Wilhelm's safe return from France in August 1919 brought the family a much-needed sense that all was once again proceeding as it should. Wilhelm looked older, to be sure. He was taller, and his youthful limbs had filled out with muscles. Instead of a goofy young grin, he most often displayed a quiet smile of contentment, although for those who knew him best, a touch of sadness now filled his eyes. His visit was short, because he was headed back to his medical studies in Cleveland.

"I may not ever go all the way and become a doctor," he told his parents. "I've seen the strain under which they operate at all times, and I'm not sure that kind of life is what I want for myself. But I definitely want to remain in the medical field in some capacity, doing what I can to ease suffering."

"Like what?" his father challenged. "I thought doctoring was your life's goal."

"I'm thinking about ancillary roles, such as administering anesthesia or directing a patient's recovery process. Maybe even research into new treatments, vaccines, and cures for diseases we don't yet understand, like last year's influenza outbreak."

"Wouldn't pay as much, would it?"

"Maybe not, but money's not my main goal. I've had my fill of trying to stuff a man's intestines back into the hole in his stomach or holding onto a jerking leg while a surgeon takes a saw to it. Sorry if that's too graphic for you, Mother, but you cannot begin to imagine—" He stopped, the muscles of his jaw popping out as he swallowed a sudden flood of gruesome memories. "I don't have to make up my mind yet. The studies come first, long before a decision on specialization, so let's leave the discussion for now, shall we?"

◈

Both Rebecca and Katerina were surprised at how quickly their lives settled down after the war. Although the major newspapers still carried stories about the peace settlements and the formation of the League of Nations, most Americans like them soon lost interest in matters that did not seem to affect them.

Katerina grumbled about the continuing controversies over what was happening in Europe. "Who cares?" she demanded. "They nearly wiped each other out over there. We had to sacrifice and send our boys over to settle matters. We put an end to the war and then we brought our boys back home. It's time to concentrate on life here. Let the French and the Germans and the rest of them squabble over treaty terms all they want, so long as we never have to go back and beat some sense into them again."

"Sounds like you want a return to Wilson's dream of American neutrality," Becca observed. "But once we've meddled in the affairs of other countries, we've already abandoned the goal of minding our own business. It shows the truth of the old observation that, if you save someone's life, you assume responsibility for the rest of that life."

"I never wanted to see us get involved in that war, and I don't want to be involved now. I'm through planting corn so that our soldiers can go and fight someone else's battles. I'm planting sunflowers this year. I want a garden that reminds me to turn my face to the sun and rejoice in the life I've been given."

Becca chuckled inwardly, thinking how true to Katerina's character that reaction was. But if truth were told, she, too, was more concerned with what was happening at home. Her interests were now centered on pending constitutional amendments that affected women's issues.

The next amendment still waiting for final ratification during the war was prohibition. Women had been at the forefront of the fight against the curse of alcohol since the creation of the Women's Christian Temperance Union in 1874, maintaining that alcoholism often led to husbands who beat their wives. Women were involved in the other social movements of the Progressive Era as well. But the Great War had also given them new arguments to support their case for prohibition. Some argued that drunken soldiers were dangerous to the war effort because they might leak damaging information to the kaiser's spies. Others pointed out that the grain used to brew beer and hard liquor could better be used to bake bread to feed the army.

The Eighteenth Amendment became law in January 1920, making Becca happy but giving Katerina a new problem to worry about: What was going to happen to Ruby? Prohibition did not forbid the drinking of alcohol, but selling it or manufacturing it for sale was a federal crime. Mike O'Malley's Tavern continued to operate as O'Malley's Corner Grill, but it was obvious that his Friday night fish fry would not be enough to keep the place in business. And if it closed, Katerina assumed, Ruby would be out of both a job and a place to live.

⁂

When Ruby wrote that she and Mike would be paying a visit that spring, Katerina was sure they were bringing bad news. But when they pulled into the yard, they were smiling and eager to talk.

"I know you must be worried about our business, Mrs. Grenville, but we're here to assure you that all is well."

Katerina eyed them silently. She knew the look on Ruby's face all too well. It fairly shouted that she was up to something.

"We've opened a new business," Mike went on.

"Really? A restaurant?"

"No, a bookstore."

"A . . . a bookstore? Not a bookie joint, surely."

"No, a real bookstore, with shelves of books—mostly used ones, for now—and comfortable tables and chairs where customers can sit down to read or gather their friends around the table to discuss the books they are reading."

Katerina was not buying a word of this, particularly because Ruby was giggling at Mike's description.

In fact, Ruby could not contain herself any longer. "Of course, we provide coffee, too, or chilled lemonade in the summer—in case the book is dry."

By now, Becca, too, was looking at them both with raised eyebrows. "How do you make money from such an arrangement? Or don't I want to know?"

"Well, some of our books are more expensive than others. If you happen to pick up the wrong book (or the right one, as the case may be) and turn to a specific page, you'll find a menu of the other liquid refreshments that we have available for our best customers."

"Ach du lieber Gott im Himmel!" Katerina exclaimed, slipping into her native German in shock. "You're running a speakeasy!"

"Some people might call it that," Mike admitted. "I prefer to think of it as a public service offering."

"And Ruby's serving?"

"No, she's still the hostess in charge of the front of the house. She's in a position to spot any prohibition agents who seek entry. So far, we haven't been bothered by the 'Untouchables,' but we're prepared for their arrival. If they show up, she will press a hidden button that flashes a warning light. Hidden in the stack of books on each table is a drawer where shot glasses can be stashed while we bring out the coffee pot or the iced pitchers of healthy refreshments. And once the agents have left, the patrons can create their own Irish coffee or Long Island iced tea."

"It's a crime. A federal crime. You'll both end up in jail."

"Nah! Not gonna happen." Mike flicked his hand as if brushing away an annoying spider web. "First, there are so many more speakeasies than there are federal agents, they can't possibly get around to everyone. They concentrate on the big operations with ties to the Mafia or those operated by illegal manufacturers of liquor. I get my supplies from little local dealers, some of them making bathtub gin or getting moonshine from a backwoods cousin. So chances are, the feds will never even hear about me. If they do, I have a great lawyer on call. And they won't be able to do anything to Ruby because she's only greeting people at the door, not selling anything."

"But she knows what's going on."

"Yes, but they can't make her talk. There's a little thing known as 'spousal privilege.'"

"What!"

Now Ruby was laughing and waggling her left hand at her mother. A plain gold band adorned her ring finger. "Yes, we're hitched," she announced. "The law says a wife cannot be made to testify against her husband, so we got married in January, as soon as the amendment passed. If Mike gets arrested, I'm allowed to keep my mouth shut. And I'll be free to tap into our secret joint bank account and bail him out. It's a great set-up. We're going to make a killing on this business."

"If somebody doesn't kill one of you first."

"Oh, Mother, don't be such a worrywart. You've wanted to see me safely married for years. Now I am. Be happy."

❧

Don't you dare gloat!" Katerina warned Becca as soon as the happy couple had left for home. "I suppose you think I'm getting exactly what I deserve."

"I'm thinking no such thing."

"Well, you should be. I've fussed at Ruby for not wanting a husband. Now I'm upset because she has one. Oh, he's nice enough. I like Mr. O'Malley, really, even if he is a redheaded Catholic Democrat. But I wish they were married because they are in love, not because it's a sneaky way to avoid the law."

"You know what you always say about wishes—if wishes were horses, beggars would ride."

"In this case, the proper saying might well be *Bedenke, was Du Dir wünschst, es könnte Dir gewährt werden.* Be careful what you wish for. You just might get it."

"In some ways, you know, I'm as guilty of that as you are," Becca admitted. "I wished that prohibition would pass so that Congress could move on to dealing with suffrage. I never expected it to have such a dramatic impact on one of our own."

"That kind of wish is fair enough. You've been wishing for a good law. You're entitled to rejoice that it has finally passed. It will save countless other people from ruining their lives."

"I don't know about the rejoicing part, but I'll settle for a feeling of satisfaction when the women's suffrage amendment finally passes. I think that one's safe enough. I can't imagine it leading one of your girls astray."

"Are you still working on the vote for women? You haven't mentioned it in months."

"Well, while the war was going on, there was no use petitioning Congress to act. They had more important matters on their minds. So our main efforts went into getting enough states on board to ratify the amendment once it passes Congress. But now that the war is over, we can actually use it as an argument in our favor."

"I don't follow your line of thinking."

"Well, first of all, women pitched into the war effort with a will. Our female supporters went to work in the shops and the factories, doing the same work that men had done and proving that they are just as reliable and capable as their male counterparts. So the war proved that all the old arguments about women as the weaker sex have been wrong. And second, President Wilson is still stressing that we went to war to make the world safe for democracy. Only now, he's using the slogan to argue for his 'Fourteen Points' that he wants to see incorporated into the League of Nations. So our people are pointing out to him that he can't make that argument if his own country is not a democracy."

"But it is . . ."

"Not if half its citizens do not have a basic right to vote."

"We're better than other countries."

"Not when it comes to women voters. Australia, New Zealand, Finland, Denmark, Iceland, Latvia, Armenia, most of Russia, Norway, and recently Germany and Austria, for God's sake—all have granted women the right to vote."

"But the vote has already been taken in Congress, and you lost."

"Then we go back and try again. Each time, we get more votes in our favor. Now we're only one vote shy. It's coming, Kat. It has to. And I want to be able to say that I was a part of the fight. I'm wishing for success. I want to see those beggars ride!"

Rebecca's Journal

December 31, 1920

*O*nce again, I pause at the end of the year to wonder what the future has in store for all of us. Somehow, this year seems particularly positioned to usher in enormous changes. First, it is the end of two decades that have been witness to overwhelming social and political upheavals. Ever since the turn of the century, we have been striving for reform. We've fought a war that promised to be the war to end all wars. We've demanded better laws to provide quality education and sanitation, fair wages, safe working conditions, and improvements in health care. We've paid more attention to those who need social welfare assistance from government. We've sought to reduce crime, lessen the burden placed on our prison system, and cut taxes. All of them are noble goals.

And we've seen some successes. Tthe Eighteenth and Nine-teenth Amendments have the potential to change American lives for the better, if they are properly implemented. But they also have a potential for the opposite effect—a result I am only now realizing. Women have led the fight for suffrage and other women's issues. Will they now redouble their efforts, or will they decide to let government lead the way once they have cast their vote? Will they keep on voting, or will they forget about the effort if it does not bring immediate results?

And what about prohibition? It has raised questions I had never considered. Will it really keep men from beating their wives? Will the lack of easy access to oblivion turn the drunk-ard into a happy family man, or will it lead him further down a path toward criminality? Will the consumption of alcohol be safer if it is in the hands of organized crime than it was when bars were operated by one's friendly neighbor? I sense an enor-mous potential for trouble there.

We seem to be headed into an age of even greater pros-perity, propelled by wide access to travel and by our country's ability to produce a wealth of luxury goods. Mass communica-tion promises cultural advances but can also encourage social unrest. Will we handle the advances wisely or be overwhelmed by them? I have no answers.

❧

Another set of questions appears when I turn my thoughts to my own family. Katerina and I have spent over thirty-five years as friends, sisters-in-law, reluctant companions, and, yes, sometimes we have fought as bitterly as the Kilkenny cats. Have we learned anything from our interactions, I wonder? From the time we were introduced, our lives have centered on the welfare of her daughters—she as their guiding parent, me in my designated role as favorite aunt, the one they turned to when they wanted to run away from home. Our goals have certainly and inevitably clashed. She wanted husbands for all of them, men they could depend upon. It took thirty-five years for them all to find husbands—some of them successfully, others, less so.

I wanted to see them develop independence, the ability to stand on their own two feet. I haven't been particularly successful with that, either. I have seen impulses toward independence emerge in only a few of them, and even those have had somewhat mixed results. Ruby's rebellious streak has led her into some unfortunate relationships. Even now I cannot fully believe that she will have a happy-ever-after with Mike O'Malley, although my hopes for them are high. Gloria, on the other hand, deliberately set out to use a career path to lead her to a rich husband. She succeeded, and I like her Tom very much, but I am less and less convinced that their relationship is based on anything more than a shared love of money. My hopes for Sally were high at one time, but her desire for a career crumbled the first time a handsome man paid her any attention. Does that mean I have been wrong about the proper life for a woman? Not necessarily. I remain single, independent, and self-supporting. And on most days, I am happy and content. My path was the best one for me but perhaps not for the young women who tried to emulate me.

Katerina's emphasis on the necessity of marriage has also seen mixed results. Nora's married life, foreshortened as it was, remained particularly joyless. Ironically, however, Henry seems to have absorbed his mother-in-law's lesson. He is about to re-marry, this time to Carrie, the young woman Nora brought in to help with the children and housework after she learned she was ill. Millie has been uncomplaining but desperately poor. Even now, she struggles to bring in some extra income from a gasoline pump in their front yard and a shed turned into a candy store for children. But what will happen to her if she loses Joseph? I cannot imagine. As for Lillian, her suitable minister has turned out to be a monster. Her only safe moments come when he is locked up for being criminally insane. And there seems to be nothing that can be done to help him—or her.

As for young Sally, she seemed determined to avoid the marriage traps of her sisters. Yet her fate seems the most unfortunate of any of the girls. Only three years into a headstrong decision to marry, and she is already embroiled in constant marital strife. She didn't know Jake well when she married him, and he has now turned out to be not only a liar but a ne'er-do-well and a drunkard with a vicious streak. To make matters worse, she now has a baby son, over whose religious upbringing the two of them fight constantly. As much as I try to avoid wishes, in this case I wish we had locked her in the cellar until that man went away.

The others are better. Martha, at least, is safe with Paul Davidson, and Fiona is the deliriously happy one. She and Lester already have two darling daughters, and there are rumors of a third child on the way. As for Katerina herself, Jamey's early death forced her into a successful career in nursing, for which she thought she had no real desire. I'm not sure how she feels about it now. I hope she at least gets some satisfaction from the comfort she brings to others.

What lies ahead for us? Here we are—two old ladies bound together forever by a shared love for the man who introduced us—her husband, my brother. What did Jamey wish for us? Did he worry about whether we would be able to get along? Did he ever fear that our different personalities would cause an irreparable family break? Did he ever remember our mother reciting The Kilkenny Cats *and worry that his Kat and I would tear each other apart? Or did he suspect that we might one day need each other and that his Yankee daughters might need us both? Did he know that our very differences would balance each other and bring us safely to the ends of our lives?*